POST AFTER
POST-MORTEM

POST AFTER POST-MORTEM

E. C. R. LORAC

With an Introduction by
Martin Edwards

Introduction © 2022, 2023 by Martin Edwards
Post After Post-Mortem © 1936 by The Estate of E. C. R. Lorac
Cover and internal design © 2023 by Sourcebooks
Cover illustration © NRM/Pictorial Collection/Science & Society Picture Library

Published by Poisoned Pen Press, an imprint of Sourcebooks,
in association with the British Library
P.O. Box 4410, Naperville, Illinois 60567-4410
(630) 961-3900
sourcebooks.com

Post After Post-Mortem was originally published in 1936 by Collins, London.
Library of Congress Cataloging-in-Publication Data

Names: Lorac, E. C. R., author. | Edwards, Martin, other.
Title: Post after post-mortem / E.C.R. Lorac, With
an Introduction by Martin Edwards.
Description: Naperville, Illinois : Poisoned Pen Press,
[2023] | Series: British Library Crime Classics
Identifiers: LCCN 2022029621 (print) | LCCN 2022029622
(ebook) | (trade paperback) | (epub)
Classification: LCC PZ3.R526 Po PR6035.I9 (print) | LCC PZ3.
R526 PR6035.I9 (ebook) | DDC 892.8--dc23/eng/20220623
LC record available at https://lccn.loc.gov/2022029621
LC ebook record available at https://lccn.loc.gov/2022029622

Printed and bound in the United States of America.
SB 10 9 8 7 6 5 4 3 2 1

Contents

Introduction

Post After Post-Mortem (the hyphen appears in the title of the first edition, published by Collins Crime Club in 1936) is a character-based mystery and one of E. C. R. Lorac's finest crime novels. Like a number of other books that Lorac wrote during the 1930s, it had vanished from sight prior to this reissue; at the time of writing this introduction, there was not a copy to be found of *any* editions of the novel on the worldwide web. Nor have I spotted any discussion of the story, either in reference books or elsewhere. Lorac is a highly collectible author these days, so if you ever come across that elusive first edition in a nice dust jacket, it's likely to be worth a great deal of money. But what matters most is the story, and here we find Chief Inspector Macdonald confronted by more than one formidable adversary as he tackles one of his most baffling cases.

In the opening chapter, we are presented with an idyllic portrait of family life at Upwood, the Oxfordshire home of Professor Surray and his wife. Mrs. Surray delights in her garden and shares with her eldest child Richard, a psychiatrist, the joy she takes in the academic successes of her offspring. They have acquired an array of glittering prizes, most recently young Naomi's first in Greats. But Richard is worried about his sister, Ruth, who is not only beautiful but a widely admired literary novelist whose latest book, their mother believes, "is going to take her name into every corner of the civilised world." Richard is particularly anxious because he suspects that Ruth is finding a remedy for insomnia in sleeping draughts, "especially that insidious barbituric group."

This scenario calls to mind W. H. Auden's description, in his famous essay "The Guilty Vicarage" of the ideal setting for a detective story: "the Great Good Place...the more Eden-like, the greater the contradiction of murder." Sure enough, the peace and quiet of Upwood is disrupted in a shocking manner, as Ruth is found dead in her bed. At first everyone concludes that she has taken her own life, and the coroner agrees that it is a straightforward case. In addition to the evidence that she had been overwrought, it seems clear that she took an overdose of her sleeping draught, confirming Richard's worst fears.

But then, after a delay in the post, Richard receives a letter (the post referred to in the book's title) that turns all his assumptions upside down. The letter is from Ruth, and was sent just before her death; it makes clear that she was not contemplating the end of her life. Deeply troubled, Richard takes advantage of a previous acquaintance with Inspector Macdonald, and asks for his guidance. Before long, Macdonald becomes convinced that Ruth has been murdered, but solving the puzzle of her death tests his resources to the limit.

The literary world plays a central part in the story, and Lorac embellishes her book with a number of neat touches. Early on, Richard tells Ruth that he is "going to write a thriller—a real, strong, juicy blood, and I shall do it under cover of a female name... All the women writers call themselves John or Anthony or Archibald. I'm going to retaliate." Given that Lorac was a woman (her real name was Edith Caroline Rivett, although many readers believed her to be a man), this remark has an appealing flavour of self-mockery. Richard also urges Naomi to come away with him to Canada and collaborate in writing that thriller: "and see if we can't catch Torquemada out by setting him a problem too subtle for him to grasp, so that he'll criticise all the wrong points!" Torquemada was a renowned reviewer of detective fiction for the *Observer*, and possibly Lorac was teasing him about a past review of one of her own novels.

Naomi recalls that shortly before her death, Ruth said to her: "Take my advice and don't go in for writing. It's not worth while. One chases the shadow and loses the substance. One's mind is always at a stretch, never at peace." Does that reflect Lorac's own view of authorship? I very much doubt it. Born in 1894, she published her first novel, *The Murder on the Burrows*, in 1931, and from then until her death in 1958, not a year went by without one or more additions to her tally.

Macdonald was her principal detective, and he is presented in rather more depth in this novel than in many of his other outings. Even before he comes on to the scene, Richard describes him as a man who "proceeded to reason like an intelligent being, and not like a policeman at all" and praises his psychological insight. We're told that he is a fine rock climber (not to be outdone, his trusty sidekick Reeves is "the best exponent of jiu-jitsu in Scotland Yard," and this skill comes in handy when a suspect attempts to resist arrest) and his shrewdness and humanity is evident throughout. As the plot complications pile up, Macdonald finds his understanding of human behaviour tested to the limit: "The motives of everybody involved in this case," he grumbles, "would take an alienist to unravel." Yet his compassion is never more evident than during his final confrontation with a murderer he has trapped into self-betrayal.

As regards motivation and theme, there are one or two moments in the story which strike me as faintly reminiscent of Dorothy L. Sayers's classic novel *Gaudy Night*, published the previous year. Even though the two books are in most respects *very* different, I can't help wondering if the earlier novel prompted Lorac to explore for herself the implications of integrity and the corrosive effects of excessive devotion to the deceased. One thing is for sure: *Post After Post-Mortem* stands on its own merits as an enjoyable period mystery that deserves a new life in the twenty-first century.

—Martin Edwards
www.martinedwardsbooks.com

A Note from the Publisher

The original novels and short stories reprinted in the British Library Crime Classics series were written and published in a period ranging, for the most part, from the 1890s to the 1960s. There are many elements of these stories which continue to entertain modern readers; however, in some cases there are also uses of language, instances of stereotyping, and some attitudes expressed by narrators or characters which may not be endorsed by the publishing standards of today. We acknowledge therefore that some elements in the works selected for reprinting may continue to make uncomfortable reading for some of our audience. With this series Poisoned Pen Press aims to offer a new readership a chance to read some of the rare books of the British Library's collections in an affordable paperback format, to enjoy their merits, and to look back into the world of the twentieth century as portrayed by its writers. It is not possible to separate these stories from the history of their writing and as such the following novel is presented as it was originally published with minor edits only, made for consistency of style and sense. We welcome feedback from our readers.

CHAPTER I

Mrs. Surray, her hands busy among the long stems of the sweet peas she was arranging, bent her beautiful silver head to inhale a deep breath of their fragrance. Each year the sweet peas from the garden seemed to be finer than their predecessors of the previous year, and these seemed to outdo all the others she had ever known. They were taller, sturdier, crisper; richer, too, in the magnificence of their many colours.

Her slim fingers busy with the task of fitting the stems into the block at the bottom of the great cut-glass bowl, she reflected that flowers had a magic all their own. Each season the garden gave her a fresh shock of joy, for there was about flowers none of that feeling which haunts middle-age: "It's lovely, but surely not so lovely as it was when I was young." This year the profusion of flowers seemed more than ever a miracle; after the May frosts, when all the gardeners had surpassed Job himself in their lamentations, the garden had broken out into a belated flowering, so that the blossoms of midsummer were ablaze late into July. The delphiniums and lilies, the roses and sweet peas, seemed intent on making up for their tardy advent with incredible richness of scent and colour. Mrs. Surray marvelled at the ardent tones of the sweet peas—purple, dusky and rich, flaming red, lilac that was almost blue. "Delicious," she said to herself, standing back to admire her great bowl of brave colour and heady scent, "and they look perfect in here."

"Here," was the drawing-room of Upwood, the square-built William and Mary house, embowered in trees, which had given Mrs. Surray's heart a shock of delight when she had first seen it, twenty-five years ago. Only to her husband had she ever admitted in words how dearly she loved the house. When other people praised it to her, Mrs. Surray only smiled, her grave grey eyes lightening softly as she replied:

"Yes, it's a pleasant spot, isn't it?"

When she was by herself, as now, she indulged her own secret passion for her home; she would stand idly, her busy hands still at her sides, and reflect. Was such and such a piece worthy of its setting? Was that colour just right to tone with the mellow brick without and the panelling within? Just now she felt particularly happy; the Italian brocade which covered her chairs and couches, which hung in supple folds by the long windows, had been designed and woven specially for her. Its cool, faint tones of tarnished silver and blue, faint jade and fainter gold, had been chosen to harmonise with the Persian carpet. This in turn had been acquired to lighten the austerity of the white-panelled walls, and to mimic the fugitive blue and green and gold of sky and trees without. The skies and trees of the Oxfordshire countryside were always delicate toned—chamber music rather than the full concert of orchestra—and the long white room reflected their philosophic beauty.

Mrs. Surray placed her precious burden of flowers upon a round rosewood table and allowed herself another long look. Delphiniums and lilies, roses and carnations—how prodigal was an English summer—and then she turned quickly as the door opened, her face taking on its most tranquil aspect, lest any one should surprise her in the impropriety of childlike gloating.

"Richard, my dear! How nice of you to come to-day!" she cried as her tall son advanced to kiss her. Richard was her first born, now a dark fellow with a sharp-cut profile and rather tired eyes, who looked his thirty-five years and a little more, in contrast to his mother, who, despite her grey hair, retained a smoothness and freshness of face which made light of her sixty summers.

"Many happy returns," he said, as he stood with one arm lightly round her shoulders. "Congratulations on increasing beauty and wisdom, too! If you'd only tell me your secret recipe, I could make a name and a fortune among neurotic patients, and retire to chew a straw and lean over a gate."

"My dear, how absurd you are, but how very charming! Recipe for what?"

"For tranquillity, happiness, and general well-being," he replied. "Ah! You've got the d'Este brocade. It's really excellent, excellent! By the way, though, Mother, did you read your *Times* to-day?"

"Not very carefully," she admitted. "I had so many letters. Have I missed something, Richard?"

He laughed. "Don't look anxious, most admirable mother in the world! It's not a disaster. It's just another triumph for you. Naomi has achieved a first in Greats. That's a distinction for anybody in this world, you know—and for a woman it's an achievement that's outstanding."

"My dear, I know it is," she cried. "Naomi! And she was such a lovely baby!"

He laughed very gently and, putting his arm through hers, he led her to the wide window seat.

"Come and talk to me, Mother. We so seldom get a chance to talk by ourselves. Tell me just what you meant by that exclamation of yours. It sounded almost like a cry of woe."

"You mustn't psycho-analyse me, Richard—not your own Mother! That would be too much."

"My precious parent!" he laughed. "Analysis is for the abnormal and pathological mind. I've told you, if everybody were as sound in mind as you, I and my fellows would go out of practice. No, I want to gossip—the sort of long chatter you and I indulged in—"

"—Before you became famous," she interpolated. "Richard, will you promise never to let me down and give me away if I tell you an awful secret?"

"Promise," he replied, his tired eyes smiling at her, while he rummaged for a pipe in his untidy pockets.

Mrs. Surray's lips twitched a little. "I don't know if you'll be able to understand, Richard, but if you can't, nobody will. I've had a shameful ambition for years, and hidden it from everybody. It would have been such a relief if one of you children had ever failed in an examination!"

He laughed, throwing back his dark head and showing

the white flash of magnificent teeth, and then his dark face grew gently grave again.

"And you feel that your last hope has gone? Naomi, the lovely baby—has got a first in Greats! You'll have to tell me some more about this feeling, Mother. I want to understand it a bit better."

Mrs. Surray laughed as she met her son's intent gaze.

"I'm being ridiculous, Richard. I shouldn't dare put my secret into words before any one but you; you may laugh at me and I shan't mind. 'My care is loss of care.' When you were all children I used to hope and to plan for you all. I was so anxious for you to do well. I needn't have worried, need I? From the time you got your Winchester entrance you went straight ahead, and after you came Robert, romping to the top of everything he ever attempted. When Ruth did the same thing I did begin to think that the family was getting stereotyped by success, and I was glad that Judith seemed such a harum-scarum when she was little."

"And then Judy got her Somerville Scholarship in the teeth of family derision," said Richard, his eyes smiling at her, and Mrs. Surray went on:

"Yes, and when Judy got married and had her baby she showed the same cool unruffled competence that distinguished her in her vivas. There was nothing she did not know, nothing she couldn't manage…and now Naomi."

She broke off for a moment, and then made a gesture indicating the lovely room in which they sat. "Take this room, Richard, and the garden. I've been planning to make them beautiful for half my lifetime. Can you remember Upwood when we first came here? Murky green paint indoors, and a wilderness out of doors? It's lovely now, isn't it?"

"It is indeed," he replied, and she went on:

"It's so beautiful that my occupation has gone. I can't plan any more because I've achieved what I set out to do. I can only sit with my hands folded and murmur, 'Nunc dimittis.' Can you understand that a little, my dear?"

"Yes," he said, "it's a solemn thought—years of thought and devotion to achieve perfection. It's rather curious you told me about all this to-day. You have a feeling—shall we call it the nostalgia of accomplishment? Your family is grown up, standing on the legs whose sturdiness you framed, whose very minds you fashioned. The house is complete—and you fold your hands and say, 'Nunc dimittis.' Not yet, I think." His voice changed. "When I came down here to-day I was considering a problem, and I was pondering whether I should discuss it with you. I hesitated. I always think of you as the happiest woman in the world. I think I'm right there, for you have a genius for life. I meant what I said when I asked you for your secret." He changed his position, clasping his long hands round his knees and leaning back on the broad window seat. "I often wonder what Gibbon felt like when he wrote 'Finis' to the Decline and Fall. Did he take a fresh piece of paper and write 'Page One' to comfort himself? Some new problem, some fresh and intricate line of thought? That's what you are going to do. Mother, I'm worried about Ruth. She needs help."

"Ruth? Are you sure, Richard? I saw her last week, and I thought that I had never seen her so triumphant. That last book of hers is going to take her name into every corner of the civilised world, and she looked so well. She's very lovely, you know."

"Yes," he agreed. "That's all quite true. Physically she is

in magnificent health, but everything is not right with her. Psychologically, if you'll apply the word in a broad sense, she's not passing her exams."

"Tell me just what you mean, Richard."

"I'm breaking a confidence in telling you this," he replied, "but I'm sure that I'm right in doing so. You can help, and you'll do it without seeming to, as you always have. I saw Ruth about ten days ago, and she asked me for some information to help her in some articles she's writing. We were discussing fatigue—physical and mental—and she let drop a fact concerning herself. She said that when she went to bed, or to rest, and closed her eyes, the thoughts which framed themselves in words took on this peculiarity; she seemed to see the nib of her pen on the paper, tracing out the characters as her mind formulated words."

"Isn't that a characteristic fatigue reaction?"

"Yes, quite, but I was struck by something in her voice when she told me about it. I asked her if she were troubled by insomnia, and she replied, 'No, not at all,' but she paused before she answered the question. You know the 'time-reaction' test? Her answer was not spontaneous, she'd stopped to think what was most expedient before she answered. I left it at that, but later during our talk I turned the conversation on to the subject of sedatives, sleeping draughts, and so forth, rather taking the line that I needed an occasional bromide myself. She knew much too much about the subject, and I was left with a very strong impression that she had been experimenting with the muck, especially that insidious barbituric group."

"Surely you warned her of the unwisdom of it?"

Richard Surray shook his head. "That would have been

worse than useless. The very fact that she was concealing the matter was an indication to me that there's some neurosis to be dealt with. The only thing I did was to suggest that she should go to have a talk with Marshall, and discuss this visualisation business with him. He's an expert on the treatment of mental fatigue. I can only tell you that she did not go, and I'm not happy about her. You see, I can't help her myself—she has begun by putting up a defence mechanism against me—and in any case it's impossible to treat your own family: that's recognised in every branch of the profession."

Mrs. Surray nodded. "Yes, I understand that. Have you any advice to give me on the subject?"

He smiled at her. "I don't think you need any advice. You have a natural facility for helping people, and a wisdom that does not falter. No, I leave it to you, because I have a great respect for your ability."

Mrs. Surray shook her head in some distress. "But, Richard, I am proved a broken reed to start with. I did not even realise that Ruth was overwrought. I thought she looked so well. I must be getting dense in my old age."

"No," he replied, "don't worry about that. I should have had no idea myself that she was other than perfectly normal and healthy in every way if she had not uttered that revealing little phrase about seeing the tip of her own pen when she closed her eyes."

Mrs. Surray pondered in silence for a while, and then she said:

"I am puzzled a bit, and surprised. I have seen Ruth working—one of the nicest compliments she ever paid me was telling me that she didn't mind having me sitting in the same room while she was writing, because my brain wasn't one of the sort that made a noise and interfered with her own while we sat silent." Richard smiled and nodded. He knew all about such "interference," and Mrs. Surray went on: "Ruth struck me as one of the type who doesn't tire at her work because she has such joy in it. She writes with a facility and delight which seem to invigorate her, as though she renewed her vitality rather than draining it by the very act of creation. Is there anything else, Richard?"

"You're very far-seeing, Mother, aren't you? You would do my job as well and better than I do it myself. I think there is something else. Ruth is feeling the wear and tear because her mind is only half free to concentrate on her work. You spoke just now of 'interference.'"

"Who is he?" said Mrs. Surray simply, and once again her son laughed. "I think I'll leave all that alone," he replied. "I feel a little bit guilty over having said as much as I have. Ruth is very acute, you know. She will realise very quickly if you know the very things she has been at pains to conceal. I'd rather leave you to find your own way about. It occurred to me that you might get her to go away with you for a bit. Weren't you talking about wanting to go to Spitzbergen, or somewhere like that, to interview the midnight sun? Ruth's very fond of you, you know, and she loves doing courier. With this book of hers safely through the press, I think that she might be glad to travel for a bit."

"I do need a change," said Mrs. Surray thoughtfully, and he chuckled as he patted her hand.

"Poor darling! Just when the sweet peas are at their best, and the rose garden is a dream, and the lilies asking to be admired by moonlight. It's a bit hard—but then you voluntarily shouldered responsibilities when you bore your children. Human beings are different from rooms—you've never finished with them. They won't stay put, and you won't be able to say your 'Nunc dimittis' until you wake up on the other side."

"If that's all one wakes up for, one might as well stay asleep," replied Mrs. Surray. "Tell me about yourself, Richard. Now, you *do* look tired."

"And I'm not ashamed to admit it," he replied. "I am. I'm dog tired. However, I can carry on until next month without loss of efficiency. We're all rather damned fools nowadays; I admitted it when I said that we strived too much. I can't be content with a good practice. I've got to write up my cases half the night after working all day, just to prove to all the world that previous conceptions on certain minute reactions are really misconceptions—and by the time I get my book through the press it'll be obsolete, I expect. We move these days!"

"Physician, heal thyself," she laughed gently, and he replied, with a shrug:

"Oh, I'm all right, my dear. I sleep—when I get time—like a log and eat like a tiger. It's only my own confounded conceit which makes me cut down my sleeping hours to five when I could do with eight, like any other fool. It will be all right next month, you know. I'm going to Banff, in the Rockies, and I shall sleep throughout the voyage like a hibernating bear. What about the rose garden? Are those new H.T.'s up to expectations?"

"Come and see, my dear." Mrs. Surray got up from her

place and led the way through a French window out on to the terrace. Before them lay a glorious stretch of turf, bounded on either side by herbaceous borders, ablaze with all the glory of summer bravery. The delphiniums and lilies predominated, the former in towering blue spires, five feet tall, faint azure to dark ultramarine, with occasional touches of deep purple. Catmint made a soft cloud of lavender along the borders, and the clear blue of flax and violet of veronica were interspersed with the royal purple of salvia.

"My Tibetan poppies have really established themselves at last," said Mrs. Surray. "Look at that mass of blue at the shady end of the border. Talking of Tibet reminds me—have you seen anything more of Keith Brandon? I went to his lecture about his climbing experiences in the trans-Himalayas."

She turned to the right along the terrace, walking slightly in front of him and reaching out her slim fingers to the doves who fluttered down from the old pigeon-house as she appeared, and perched on her outstretched arm until she threw them lightly into the air again. Richard raised his eyebrows a little at her question about Brandon. Was this chance, guesswork, or intuition?

"No. I haven't seen him—or anybody else save patients—for weeks," he replied. "Brandon's being lionised a bit; of course, that's only natural considering the remarkable things he did in the climbing line. I didn't know you'd been to hear him lecture. What did you think of him?"

He drew level with her as they left the terrace by a flight of shallow steps at one end, and went through an arch in a tall hedge of sweet briar which led to the sunken rose-garden. The sight of it made Richard forget everything else for the moment; the flaming gold and orange and crimson, the veritable cascade of white and yellow and red, all fragrant in sunshine, was an unforgettable sight. Tea roses tumbled from pillar to pillar of the Ionic pergola—deepest orange to palest cream, and their scent made him catch his breath.

"Gad, it is glorious!" he said. "Look here, surely Spitzbergen's not necessary. Get Ruth to stay here. Nobody could feel out of tune for long in this place; it's too lovely."

Mrs. Surray looked lovingly at her roses, and at the water lilies floating in the circular stone basin in the centre of the lovely little plot. Above them a slender bronze nymph was poised with beckoning finger.

"It is heavenly, isn't it?" she said wistfully. "I wish you could come down more often, Richard. You haven't been here since Easter. But about Ruth—I'm sure you were right in your first suggestion. She wants something new to occupy her mind to the exclusion of other things, and she loves the sea, too. This is too familiar; a garden is a place to be contented in, but it wouldn't take her mind away from everything."

She sat down under the burdened pergola and patted the seat beside her in invitation, but her son sat down on the grass at her feet and began to play with the creamy rose petals which fluttered down on the breeze.

"You can decide for yourself," he replied, "only it does seem rather bad luck that you should have to go away just when you're enjoying all this so much. By the way, talking of Brandon—what did you think of his lecture?"

"It was good," she replied. "Clear and concise and well delivered. The man himself surprised me a bit. Most men who have done anything outstanding in the way of exploring or climbing have a peculiar sort of diffidence when they talk about their own doings. The bigger the achievement, the less tendency is there to brag about it."

"Brag? That's rather hard, isn't it?" he put in, and she went on:

"I don't mean that he bragged. He didn't; but there was a suggestion of condescension about him. One was left with a vague feeling that had Brandon been with the last 'Everest' expedition things might have ended differently. Perhaps I'm not being fair," she added, "it may be that that extraordinary vitality of his gave me the impression of abounding self-confidence, and from that it is only a small step to egoism. He's a magnificent specimen physically. I've never seen a man whom I was more disposed to admire."

Richard chuckled a little, shifting the rose petals from hand to hand, as though enjoying their delicate texture.

"I like the way you phrase your antipathies," he replied. "Your point of view about Brandon is rather original. Most women fall at his feet, and most men say, 'Splendid fellow,' either because they admire what he's done, or are afraid of being thought mean-spirited if they don't."

"And you, dear?"

"I told you, I haven't seen much of him lately, so I haven't had a chance to observe if lionising has gone to his head. It oughtn't to have—he's got one of those long Norse skulls which are generally impervious to that sort of thing."

"Like Nansen? I think your friend Brandon is a bit like Nansen obscured by mental adipose."

"Their minds are swollen with fatness," chuckled Richard. "He's not really a friend of mine, Mother, only an acquaintance. Hallo, here's the pater."

He jumped to his feet as Professor Surray's long figure appeared through the briar rose arch.

"Morning, Richard. Nice to see you doing nothing for once. I didn't know you were coming, but now we shall have the family in force. I never knew a more independent set of units who described themselves as brothers and sisters. You, presumably, have come by yourself. Ruth is driving down by herself. Robert is coming by train to Oxford and then driving. Naomi has been out at Burford, and is coming by bus. Judith is also coming by train to Oxford, but not by the same train as Robert."

"They're always like that," said Mrs. Surray. "Don't you remember when Ruth and Judith were both up together, if mutual convenience urged them to travel by the same train, one would travel in the front of the train and one in the rear, just to demonstrate that there was no sentimentality about them."

The Professor twinkled at Richard. "Read your *Times* to-day?"

"By jove, I have! When you took Greats, sir, would it have given you a blue fit if some Cassandra had told you with authority that in due time your youngest daughter would nab a first?"

The Professor gave a deep rumbling laugh of purest enjoyment. "Daughters didn't, not in my day," he responded. "Your mother's arts degree was considered very undesirable. I thought Naomi would pull it off, though. Got the soundest head of the lot of you, has Naomi. To hear her giving Kant and Hegel beans is as good as a play. We ought to have something worthy to toast them in—your mother and Naomi. None of your cheap cocktails or champagne. It's a low drink, only fit to comfort elderly virgins at wedding breakfasts. I've still got some port that's worthy of the occasion. What about it? Though I'll drink my toast in brandy that makes that port feel juvenile."

"Don't ask me," replied Richard. "They drink the vilest brews nowadays—mix gin and champagne and orange juice and God knows what else, whisky, too, I expect. Make it port, sir, and educate their palates. Are you going a-jaunting next month, or staying here in peace to enjoy life?"

"I thought of going to Heidelberg if British nationals aren't verboten," the Professor replied. "It's good for the elderly to travel—makes 'em appreciate their blessings at home."

"I'm seriously thinking of going to Spitzbergen, John," put in Mrs. Surray. "I've always wanted to penetrate the Arctic Circle, and if I wait much longer I shan't have the courage."

"If I go to the Rockies, and Robert goes to the Dolomites, and Judith goes to the Pyrenees, and Naomi goes to the Outer Hebrides, we should be keeping up the tradition of the united family front very efficiently," murmured Richard.

"And Ruth?" inquired the Professor.

"I don't know about Ruth—somewhere strange and remote, I imagine," replied Richard.

"We can't have your mother jaunting off to the Arctic Circle alone," said the Professor, but his wife only laughed.

"Leave that to me, dear. I'm quite good at my own devices. I'd better go in and see about lunch. There's plenty of everything, and it's all cold. Richard, shall I have cocktails or sherry?"

"Both, my love," chuckled the Professor, "but tell the children that they're not to be mixed. I believe in keeping the family respectable."

CHAPTER II

Despite their academic achievements, the Surrays made a merry luncheon party. Over the cold salmon and the lobster salad, the quails in aspic and the pigeon pie, their voices rose in a crescendo of mirth and enjoyment. From Richard, dark and tired about the eyes, to Naomi, fair-haired almost to whiteness, and fresh-skinned as her favourite "Irish Elegance" rose, they chattered and laughed, challenged and riposted, derided and encouraged, until the long dining-room fairly echoed with their cheerful voices.

It was after they had toasted their mother, crying congratulations and good wishes with a vociferous sincerity and delight that nearly brought tears to Mrs. Surray's grey eyes, and then had raised their glasses to acclaim Naomi's achievement, that Robert (the only red-headed member of the family) demanded:

"Well, kid, what are you going to do about it? A career seems indicated, but what? Do, for the love of Mike, strike out on something original. We're all so damned obvious in our high-browed callings—"

"Sconce him? That word's *défendu*," groaned Judith.

"A proof of my correct use of it," said Robert. "It's a popular word, wherefore we bar it. You know they say that Mr. Selfridge gives quite good jobs to people with passable degrees—or that new store in Regent Street with alabaster fitments. Culture for the counter, Hegel in the Haberdashery and Comte in the counting house. What about it?"

"Don't take any notice of him; the lobster's gone to his head," said Judith, nibbling a salted almond. "All the same, what are you going to do, Naomi? Have you decided?"

Naomi shook her fair head. Her hair was bobbed with a straight fringe, and its shining folds framed a face which looked impossibly young and serene for one of such erudition.

"I don't know the least bit," she replied. "After my viva I was rather pleased with myself, and I know that's considered fatal, so I took ploughing for granted, and decided I'd become a Games coach. If my philosophy's bad, I know my Lax is good."

"Gawd! No school-marming!" groaned Robert. "That's N.B.G., anyway. No Head would take you lest you found out her ignorance. I know, kid. I'm sick of my job. Let you and me take a pub at Bletchley, and run it in the modern method—Plato in the bar, Plotinus on bedside tables, and drinks fit for heroes."

"Why Bletchley, of all rotten places?" inquired Ruth, and Robert retorted:

"That's why—and if you'd ever played in a match against the Tabs while you were up, you wouldn't ask such footling questions. The railway authorities specially arrange for all the Oxford trains to lose the Cambridge connection, so consequently all the best people inevitably spend a certain portion of their youth in Bletchley. As things are, they can't help it, but if we started a pub they might spend longer."

"I've only one suggestion to make, Naomi, and that's a negative one," said Judith. "Don't do anything which involves writing a book at the end of it. The number of Wentworth-Surray books already published is quite overpowering. Father and Richard write scientific treatises, Ruth writes books which are just books, Robert was involved in galley slips last time I paid him a surprise visit."

"Here, confound you, that's not public property yet," complained Robert. ("Just a few words on the unfilterable viruses," he explained to his father). "Look here, Judy, what's yours about?"

"It isn't," she replied. "I burnt my manuscript when I'd finished it, to save the world more confusion. I've seen wretched people tie themselves into knots because they thought they were reading J. S. Haldane and they'd got hold of a J. B. S. by mistake. If in addition to R. Wentworth Surray being Robert, and R. C. Wentworth Surray being Ruth, and R. S. Wentworth Surray being Richard, and J. Wentworth Surray being father, we add J. M. Wentworth Surray, being me, the librarians will ban us *en bloc*—and quite right, too. It's not decent. So no more books!" she laughed at Naomi.

"Do you know, Judy, I'd thought of that, too," said Naomi, "and it's very difficult. There's a Maguire travelling scholarship going—a real snip, £500 a year for three years and no restrictions—but you've got to write a book at the end of it."

Professor Surray laughed. "I know, infant. The Bantus, their tribal culture; the Samurai, their unpublished laws; the Americans, their attitude to State Insurance. Don't you do it! If you want to travel you can, but forget the note-book habit for a while."

"Just go gay," murmured Robert, and then Ruth put in:

"Why not explore, Naomi? You're interested in unmapped regions, and you've got the right physique for roughing it."

Richard pricked up his ears. Was there acrimony behind that low pleasant voice? Was Ruth so edgy that she was ready to be cattish to her sister—a failing almost unknown in that curiously friendly family of theirs.

"That's no go either, Ruth," he put in. "If you do an exploring stunt you *have* to write a book about it, just to defend yourself from the lies the journalists write. It's inevitable, like waiting on Bletchley platform."

"Isn't it awful?" groaned Naomi. "I'm game to do anything and every prospect is barred by pen and paper at the end of it. There's beauty culture, of course—and feet!" she ended despondently. "I *won't* be a don. I'd rather sell hats. Donnishness is devastating."

"Don't be a don, darling," put in Mrs. Surray. "You don't look like one, though I have seen some very snappy-looking ones wandering Woodstock-wards once or twice lately. If you want to write a book, don't be put off by Judith's exclusiveness— write one and call yourself Surray-Wentworth, Naomi, with a foreword to explain why."

"Why not a pseudonym?" inquired Richard. "That's what I'm going to do when I produce my first novel."

"Your what?" gasped Ruth, looking quite upset.

"My novel," he said placidly. "Now don't get all agitated about it; I'm not competing with you, neither will any one ever know who is the guilty party. I'm going to write a thriller—a real, strong, juicy blood, and I shall do it under cover of a female name—Lucy Lockett, or something nice and alliterative like that. All the women writers call themselves John or Anthony or Archibald. I'm going to retaliate."

"Pig and beast!" said the most recent adornment to the "Greats" list. "You've bagged my last idea. What a ghastly family this is. One can't do a thing without being anticipated by one of you. It's a rotten position being youngest in the family. All the others bag everything before one starts."

"Don't worry about that," said the Professor. "Richard isn't being original, even so far as this family's concerned. I wrote a blood once. I was twenty-five at the time, and I got twenty-five pounds for it, quite appropriately. It sold three hundred and seven copies altogether, and the publisher went bankrupt the following year."

Richard pulled out a pencil and a note-book. "Name, sir, please. This is a new one to me."

"No, my lad! You're not going to get the chance to giggle over my youthful optimism. Nobody but your mother knows about that little excursion, and she won't tell you. That £25 came in very handy," he chuckled. "Now tell us about your crime. Take my advice and don't try to be intellectual over it. What the public likes is blood."

"Oh, I can do that all right," said Richard cheerfully. "I can't tell you the plot, because I haven't made one yet, but I'll tell you what gave me the idea of writing it. Last Wednesday, at the end of a grilling day with more patients than I'd patience for, the final effort walked in for his consultation at seven-fifteen. I'd kept him waiting half an hour through no fault of my own, and when I saw him he got my goat. He was a big, lean chap, tanned, and straight as a guardee, and looked so loathsomely fit that the sight of him made me terse. I don't mind missing my dinner for a nice pathological case, but to be asked to be patient with this lad was too much. 'Look here,' sez I, 'if you want to know what's the matter with you, I'll tell you. Nix. Got that?' 'Thanks,' sez he. 'I'm disposed to agree with you. I didn't come to talk about myself.' And he shoved a card under my nose. He was Chief-Inspector Macdonald, the cove who got himself talked about over the to-do at Waldstein's Folly."

"Really, Richard," said Robert, "this is a revelation. Hyde Park, my bonny lad?"

"Have we a crime in the family at last, or has your last cargo of books from Germany proved too much for the susceptibilities of His Majesty's Customs?" inquired Ruth, and Richard lighted a cigarette before he replied:

"Sorry to disappoint you. No. The bloke had come on quite bona fide business to ask me to take a case. It's a damned remarkable story!" he exclaimed. "Would you believe that anything that once wore constabular boots would walk into a consulting psychologist and say, 'Yours, I think,' with reference to a criminal case? I can't get over it."

"What's the story, old boy? Tell me more!" demanded Robert hopefully. And his brother went on:

"Put briefly, something like this: The local police force had been flummoxed in a certain district by a series of incomprehensible attacks on a boy of 18—wounding, batting over the head, and other items—and they got Scotland Yard on to the trail. This Macdonald fellow examined the evidence and came to the only sane conclusion—the boy had damaged himself. He'd never been attacked at all. Now there's nothing remarkable in the fact of a trained C.I.D. man reading evidence aright. It's his job. What is remarkable is that this one proceeded to reason like an intelligent being, and not like a policeman at all. He took the trouble to find out that the boy had failed Matric twice running, and couldn't get the job he wanted as a consequence. Result, complex over his own failure and a subconscious desire to assert himself and get notice taken of him, which resulted in this self-wounding game."

"Your diagnosis, or the Inspector's?" put in the Professor.

"His, bless you! He didn't stop there. He came to the conclusion that if he faced the boy with the facts himself, being no psychologist, he'd probably make a b—hash of it, and drive the chap clean over the border line and make a raving lunatic of him, and if he handed him over to a magistrate on a charge of misleading the police and wasting the time of the police force, he might as well chuck him in the Thames straight away. Better, in fact. His phrase, not mine. Can you beat it? A Chief Inspector, who'd once been in the ranks, applying a psychological yardstick to a young offender? I call it rich! He asked me to see the offender and put him straight. Quite renewed my faith in law and order. I'll pay the police rate with a happy smile after this."

"All included in income-tax, damn it!" said Robert; but Ruth put in:

"You can't get a plot out of that, Richard. There's no point."

"I'm not suggesting there is," he replied with a grin; "but see what a pull I've got! I'll take this Chief Inspector out to dinner and get him to prime me on all the howlers these thriller merchants slip up on. I'll provide the blood, as per contract, and he'll supply the local colour. What's wrong with that?"

"First," said the Professor, "you've limned the wrong man. Macdonald's a Scot, and they've got their own notions of being funny. If you try to pump him he'll hand out the dope—all wrong—and every bantam in the Police College will crack his sides at the expense of Lucy Lockett."

"Look here, Richard," said Naomi anxiously, "be a sport and ask me to dine with him—the Macdonald, I mean. You haven't time to write a blood, and I should simply adore to. Besides, Macdonald wouldn't hand *me* the dope all wrong. I look so virtuous, when I try, that his better feelings would prevail. Give me this one—call it a birthday present," she pleaded. "I won't write it under the family name, honest to God I won't."

"Oh, Lord! That's what comes of telling stories in the bosom of the family," groaned Richard. "I can't, infant. If I mentioned I'd a sister to that bloke he'd run miles. Sorry and all that, but there it is. I'll show you to anybody else you like to mention, but not to this one."

"And that's what brotherly affection amounts to," groaned Naomi. "The only other thing for me to do is to develop a defence mechanism and start shooting myself and hope they'll put your Inspector on the job because the local cops are stymied. It's an idea," she said thoughtfully.

"No go, poppet," said Robert. "Your eldest brother would go into the witness-box and give evidence against you—malice aforethought and all that—just to prove the integrity of the scientific expert. Headlines in the Sunday papers: 'My own sister, but Science comes first.'"

"Funny, aren't you?" said Judith. "Frankly I'm disappointed. I thought Richard had a really good corpse up his sleeve, and it all boils down to shop, and poor Naomi's left on the dole without hope of employment."

Mrs. Surray got up at this juncture, saying, "If any member of the family would like a little fresh air, they can take their coffee to the rose garden. I'm assuming with my usual optimism that you'll all stay to tea."

"Will there be beds for all?" murmured Robert. "If so, count me in. Judy, come and talk to me *sub rosa*. I'm thinking of getting married, and I want to be told the snags before I go too far. Facts of life, by one who knows!"

The family wandered out into the garden, arranging themselves into groups. Robert and Judith, Mrs. Surray and Ruth, Richard and Naomi, paired off together, while the Professor produced a book from his pocket and settled down in the strategic shade of an immense flame-coloured rambler, on a seat which held one, and one only.

"Come down into the paddock and see old Charity," said Richard to Naomi. Charity was a pony who had been ridden by most of the family on occasions. Her name indicated her nature. "Charity never faileth. Beareth all things, endureth all things," had been inscribed over her stall by Naomi, long years ago, and Richard slipped his arm inside his youngest sister's, and they walked together over the smooth lawns, through the walled garden where peaches ripened on the warm walls and into the fragrant paddock, where the ancient pony came ambling happily towards them.

"It's all rather difficult, Richard," began Naomi without further preamble, as one who is certain that she will be understood at once. "Ruth has got all tetchy these days. She and I were staying a week-end with the Downings at Steyning, and she seemed to resent my existence. I've never known her like that before."

"She's tired, although she doesn't know it," replied Richard. "She wouldn't admit it, but it's a greater strain for a woman to live up to a peak of intellectual endeavour than it is for a man. Ruth never condescends to the commonplace."

"Perhaps that's why I annoy her," said Naomi, and he laughed and gave her arm a squeeze. "Won't wash, my child. Tell me about the Downings. They give rather good parties."

"This one was a corker, but they made a mistake in asking me when Ruth was there. Arosio was the lion—you know he sang 'Walther' at Covent Garden this year; and Wilford Hanks, the Communist—terribly amusing; and Setterby, the economist, and Keith Brandon. You know him, don't you?"

"A bit, yes. Was it you who sent Mother a ticket for his lecture?"

"Yes. I wanted to hear what she thought of him, but she wasn't very forthcoming."

Richard looked at his sister with troubled eyes.

"You don't really worry about him, do you, Naomi?" It was characteristic of their attitude to each other that neither beat about the bush.

"I do!" she cried passionately. "I worry a whole lot! I got to Steyning a day before Ruth did, and during that day I got to know Keith all of a sudden—plop! like diving into a pond. How was I to know that Ruth considered she had vested interests in him? It's not fair. Ruth's got half London prostrating itself at her feet. She's an intellectual; she'd shrivel up and die if she had to spend an hour in company with a commonplace idiot. Keith isn't intellectual; he's not a fool and he's not commonplace, but he can't live in that rarefied atmosphere Ruth breathes."

"That being so, how was it that he ever came to be on such intimate terms with her?" asked Richard quietly. "I don't know anything about their friendship, Nummie, but I do know that Ruth isn't the woman to assume what you call 'vested interests' in a man without some expression of reciprocity on his part."

Naomi flushed unhappily. "Whatever there was, it was only on what Ruth would call 'the plane of intelligence,'" she replied. "Can you imagine Ruth responding to any man's passions? If she went away with anybody she'd spend the night discussing the emancipation of the intellect!"

Richard's lips twitched a little. "You're only arguing with yourself on those lines to convince yourself about something which you know isn't sound," he replied. "Men and women aren't intelligent beings in their inner consciousness. Far from it. Ruth's as human as a gipsy underneath. I'm sorry about all this, Naomi. It's bad luck. Tell me—can't you cut it all out?"

Naomi's white forehead showed lines which seemed unnatural to that smooth young face, and her square jaw set itself in a manner which altered her curiously: the child was gone, and it was a woman's eyes that met Richard's.

"Can't *I* cut it all out?" she cried angrily. "Ask Ruth that, Richard! Why, because I was born later, should I have to accept only what Ruth has rejected? I mustn't write—not because there are too many Wentworth Surrays in the *Times* catalogue, but because Ruth might be embarrassed by her younger sister's publications! She wouldn't know what to do about it. If I didn't come up to her standard she'd live in constant fear that people would muddle me up with her, and if I *did* succeed she'd live in a nightmare that some one would congratulate her on having written my book! It's true, Richard! Ruth's got ten years' advantage of me! She's got there before I've begun, and yet when it comes to Keith Brandon, you turn to *me* and say, 'Can't I cut it all out? Stand down, be a good child and behave nicely. Ruth must have a clear field!'"

"My dear, I'm so sorry. I didn't realise it was as bad as this," said Richard. "Never mind about the books—that'll settle itself—but we've got to get to the bottom of this other thing. You're utterly wrong in one of your arguments, you know. Ruth hasn't ten years' advantage of you—*you* have ten years' advantage of *her*. Youth is a complaint that cures itself automatically, but there's no cure for growing older, Naomi. I only remind you of this that you may bear in mind that the grievance isn't all on one side, as you are assuming. You speak of Ruth bitterly; perhaps she feels a little bitter when she sees a young thing like yourself sailing in and grasping what she thought was her own. There's this about it, too: Ruth has been very late in awaking to the emotional nature of life. She spent her girlhood in writing about the things which she was too fastidious to touch experimentally."

"Isn't it awful?" groaned Naomi. "Why didn't somebody warn us about the dangers of intellectuality? Judy was the only sensible one of the family. She burnt her manuscript and had a baby instead! Ruth ought to have got married young like that! I see all the awfulness of complex-ridden middle-age in front of me, and *you* say, 'Cut out the other thing.'"

Richard laughed a little and squeezed her arm. They were

both sitting on the gate of the paddock now, while Charity butted them affectionately at intervals.

"I don't," he replied. "Produce the right young man and I'll urge you into matrimony at top speed, and congratulate you on an infant—in wedlock or out of it!—as a most desirable appendage—or antidote—to your degree. I've nothing to say against Brandon except that I don't think he's a suitable husband for either you or Ruth, but I do say this: if you go on your present line you'll ruin the whole of our family happiness. Do you realise that a family of grown men and women who never quarrel amongst themselves is rather remarkable? Would it please your fancy to go to Mother and say, 'Do you back Ruth or me in this? Because you've got to hate one of us!' What about me? Am I to acquiesce in Ruth being unhappy because *you*—who have never known a heartache—must swallow the whole oyster of your newly-opened world at a gulp? Think again, Nummie! I'm not asking you to make heroic renunciations, but I do ask you this. Come away to Canada with me next month, and let this business simmer down. We'll write the Lucy Lockett novel between us, and see if we can't catch Torquemada out by setting him a problem too subtle for him to grasp, so that he'll criticise all the wrong points!"

"That's really nice of you, Richard, but you don't want me while you're on holiday. You'd be much happier without any skirts hampering your activities."

"Wear shorts, then, you mutt," he replied. "I shall like having you, Nummie. You're much too hefty a lass to need any consideration from me. Promise me one thing. Leave any decisions about this Brandon business until you haven't seen him for three months, and then talk to me about it again. Don't go rushing into something that may upset all our apple carts without pausing to consider if it's worth while first."

She pushed Charity's inquiring nose away, saying, "You mean don't see him, don't write to him?"

"I mean don't commit yourself to anything which will profoundly affect your future until you've had time to weigh the pros and cons dispassionately first. I was wrong to ask you to promise anything—that's not fair. Just think it over. We'd better go up to the rose garden again; Mother will think we've deserted her. By the way, what are you doing for the next few weeks? I sail on August 20th—can't get away before. I'll see about getting you a reservation. But meanwhile?"

"I'm going to stay here for a week, and then I'm going with the Underwoods up to the Hebrides. I'll join you whenever your ship sails—if you really mean it. I've always yearned to see the Rockies."

"Good! That's settled, then. By the way, if Ruth stays here, too, for next week, try not to mind her if she's edgy. It's a pity, in a way, that you're both here together."

"Oh, we shan't scrap," Naomi replied cheerfully. "That's one thing about an academic training: it gives you marvellous facility in being polite under difficulties."

They found Mrs. Surray and Ruth still sitting in the rose garden, surrounded by maps and travel books and steamship publications. Robert was reclining on the grass, smoking placidly.

"Hallo," he said as his brother and Naomi appeared. "I've decided not to get married after all. Judy told me too many snags. Some one told me the other day that all young doctors ought to be married; but I question the soundness of their premises. I say, Ruth, is it true what a bloke told me, that you're going in for reviewing? If my viruses come your way you might bend the sisterly eye on them."

"Robert, you're getting fatuous, and as a habit it's tiresome. It's like the obesity that creeps on some men unawares when they give up playing rugger. I don't review, and if I did, semi-popular science is hardly my province."

"Whoopee! For a real deflating commend me to a loving sister," he replied. "I think I shall get married after all. A man's wife is bound to listen to her husband with some show of respect. What's this paper I was reading in the train—the *New Chancellor*? It's a review, isn't it? And you've got a whole page to yourself. Isn't that reviewing? Or is it a journal, in which case do you call it journalising?"

Mrs. Surray laughed. "Don't take him seriously, Ruth, he likes to be childish occasionally. I was particularly interested in your article in the *New Chancellor* this week. This man Stanwood whom you were writing about is a new name to me. You think the world of him, it seems."

"I'm so glad you read that article," said Ruth; "and in a way I'm glad that you said you had never heard of him before. It proves the very point I was making. Geoffrey Stanwood's work is outstanding, and his prose is the finest I have read since Hardy died, and yet no one has heard of him. I picked up his book by chance in Hatchard's, and started reading it, and I was simply amazed! It's an awful indictment of the average reviewer that such work should not have been recognised and acclaimed at its true worth before. His books are sheer works of art—"

"Well, you've given him a boost, and no mistake," put in Robert flippantly. "The poor devil must be ready to lick your boots. Recognition is precious to the artistic soul!"

Ruth shot a glance at her brother, but ignored his sally. To Mrs. Surray she said:

"I got into touch with Stanwood, of course. He has a most interesting and original mind. Mother, would you care to have him down here—say for a week-end? Upwood's looking so lovely, I'm certain he'd revel in it. I thought we might ask Leon Tracy, too—he ought to meet Stanwood—and perhaps get Vernon Montague to come. Would you mind?"

"I should be delighted," said Mrs. Surray warmly. "It would be most interesting. I must get Mr. Stanwood's book, Ruth, and read it before he comes."

"I've brought you a copy. I know you'll love it," replied Ruth. "You'll tell people about it, too, won't you? I'm so anxious to do all I can for him. It's belated recognition, I know, but I do feel that all intelligent people should do something to make up for their previous neglect."

"How nice all this is!" chuckled Robert. "And they say writers are a jealous crowd! This'd larn them—one literary star simply polishing another in the jolly old authorised firmament. Still, you're a bit late in the day, Ruth. I read Stanwood's first book a couple of years ago. Corking good, I grant you. In fact, so good that like the Scriptural liquor it needed no bush. Humorously enough, I believe I found the book in your bookcase. Naomi, come and play me a single. I'll give you what points you like, but I've got to consider the shadow of my imminent adipose. Where's Judy, by the way. Would she like to hit a ball about?"

"She's in the library with Father," replied Naomi. "Leave them to it, and come and be licked by me."

Robert Surray, with his arm tucked in Naomi's as they walked towards the tennis courts, observed:

"I should like to come down if Ruth fixes up her week-end party with Stanwood and Montague."

"Why?" said Naomi. "It seems to me that it might be an uncomfortable sort of party. I met Mr. Montague at Ruth's flat and the sight of his face when he was watching her made me feel unhappy. He's deeply in love with her, and she just keeps him hanging round and discusses literature with him. He's an odd creature, but awfully likeable. He's big and ugly and clumsy, and it's said that he's the most unbusinesslike publisher in the world, but he's just got this extraordinary flair for spotting good work."

"I don't think you need waste any tears over Montague," said Robert. "If he trails round after Ruth you may be quite sure he gets more pleasure than pain from the process. I wasn't thinking about him; I was thinking about Stanwood. Some one was talking to me about him the other day. He's one of the writers who couldn't get recognition. You remember how very poor W. H. Hudson was—poor to the hunger line. Stanwood was like that. He's the son of a poor provincial printer, and he turned up his father's business and came to London. He couldn't get his work published for years. The poor wretch got married, and his wife went T.B. She died a few months ago, just when he'd attained the success which might have saved her life if it had come earlier. Pretty damnable. A man who's been through the mill like that is more worth knowing than the people who reach the top straight off."

"Like Ruth?"

"Look here, kid, don't get feline. Incidentally, if you feel like writing, write. There's no reason why you should have your style cramped by previous successes in the family. You might as well decline to have a baby because it isn't original, Judy having done it rather well with John Michael."

Naomi drew her arm from under his and executed a wild leap in the air. "Sorry. I didn't mean to be cattish. I just feel over-full of *élan vital*, and Ruth's a spot languid and sophisticated. She's been admired too much, and too often, and too young. I'm going to beat you with a love game in every set."

"At-a-ball!" chanted Robert.

CHAPTER III

MRS. SURRAY, CALLED UP TO RUTH'S ROOM BY A WHITE-faced maid, had put her hand gently on to her daughter's shoulder as though to waken her, but before she felt the rigidity of bone and muscle, the cold unyielding stiffness beneath her hand, she knew that Ruth would not answer to her voice. In the overwhelming sorrow and desolation of that moment a voice within her said bitterly, "I thought I could help her—Richard trusted me to help her, and I was no good." For a few seconds blackness overcame her, a desire to cry out in agony, in fierce protestation against this cruelty to herself, and then she made an effort and spoke quietly to the frightened-faced girl who had followed her into the sunny bedroom.

"I must go and fetch my husband, Gladys. Go and sit in my room for a minute."

"Oh, ma'am, she looks so beautiful, just like a child asleep," sobbed the other. "When I touched her…"

"Yes, yes," said Mrs. Surray gently, taking the girl's arm and drawing her away from the white bed. "Don't cry—we mustn't cry." Her voice was shaking, but she drew the girl out of the room and closed the door. "Go and sit down for a minute... John, come quickly, dear."

As though something had told him that there was trouble at hand, Professor Surray was coming upstairs, and he took his wife's hand and they went together into the sunny bedroom where Ruth lay like a child, still and untroubled, her white face smiling the strange peaceful smile of death, and a box of sleeping-draught tablets on the table beside her.

It was half an hour later that Doctor Saunders, the friendly practitioner from the village, who had so often laughed at the Surrays for being an unprofitable family from the "professional" point of view, said sadly to the mother and father, "I am more sorry than I can say, but I can't sign a certificate. You know I would if I could—I would do anything to save you further distress."

But he could not do it, and both Mrs. Surray and her husband knew it. In addition to the heart-breaking sorrow at the death of their daughter was to be added the horror of a coroner's inquest, the inevitable gossip and surmise of popular curiosity, the raking over of intimate things which supplied paragraphs for the popular press. White-faced, but self-controlled, Mrs. Surray bent her head in acquiescence.

"I know," she replied. "It's got to be faced. This means the police, too... Dr. Saunders, you are an old friend and a tried friend. I can trust you, and you will not misunderstand me. I am not afraid of breaking the law: it exists in this case only to hurt us more—and to hurt Ruth's memory. If I take it into my own hands to destroy those papers we found on the table beside her, would there be more hope of a verdict of death from misadventure? Could we prevent that ghastly verdict of suicide? It hurts; I can't tell you how it hurts."

Dr. Saunders shook his grizzled head sorrowfully.

"We can't do anything. However much we long to, we are all helpless. If you destroy evidence you may make things worse—far worse. Those papers prove, so far as proof can be taken to exist in circumstantial evidence, that Ruth ended her own life. In the absence of that evidence, the police would be bound to make a far wider and more searching inquiry. The question would immediately arise: Did she die by her own hand? Forgive me if I hurt you, but you must face the facts. Moreover, at present the cause of her death is merely presumptive. I don't *know*; I can't be positive until after the holding of the post-mortem."

"Yes," said Professor Surray. "Saunders is right, my dear. However hard it may seem, this inquiry must take its course. We are helpless—the thing is beyond our power to alter." He turned to Saunders with quiet dignity. "It is your duty to acquaint the coroner with the facts. We have guests in the house. Is it necessary for them to stay, or can they leave us, as, in the normal course of events, they would be doing?"

"I think that they had better stay for the present," replied Saunders. "The police will wish to establish who was the last person to see Ruth alive. It is a bitter business, but their inquiry has of necessity to be wide. I think that you would do well to let me lock the door of her room and leave everything as it stands. I will save you as much distress as I can," he added gently.

"I know you will," replied Mrs. Surray, and she choked back a sigh which would have become a groan had she been by herself, and continued with the same self-control she had shown throughout: "I must tell Naomi when she comes in from riding. John, will you tell Mr. Stanwood and Mr. Montague, and telephone to Richard? I think that he ought to be here."

It was several hours later that the Professor and his wife had the chance to talk together alone. There had been a series of interviews with the police, in which the courteous and sympathetic Superintendent did his best to do a painful job as humanely as he could; there had been Naomi to deal with—a new, wild-eyed Naomi who uttered the strangest self-accusations, whose distress at the loss of her sister was fraught with a terror and agitation which poor Mrs. Surray could not understand. Of one thing she was determined: Naomi should not be called upon to give evidence by the police if she had any power to prevent it. At last, after many weary hours, she went with her husband to his study and sat down beside him on the big leather-covered chesterfield. She could not bear her beautiful panelled drawing-room just now, and the rose garden was equally intolerable; they seemed to be full of Ruth—her tall figure seemed to be flitting like a shadow through the brier arches, across the terrace, and about the long white room which she had said was the most restful place in the world. Only in the austere, book-lined study, with its long windows facing the little sunlit rock-garden, could she bear to sit down and think.

"Rest a little, my dear. Put your feet up, and let me read to you," said her husband. "You're tired out, Nell. I wish I could bear this for you," he said.

She shook her head. "I can't rest, John. I can't stop

thinking—not yet. If you and I were to go over things quietly together it would help most. I've got confused with answering so many questions, and I'm afraid of making things worse tomorrow if I don't get things clear. All those questions have got to be answered clearly, and I want to go through everything now, before I muddle myself afresh."

Just as she spoke, the door opened and Richard came quietly into the room. "I'm sorry that I didn't get here earlier," he said. "I was out in Essex at a consultation."

"Come and sit down, Richard," said his mother, after he had kissed her. "I was just telling your father that I wanted to talk things over, and try to arrive at some statement that isn't muddled or garbled. Since we have got to be questioned at the inquest I want my answers to be clear. All the world will be watching our distress, and I don't want to make things worse by having to be asked the same thing twice over and exhibiting my own confusion."

"If that is what you wish, let us put all the facts we have gathered before Richard," said the Professor, his deep voice as quiet and calm as though he were giving a lecture. "Your evidence," turning to his son, "may make all the difference to the verdict. You will want all the available facts we have gathered."

Richard bent his head in acquiescence, and Professor Surray went on: "Ruth has been staying here since she came down last Monday week—on your mother's birthday. She seemed tired, or at least disturbed in mind, for she alternated between periods of intense activity and periods when she was very silent, and, as far as I could judge, idle. She said that she was not writing anything for the time being, but I took it for granted that she was busy thinking—working out some new matter for a fresh book. I did find her unlike herself, less prone to start a discussion, less prolific of ideas than usual. However, early in the week she told your mother that she was writing to Mr. Stanwood, to invite him to come down here for this week-end. She also invited Mr. Montague, and a young essayist whom she had not previously met—a man named Charlton Fellowes. She seemed to be looking forward to their coming, and herself suggested that Mrs. Trant should be invited to round the party off, so on Saturday evening eight of us sat down to dinner, the three literary men, and our four selves, Ruth, Naomi, your mother and myself, and Mrs. Trant, who, you remember, is a painter and illustrator. So far as I could judge then, Ruth was perfectly normal. She talked well at dinner—in her most witty vein—and seemed to have thrown off the abstractedness of the previous week."

"Tell me a little about the visitors," said Richard. "Montague I have met—Stanwood?"

"He's a quiet, likeable man of forty, more given to listening than talking, but when he talks he's worth listening to. The chief point about him was that Ruth took any amount of trouble for him: she did her best to keep him in the conversation and to get him and Montague on to topics of mutual interest. I was glad to see her so alert and so enthusiastic over Stanwood. He is obviously a man who has seen a good deal of hard luck, and she took an obvious pleasure in paying him a sort of homage—nothing in the least exaggerated, but with a determination to show him every possible courtesy and to greet him as a fellow writer."

"You remember hearing her talk about him, Richard," put

in Mrs. Surray. "I was glad that she was so interested in his work. It seemed to take her out of herself a little."

"I remember," replied Richard, "and the other man—Fellowes?"

"A cheerful lad, under thirty, I should say: devoted to Ruth and rather inclined to hang on her words. I welcomed him because he had a touch of originality about him—he's not of the academic pattern and thinks along fresh lines. Mrs. Trant—as you know—is an established painter, but somewhat too heavy in her dogmatic assertions about topics of which she knows little or nothing. You wanted an idea of the party, Richard. That's the best I can do; but I'd add this: they all revolved round Ruth and admired her. Montague, as a publisher, would be only too glad to have got a contract with her; Stanwood owed to her his first genuine recognition; Fellowes obviously adored her; and Mrs. Trant wanted to paint her."

"Let me go on here, John," said Mrs. Surray, "and tell me if I make any mistakes. At dinner on Saturday evening everybody seemed happy and jolly. I may have been dense, but I could not sense the least undercurrent of nerviness. I had been watching Ruth pretty closely, too, and I felt perfectly happy about her. After dinner we sat in the rose garden and everybody talked—talked furiously, as is the way with literary people. Naomi and Mr. Fellowes bantered away at one another, your father argued with Mrs. Trant, and I chattered to Mr. Montague, while Ruth talked to her new discovery. You couldn't imagine a more jolly, sociable evening. Then on Sunday morning Ruth drove Mrs. Trant, together with Montague and Stanwood, over to Sudeley Castle, where she'd got permission to take them over the grounds. Naomi and Fellowes stayed at home and played tennis. Lunch was especially arranged as a movable feast, so that people could come in when they liked, and I didn't see most of them again until tea-time. Once again every one seemed perfectly happy, and Ruth seemed in her element. We had a cold supper served on the terrace; after it was over I left them all to themselves, thinking that they wanted to talk shop or business. Your father was here in his study, and Naomi took the two-seater and drove herself over to see the Langs at Stow. I went into the drawing-room just before ten o'clock. Montague and Stanwood were both in there, talking to Ruth, Fellowes was on the terrace, Mrs. Trant had gone to bed with a headache—it had been very hot all day. I said good-night, because I was tired, too, and Ruth said, 'We shall none of us stay up late, we're all yawning already. I expect it's the sun.' She walked out into the hall with me and said, 'Good-night, darling. Everybody's loved it all. Thank you so much.' Then I went up to bed. Montague and Stanwood say that Ruth went up about half an hour after I did."

"I talked to Montague and Fellowes in the garden for a bit, between half-past ten and eleven," put in the Professor. "They went up when I did. Stanwood went up a bit earlier, saying that he had some letters to write. All three of them have given it as their opinion since that Ruth seemed perfectly well and normal, perfectly happy, in fact, during the whole day."

"At half-past nine this morning Gladys, the housemaid who does Ruth's room, came to fetch me and asked me to come up to Ruth," went on Mrs. Surray. "She—Ruth—had said that she was coming down to breakfast (she usually had it in her room), as she intended to drive Stanwood and Montague into Oxford before they went back to town. Gladys took Ruth's tea in at eight o'clock, but did not like to wake her because she was so fast asleep—the girl knew that Ruth liked to have her sleep out. It was I who sent Gladys up again to wake her—and then I went up. When I saw Ruth—and touched her—I knew she must have been dead for hours."

Mrs. Surray's voice broke, and a spasm of pain passed over Richard's face, but the Professor went on:

"We have got to face this. On the table beside Ruth's bed were two papers, lying under a box of sleeping-draught tablets. One paper was a draft of her will, dated overnight, signed but unwitnessed. It made disposition of her property and appointed Vernon Montague as her literary executor, with certain precise instructions about destroying some of her manuscripts. The other sheet of paper was headed by a couplet of Spenser's:

> 'Sleep after toyle, port after stormie seas,
> Ease after warre, death after life doth greatly please.'

Beneath it she had written, 'I am tired—too tired to care any more. Good-bye.'"

There was silence for a moment after the Professor's voice had died away, until Richard said sadly:

"I am afraid there is only one interpretation of that. The papers were both in Ruth's own writing?"

"Yes; there can be no question about that, nor about the fact that both had been written recently."

"But why?" cried Mrs. Surray. "Richard, I shall ask myself that question until I die. What happened after Ruth went up to bed, to make her suddenly despair of life and decide to end it—without a thought of us, without a care for our distress? I *know* she cared for us; I know, too, that she was feeling more rested, less troubled in mind."

"We can't answer those questions," he replied gently. "None of us can probe another's mind against their will. What we have got to face now is a practical problem. If it be proved—as seems certain—that Ruth died from an overdose of an opiate, the discovery of those papers by her bedside make the coroner's verdict a foregone conclusion. If a coroner considers that the facts germane to his inquiry are so clear that no problem arises, he can sit without a jury and return his own verdict. If any question arises as to the interpretation of the facts, the inquiry becomes wider in scope and consequently more misery is involved for those who care. I would say this—out of consideration for you especially—that once the post-mortem has settled the cause of death, the briefer the inquiry, the better. It will not help Ruth—nor anybody else—if a searching scrutiny is to be made of every detail of her life. If we can avoid the horror of unnecessary probing, let us do so. On the face of it, I don't think that there can be two interpretations of the facts. There is not the remotest vestige of suspicion of any foul play. Ruth chose to end her life because her mind was weary and she could not face the effort of living: she chose 'sleep after toyle.' For God's sake let her memory rest in peace. We don't know her motive— but there is that clear explanation of overstrained nerves, of an overworked mind which reached a breaking point that no one could have foreseen. Don't ask why or wherefore. It won't help you, or Ruth, or any of us."

"So far as publicity is concerned, God knows you are right," said the Professor, "but your mother has the right to know the answer to her question, if answer there be. Do you know it, Richard?"

"No, I do not," he replied quietly, and put all the will-power he had into controlling his voice to express the certainty he was very far from feeling. Richard Surray's one desire at that moment was the instinct of a physician to prevent the spread of a deadly disease. He feared desperately that other lives might be involved in this web of emotional confusion, and he foresaw fresh misery—for his mother and father and sister—if certain possibilities were made public, were dragged into the searchlight of popular curiosity, and his voice was quite steady as he continued: "Ruth was a mature woman, no child to be cross-examined as to her actions and motives. My attitude towards her was that of a brother to his sister. She was not my patient. I respected her reticence concerning herself, and I made no inquiry into her psychic condition, barring what you already know. I did not realise that the mischief of overstrain had gone so far in her case. I thought it superficial. True, I asked her to seek advice, but my main anxiety was concerning the matter of opiates. I know only too well how a habit easily acquired can sap the very foundations of mind and will-power. The blame is mine; I am willing to take it."

He got up as he spoke, adding: "Will you not both leave the immediate problem to me for the time being? I know— better than yourselves, even—the burden of strain and fatigue which has been put upon you. The main evidence is clear. Try, both of you, to rest your minds from grappling with further implications. I think, or like to think, that I can help you a little."

Mrs. Surray was about to answer, but her husband put his hand over hers and said, "Richard is right, Nell. You must try to rest, and try not to go over this weary interminable treadmill of supposition. Ruth—don't think I judge her! God knows I do not—she laid down a burden for others to pick up. Richard has come to share it with us."

When Richard Surray left his parents together, his first thought was of Naomi. All through the preceding conversation he had been waiting for her name to be mentioned, and the only time he had heard it was when Mrs. Surray said that Naomi drove over to Stow on Sunday evening. Richard was apprehensive in his own mind that the very fact that no more had been said about her boded no good. As he crossed the hall he saw a door open—it was the door of the room which the family called "The Call Box," because it was used only for telephoning, writing brief business letters, and so forth—and Judith beckoned to him.

"I'm sitting in here muffling the damned telephone," she said. "Half the county considers it necessary to ring up and ask if it's true. No one would ever commit suicide if they had enough imagination to foresee the results. I've always maintained before that one's life was one's own and one had the right to end it. Now I know better."

"The hardest part of this life is that one can't do a thing without affecting other people, Judy," he replied. "Do you know where Naomi is?"

"On her bed, I hope, fast asleep. I gave her enough aspirin to keep her quiet," replied Judith, speaking with the elaborate casualness which was only a cover to strong feeling. "I shall get old Saunders to sign a certificate that she's dangerously ill if the police try to get at her. The kid's in an impossible state, and God knows what rubbish she'll blurt out. Is it possible to keep this inquiry 'localised,' Richard?"

"I'll do my best," he replied. "Look here, I want to see Naomi when she wakes up."

"I'll see that you do. I've locked her room door so that no one shall go in; but I'm prowling round pretty wakefully, one eye on the hall and one ear... Oh, that blasted phone. Go and talk to Montague and Co.—they're in the rose garden trying to look non-existent, poor wretches!"

Richard walked out into the garden. He understood Judith perfectly well: whatever her feelings, nothing would induce her to show them—save by this added brusqueness which she assumed as a shield, and he guessed from what she had said that she was as anxious as himself to avoid spreading the family troubles to the public gaze.

Vernon Montague was stretched out in a deck chair, immersed in a bulky manuscript; beside him sat a younger man, whom Richard knew must be Charlton Fellowes. Both men got up as Surray walked towards them, and on another occasion he might have been amused at the contrast they presented. Montague, the publisher, was an immensely long, lean creature, his height lessened by a pronounced stoop, his clothes loose and baggy, hanging untidily on to his shoulders, and giving the impression that there could be nothing but a skeleton beneath their amplitude. His hair, black and untidy, fell forward in a lock over his high narrow forehead, and his dark eyes were set beneath penthouse brows, the dark eyebrows shooting up at an odd angle away to the sides of his hollow temples. Fellowes was a square-built, compact fellow, fair of skin, noticeably erect and neat; he looked a very short figure beside Montague's sprawling six-foot three, and his fair skin seemed as fresh as a girl's in contrast to the other's pallor. Montague, pulling off his glasses with a characteristic nervous gesture, fumbled the loose sheets of his manuscript together as he hitched his long limbs awkwardly out of the deck chair, but as Richard Surray came up to him he spoke with a simple sincerity which betrayed no awkwardness at all.

"I'm so sorry, Surray—so very sorry. It would be easier for you if Fellowes and I were out of the way, but your father seemed to wish us to stay on here for to-night at least. I don't think you know Fellowes?"

Richard nodded to the younger man and replied, "It's a difficult position for you both, I know. Montague, I'd be glad of a few words with you—and with Mr. Fellowes a little later."

The younger man said, "Of course. I'll stroll down towards the paddock. You'll find me thereabouts any time you want me."

Richard sat down beside the publisher, saying, "I needn't beat about the bush with you, Montague. You knew Ruth pretty well. Is there anything you can tell me which bears on her death? You can be quite frank with me. If there is anything to tell, it's easier for you to say it to me than to my father and mother."

The other twiddled his glasses in one hand and pushed back his forelock with the other. "I was told about the will, of course, with myself as literary executor. It came as a shock—a complete surprise. Never thought of such a thing—your sister never mentioned it. God knows what made her do it... she was young enough... Is there such a thing as a brain-storm,

Surray? Some sudden submersion of reasoning? She had everything before her—everything."

"Then nothing which she said to you at any time suggested that this was in her mind? You had no inkling that she was overwrought, or distressed?"

The other dropped his glasses and twisted his long nervous fingers into knots. "When I last met her in London, a month ago, I thought she was at the very top of her form. On Saturday I thought I detected a sort of nervous tension, some sort of anxiety to keep up to concert pitch. Yesterday, I don't know. I don't know. I haven't said anything to anybody yet. You're the best judge, perhaps. We were discussing this vexed question of a hereafter, the wish of man to survive, his *will* to survive and project himself into eternity. She said something to the effect that the desire for a future life was primitive—the more developed a man's intelligence, the less he wished for immortality. For herself she expected—wished for—annihilation, blackness. Those lines of Davies's: 'Take me in my sleep, oh death, and do not wake me.' All philosophic, I thought, not impinging on reality. I don't know."

"Then there was something in her mind, or on her mind, yesterday," said Richard slowly. "You've no idea what it was? You don't know of anything which happened later in the day to upset or distress her? It's like this, Montague: If Ruth was as normal as she seems to have been yesterday, I can't understand what precipitated this. It's unlike her. You may think it's trivial reasoning, but I can't see Ruth, who had a nice sense of conscientiousness and hospitality, choosing to do a thing like this when she had the well-being of guests on her mind. I've heard her discuss suicide, quite coolly and thoughtfully, and she said, 'It's an unmannerly business. If people wish to put an end to themselves they've a perfect right to, but they might take the trouble not to inflict themselves on other people more than is necessary. It's not decent.'"

Montague shook his heavy dark head. "Can't tell. If a woman gets to that stage she doesn't reason. It's like possession. The normal faculty goes. Do I mention that conversation or not? It's just as you think. Utterly beastly, all this inquest business. No sense in it. The thing's done. Better leave it at that."

"Much better, but one can't," said Richard bitterly. "I spend my life trying to eliminate consequences of previous mistakes and accidents. So far as that conversation goes, I think you'd better give it in evidence. I shall attest myself that Ruth had been overwrought; her brain was fatigued, though I didn't realise how far the mischief had gone. About this man Stanwood. Was he there when the conversation took place?"

"Yes. We were out at Sudeley. He's all right, Surray. A reticent fellow. Not given to spreading himself. He only wants to do what he can to help you. He owed a lot to Ruth. I was fixing a contract with him. I told her. I'm glad, because it was what she wanted. The last thing I said to her."

His abrupt staccato voice sounded utterly miserable, and Richard thought again how many people had wanted to please Ruth. This big lean ugly fellow—it wasn't only the homage of a publisher to a successful writer, it was something far more intimate, a devotion which the big man would not express in words, but which showed in every twitch of his queer expressive face.

"The verdict's a foregone conclusion, isn't it?" he asked.

"Insane, they always add. A queer idea of charity. Those whom the gods wish to destroy. I'm sorry, Surray—I'd have done anything. I ought to have done something. I was here, but I just didn't see."

"No one could have done anything. Don't distress yourself with regrets. I hope the inquest will be brief—and merciful. They'll go through Ruth's papers, of course, but I'm hoping that will only be a formality. I know she destroyed letters as they came, and she didn't keep a diary. Ghastly to have one's secret thoughts paraded in the press. God! How I do loathe those papers that batten on people's miseries."

He looked up with a start as he became aware of a figure between himself and the light, and Montague, looking up also, said, "This is Stanwood, Surray. You were asking about him."

Richard got up as the other man hesitated, and went towards him, and Stanwood murmured, "I'm sorry—I didn't realise that you were here talking to Montague. I'll..."

"Won't you come and sit down?" said Richard, feeling again that anti-climax of discomfort which he had mentioned to Montague. The fact of these men being in the house, involved in the wretchedness of this inquiry—wasn't it the very thing Ruth would have hated? Stanwood looked embarrassed, as well he might—a stranger brought into close contact with a sorrowing family. He was a nondescript-looking man, with mouse-coloured hair, grey eyes, and a pale face, but he had a fine head and a certain poise that gave his figure dignity, for all his ill-fitting clothes. He sat down beside Richard, and spoke with an obvious effort:

"Sympathy at a time like this can't be expressed adequately. I've been through some bad times myself—I know. Words are useless. We only use them with our minds, and it isn't only the mind that feels."

"Thanks," said Richard, replying rather to the effort than to the words themselves. "As you say, the mind seems singularly unable to meet some demands. I was talking to Montague, and he mentioned a conversation you two had with my sister yesterday—about her own attitude to a future life."

"Yes," said Stanwood slowly. "I have been thinking about what she said. She had her own convictions on the subject. Montague was wondering whether that conversation were best forgotten. Thinking back to it, one realises that her mind was preoccupied with the subject of eternity—in the sense of eternal peace and rest. She was saying, a little bit earlier, that the mind of the writer—the creative, imaginative mind—has moments of intense depression, when inspiration fails and there is a consciousness of frustration, uselessness, as though the well had gone dry, and nothing is left but a mechanical ability to spin words. We all feel like that sometimes."

Richard nodded, his face sombre. "You and Montague, then, can both give evidence that my sister was suffering from mental depression and exhaustion. I think it is better that you should do so. For the sake of my father and mother it is best to have this inquiry as brief and simple as possible. I understand that both of you were with her in the drawing-room just before she went up to bed?"

"We were all three there—Fellowes, Stanwood, and myself," said Montague. "I was the last person to speak to her. She said, just at the door, 'I am glad you were able to come down this week-end. I feel as though I have accomplished something useful. It's a good thought—so many impulses are barren in their results. Sleep well.'"

"Miss Surray used the last of her energies to help me," said Stanwood. "I shall never forget it. She, to whom success came so easily, as her birthright, sought to share the fruits of fortune with one less happy. I owe her everything. It's not easily realisable…" Stanwood spoke awkwardly, but with intense feeling, his voice shaking, and Richard, himself reticent, shrank from the emotional element in the other man.

"By no means everything," he said quietly. "The quality of your own mind was the factor. My sister only recognised it. She had great perception."

"Without her I might have gone on—groping," replied Stanwood. "Life is like that. Ability is not enough."

Richard got up. He felt edgy and exhausted, and the intense feeling in the writer's voice grated on him. There was an emotionalism in it which had a morbid quality, and the psychologist felt that the very intensity of Stanwood's gratitude to Ruth had that tinge of excitability which was just what he—Richard—wished to avoid catching. The atmosphere was tense enough already, without further charging.

"I want to go and see my younger sister," he said abruptly. "Meantime, will you two regard yourselves as perfectly free to do what you wish? If you care to stay here until the inquest, please do so. The house is absolutely at your disposal, but since the preliminary inquiries are through, I imagine there is no reason for you to stay if you would rather go, but since you must both be here for the inquest, it may be more convenient to you to stay. I am only saying this so that you need not feel it incumbent on you to stay. I realise that the atmosphere of this place must be distressing for both of you, and though I should be glad to talk to you again later, I don't want you to feel tied. In any case, I shall be seeing you again at tea-time; but I must just go and have a word with Naomi."

He went away towards the house, and Stanwood said:

"What's the best thing to do, Montague? It's the very devil for Mrs. Surray to have visitors here now, yet she asked me to stay. She said that she wanted to talk to me again later."

"We'd better be at hand, in case Richard wants to go over the evidence, and lest there are other questions which have not yet arisen," replied Montague. "We could move our traps down to the inn: we should be near at hand if they wanted us, but not too much in the way. Will that suit you? I'll mention it to Richard later."

Richard, after another word with Judith, went up to Naomi's room. She had just woken up, and was sitting on her bed with her hands round her hunched-up knees, her eyes still dark from sleep, blue-ringed and distressed, her fair hair tumbled like a child's.

"Richard!" she cried. "This was my fault! I shall always know that I killed her!"

He came round and sat down on her bed and took her hand in his own. "Listen, Naomi, and try to understand. By giving expression to morbid and extravagant thoughts you are only making more wretchedness, when there is too much for us all to bear already. Before I let you say anything else you are to answer the questions I ask you, and to answer them without exaggeration." His voice, steady and emotionless, startled her to attention, and he went on: "We can assume from what we know that Ruth died of an overdose of an opiate. Did you administer any opiate to her? Answer that question by yes or no."

"No," she replied indignantly. "How could you…?"

"Did you know, by direct information, that Ruth intended to end her life?" His dry voice was having its effect now.

"No," she replied. "I did not."

"Did Ruth ever mention to you that she contemplated suicide, or give you any reason or indication to suppose that she contemplated it?"

"No."

"Did you have any quarrel with her, or any outspoken argument which caused the rupture of your habitual relations?"

"No."

"I know you were out of the house on Sunday evening. Did you have any conversation with Ruth earlier in the day which may have caused her great distress of mind?"

"No."

"Then in saying that you were responsible for her death, you seemed to have been talking very great nonsense," said Richard quietly, "and nonsense which is calculated to cause further unhappiness, Naomi. I am not going to let you explain to me what you meant until I have put certain points to you. Then it will be your turn to confide in me, if you wish. You see," he added, and his voice was gentler now, but still very firm, "at times like this the main point to remember is to avoid giving occasion for greater distress to others. You have got to forget yourself for the moment—and fight other people's battles."

Naomi sat very still, watching him, and he went on:

"You know that there will have to be an inquest? The verdict can only be suicide, but there will be some inquiry into

Ruth's state of mind prior to her death. You know, as I know, how much distress is caused when a dead person's intimate history is published for all the world to conjecture upon. I want to avoid that in Ruth's case—if I can. She did confide in me to the extent of telling me of her own fatigue, but beyond that she did not go. Neither, to the best of my belief, did she tell either Mother or Father about herself or her own troubles. I want you to understand my point of view, Naomi, because I am sure that you will share it. There is enough evidence to satisfy the Coroner that Ruth took her own life in a moment of mental depression, following the overstrain of months. Don't complicate things, if you can avoid it, by causing to be related in court things which Ruth tried to conceal from us all."

"Yes, I understand," she said, her brows drawn together in the frown of attention which aged her youthful face so much. "Then it would be better for me not to talk to you, not to tell you anything, lest you in turn are forced to repeat it as evidence."

"Hearsay is not evidence," he replied. "You can now tell *me* anything you wish to, Naomi, but let it be only that which can have direct bearing on Ruth's death. Stripping your words of any verbiage, getting down to cold and sober facts, is there anything which you can tell which sheds any light on it? I haven't forgotten our conversation down in the paddock, but is there anything to add to that?"

She sat brooding, looking beyond Richard and out of the sunlit window, and then turned her face to him again.

"Remembering what I told you, you would still say that Ruth's death was not my fault?"

"No one in their senses could imagine it was your fault," he replied. "You might as well say that it was mine. You haven't answered my last question, Naomi. Is there anything else that I ought to know?"

She pushed back her hair from her face with the gesture of a child and her unhappy eyes turned again to the window.

"No," she said at last. "Some time I should like to talk to you a bit more, but not now—not after what you have said. This morning, when I heard about Ruth, I think I went a little mad. I'd been dreaming, too. Is there such a thing as telepathy?"

"I don't know. Nobody knows," he replied. "It's not established, nor, perhaps, refuted. Why do you ask?"

"Because I felt as though Ruth had read my mind, and this was her answer to me—her way of beating me."

"Don't give way to thoughts like that, Naomi," he replied. "It's up to all of us to keep our heads, keep our balance. I think, though, that you'd better answer one more question. When you came in last night, did you see Ruth?"

She shook her head. "No. I came in just after half-past ten. She had gone to bed. I saw Mr. Stanwood in the hall and asked him. If I have to give evidence at the inquest, what am I to say?"

"You may be asked if you had noticed any signs of abnormality in her," he replied. "Apart from that, I doubt if you will be questioned. You were hardly with her at all yesterday, and you were out after dinner."

"She said to me last week—after you had gone, 'Take my advice and don't go in for writing. It's not worth while. One chases the shadow and loses the substance. One's mind is always at a stretch, never at peace.' Do you think she's at peace now, Richard?"

"I'm certain of it," he replied. "It's not Ruth who is to be pitied now. Her troubles are over, but Mother is terribly unhappy. You can help her, if you try."

Naomi hid her face in her hands for a minute.

"I was mad this morning," she said. "I'll go to her now, and try to make things right. I'll be very careful, Richard. I do understand."

"I think the same thing will be in all our minds," he said. "It's bad enough to have lost Ruth. She was a reticent person, when she was herself. I want to keep her dignity alive. She hated publicity. We can only do our best to save her memory from the very thing she would have hated most."

CHAPTER IV

THE INQUEST ON RUTH SURRAY HAD BEEN HELD ON THE Wednesday, two days after her death, and the verdict had been suicide. Every effort had been made by the local authorities to spare Professor Surray and his wife as much further distress as was possible, and the Coroner—a well-known medical practitioner named Wonter, who had some fame as a medical jurist—had sat without a jury, since he held the opinion that the facts were so straightforward that there could be no two opinions about them. Death had been caused by an overdose of thalmaine, a well-known drug of the barbituric group. The tablets, of which a certain number were found in the box by the bedside of the dead woman, had been supplied to her by a London doctor named Blake, a personal friend of Ruth Surray's. Giving evidence, Dr. Blake said that Miss Surray had consulted him over a month ago, saying that she suffered from sleeplessness owing to the intense mental activity of her recent work. She had eased off from that work once her book was safely in the press, and had been leading a healthy, normal life, with plenty of exercise and fresh air, but she could not sleep. She had got into the habit of working until the small hours, and now, when she needed sleep most desperately in order to recuperate, she lay awake for hour after hour and was getting ever more weary and irritable in mind. Dr. Blake had been unwilling at first to give her a sleeping draught, but eventually had done so, agreeing with her point that what she needed was to break the habit of sleeplessness; given some nights of unbroken sleep, he believed that her excellent constitution would recover its normal working. He had warned her of the nature of the drug he had given her, telling her clearly that an overdose would be fatal in effect. In reply to a question from the Coroner, he said that he had examined deceased carefully and found her general health to be sound; her mind seemed to be perfectly clear and untroubled, and he had had no apprehensions whatever of the development of any abnormality or morbidity in her nervous state. He said that he had discussed with her the whole matter of sleeping draughts, expressing his own general antipathy to their habitual use, and that Miss Surray had shown the utmost intelligence in her own comments on the subject.

At her request, he gave her the medicine in tablet form, as she had said that she might be travelling, and that tablets were easier to pack than a bottle. He had seen her again only a fortnight ago, when she had told him that she was now getting back to the habit of normal sleep, and hoped to be able to dispense with the tablets, whose occasional use had been very helpful. He had then judged her to be in good health and entirely normal in mind.

Apart from the formal evidence as to the finding of the

body, and the time of death, those who had been staying at Upwood House gave evidence concerning Ruth's state of mind immediately previous to her death, and Richard Surray described his own observations of her fatigued mental condition, and the fact that he had asked her to consult a fellow psychologist. He stated frankly that he blamed himself for not having appreciated the fact that his sister's mental state was serious. He had thought that immediate rest and change would restore her to normality, and he had not judged her to be in a pathological state. He said that he would not have believed it possible that she would commit suicide, but qualified this opinion by the statement that his sister was an unusually reticent woman whose mind was difficult to fathom. He had not examined her as he would have examined a patient who was consulting him—in fact, his sister had told him that she was perfectly well, and it was only by his own observation that he had gathered there was anything amiss with her. He had thought that a rest in the peaceful atmosphere of Upwood would restore her normal vigour and poise.

After Richard Surray had given evidence, Inspector Green stated the findings of the police. In examining the papers in the dead woman's study in her London flat, the Inspector had found a series of notes and a completed essay dealing with the subject of suicide, and making out a case for the right of the individual to end his or her life. These papers were handed to the Coroner, together with a copy of an earlier will, the latter duly witnessed and signed. In this document the disposition of her property was the same as in the will found by Ruth Surray's bedside. All money in her possession, or any sums accruing to her from royalties after her death, was to be invested to form a trust, the income from which was to be expended in a biennial prize to the writer of a first novel published within two years after her death, and every subsequent two years. James Vaughan and Hilary Woods were appointed as arbiters of the award, with a request to them that they should name their own successors in order that the scheme might be perpetuated. In the first will Richard Surray was named as literary executor, and given a free hand to deal as he thought fit with his sister's unpublished MSS. In the second will, Vernon Montague was appointed to the office, but with definite instructions as to destroying the greater number of Ruth's papers.

The Coroner finally summed up very simply, stating his reasons for his verdict, and ending on a note of intense sympathy with the family of deceased, and a word of sincere regret at the loss of a writer whose work was valued by every lover of literature.

The inquest over, Richard Surray was aware of a tremendous sense of relief. The thing he had dreaded had not come to pass, and the material facts dealt with had given no loophole to scandalmongers or gossips. The tragedy had been bitter enough, but the family had been spared the indignity and horror which so many people suffer under like circumstances, when the words "Sensational Revelations at Inquest" plaster the sheets of newsvendors throughout the country.

On the Saturday after Ruth's death, Richard went back to his rooms in Bloomsbury. Judith, with her baby, was staying at Upwood House. Naomi had gone with her friends to the Hebrides—this on Richard's advice. He knew the Underwoods with whom she was staying, and he judged them to be wise and sympathetic companions for her. He had arranged for her to join him later on his journey to the Rockies, and felt that the present arrangement was the wisest one that could be made.

Settling down at his study table, he looked at the pile of letters awaiting him. During his absence from town he had given his secretary, at his Harley Street rooms, instructions to deal with letters delivered to him there. The private correspondence sent to his flat in Berry Street had not been forwarded, and it was to this he now turned his attention. Letters of sympathy—Richard sighed as he began to open them. It was good of people to write. What could one's friends do but write? And yet it meant that these letters had to be opened, read, and acknowledged. He almost wished that he were friendless, that he could light his pipe and open a book, and try to forget all the distresses of the preceding week, and then, as he lifted another letter and glanced at the writing on the envelope, his heart seemed to give a jump upwards and then to stop. This was Ruth's handwriting. The letter was addressed to "Richard Surray, Esq., 29 Gower Street, London, W.C." It was scrawled over with "Not known here." "Not known at 19, 39, or 49." "R. Surray gone away— left no address," and "Try 29 Berry Street." The letter had been wandering for days. He knew just what Ruth had done. He used to live in Gower Street. She had put the number of his present address in Berry Street and the name of the street where he had lived for several years, and this letter had been handed in at one address after another by the painstaking postal authorities until some one had recognised his name and written "Try 29 Berry Street." With a mouth that was dry and hands that were steady but very cold, he slit open the envelope.

That same Saturday afternoon, Chief-Inspector Macdonald was at home in his rooms in the Grosvenor Road. Looking very unlike a policeman, and, feeling at peace with the world, he was playing over Toscanini's rendering of the "Haffner" Symphony on his gramophone, a miniature score in his long capable hands, his feet up on the top of another chair while he reclined in the depths of a capacious "Minty," when his telephone bell rang. With an expression of extreme disgust he got up, lifted the needle carefully from the disc and went to silence the intruding noise. It was certainly not possible to listen to Mozart and ignore the telephone. Neither was it possible for a C.I.D. man to cut off his telephone, even on a peaceful Saturday afternoon when he had earned his leisure by many hours' overtime in the previous week. He lifted the receiver and listened. "Surray? Yes, of course… Certainly, if you think I can help. Oh, I'll come along to you. I'm quite free. I shall be glad to help if I can. You were very helpful to me. In about twenty minutes? Right."

It was rather less than twenty minutes later that Macdonald was shown into Richard Surray's study. The Chief Inspector had thought when he first saw the psychologist that the man looked tired and worn, but on this occasion he looked really ill; his pale face was heavily lined and the dark eyes seemed to have sunk back into their sockets.

"It's good of you to come," said Richard. "I'm in trouble, and I want your advice. You heard about my sister's death?"

"Yes. I was very sorry," replied the other.

"Did you read the evidence at all?"

"Yes. Fully."

"That's a great help. I shan't have to go over it all again." He took up a letter and handed it to Macdonald. "This was written to me by my sister and posted, presumably by her, some time on the evening before she died. It has only just reached me; you can see for yourself that it's been wandering about, owing to being misdirected. Will you read it, please?"

Macdonald, after examining the envelope, drew out the letter and read it. It was headed "Upwood," Sunday evening.

"DEAR RICHARD," it ran, *"I've had you on my conscience, rather. I know you've been worrying about me although, like the sensible creature you are, you didn't fuss. You looked so tired yourself that it's not fair you should be burdened with unnecessary worries about me. I did feel pretty poor a week or so back; life had been rather wearing one way and another, and insomnia always pulls one down. I feel marvellously better now. Upwood is lovely—I can't think why I don't spend more time here, and Mother has been the ideal companion for a work-worn 'intellectual.' (How Judy loathes that word!) We (Mother and I) have got the Spitzbergen jaunt well planned out. I'm coming up to town on Tuesday to see Cook's. Could we lunch together? A picnic would suit me, either in your rooms or my own. Phone me here on Monday evening if you can manage it—after all, you must eat somewhere and some time. Take care of yourself—and bless you.—RUTH."*

Macdonald looked up as he finished reading and met Richard Surray's eyes. "Before we go any further," said the latter, "I should like to tell you what has been the chief thought in my mind since I heard of my sister's death. I wanted to spare my parents any more distress. Ruth was dead—I ought to have been able to help her, but I failed. She was beyond my help. They were suffering, and I tried to manage things in such a way that they were not called upon to endure fresh pain. Let me make this quite clear: I believed that Ruth killed herself, and that her mind was deranged when she did so. The papers she left by her bedside, and what I knew of her previous state of mental tension, seemed to indicate only one thing—suicide; but I *did* endeavour not to have her emotional distresses published for other people's entertainment. To my mind that was irrelevant from the point of view of justice, and intolerable from the point of view of our father and mother. This"—pointing to the letter—"proves that I was wrong."

"Let us go into things more fully," said Macdonald, deliberately refraining from any comment on what the other had said. "This letter is dated 'Sunday evening' by your sister. The cancelling stamp is Monday morning—8.45 a.m."

Richard nodded. "Yes. The Sunday post goes out from Upwood at six in the evening. The letters at home are taken down to the post box in the village by one of the servants, about half-past five. That letter was posted some time between the clearance of the box on Sunday evening at six o'clock and its clearance on Monday morning at 8.45. Now I know that Ruth did not go out to post a letter herself between six o'clock and half-past ten. I have been told exactly what she was doing during those hours; she had no time either to write or post a letter. That one must have been written after she went up to bed at half-past ten, and it is probable that she came down and went to the post with it herself. It was a fine night, and I have often known her walk to the post just before going to bed; she liked the walk, and said that it freshened her up. Now can you imagine any woman—especially one of Ruth's type—writing and posting that letter, and then going home to write out her will and a farewell message and deliberately to take an overdose of thalmaine?"

"On the face of it, no. I can't believe it," said Macdonald; "but there are other points to consider. You don't know that she posted the letter herself, neither can you be quite certain that she had no time to write it earlier in the evening. One can assume that Miss Surray went to her room to dress for dinner. She may have written this letter then, and have asked somebody to post it for her."

"I know that she did not ask anybody to post a letter for her during the evening, because I asked, for reasons of my own," replied Richard. "She actually stated on Sunday evening that she had written no letters for a week, and that her correspondence was all in arrears."

"Then what conclusions do you draw from this?" asked Macdonald quietly. "You had better express your own view first, and we will examine all other possibilities later."

Richard put his hand up to his eyes with the unconscious gesture of a desperately weary man.

"I assume that she went upstairs and wrote that letter," he said. "Later, when everything in the house was quiet, she came down, let herself out by the conservatory door, and walked to the post, in order that her letter should reach me (as it would have done had it been properly addressed) by tea-time. Then she walked home again. Her death occurred about three o'clock in the morning, as far as can be judged. After Ruth posted that letter, either something happened which altered her state of mind completely—or she did not kill herself at all."

He sat up here and looked Macdonald straight in the face. "It is because of that last possibility that I asked you to come and talk to me," he said. "If I were still certain—as I was previously—that Ruth killed herself, I could justify myself in destroying that letter. She was by nature a reticent woman; she hid a great deal of herself from the world, even from those whom she loved and trusted. I don't want to outrage her reticence now that she is dead." The eyes that met Macdonald's had a look of appeal in them now. "I have been sitting for the past two hours arguing this thing with myself. I've been on the point of burning that letter a dozen times. If Ruth *did* kill herself, what earthly good can arise from opening the whole wretched problem again? It can't help anybody, and it will inevitably cause more misery. I'm putting this matter to you because I know that you will look at it with humanity and intelligence, not only with the mind of the official. If it had been your sister who had died, your mother who would suffer from the reopening of an inquisition, what would you have done?"

"I can only say that the problem of your own behaviour is settled for you by your use of the word 'if,' in reference to your sister's death," replied Macdonald. "It is not for me to judge the wisdom or unwisdom of your previous reticence concerning her when you were convinced that she had taken her own life. Once the faintest suspicion of uncertainty has crept in, there is only one course open to you—the one you took when you showed me that letter. Against your own reason you hoped that I might say, 'Destroy it.' You know that I could not say it, neither could you bring yourself to do it. I realise perfectly well the pain which this must cause you, but there is no choice."

"No," replied Richard quietly. "I suppose there isn't."

When Macdonald spoke again, the latter deliberately cut all sympathy out of his voice, and proceeded as though he were stating a case to a jury.

"It is the business of the Coroner to gather all the facts having a bearing on the death whose cause he is investigating, particularly the last known actions of the deceased. At the inquest, in the absence of other information, it was assumed that Miss Surray went straight to her room and stayed there after she had said, 'good-night.' You have proved to your own satisfaction that she did not do so; she came downstairs again and walked to the post. She may have met some one out of doors; she may have talked to some one who was staying in the house, or even have admitted a visitor. You argue—quite rightly, to my thinking—that something happened to her after she had written that letter to you. It might have been something which altered her whole outlook, and caused her to commit suicide. It might be something totally different which alters the entire case, so that the verdict of suicide is no longer tenable. One thing is certain—the evidence produced was incomplete and consequently misleading. It has to be reconsidered."

"That being so," replied Richard, "is it possible for you

to help us in this way? If I put before you every scrap of evidence obtainable, giving you access to every material fact, and putting before you every idea which may have occurred to me, could you personally put the investigation through and report it further if need arise? I still grasp at the hope that the verdict can stand without our being subjected to publicity. If Ruth did kill herself, even though further evidence be forthcoming, there is surely no necessity to publish every particle of it immediately, to focus the attention of everybody by a renewal of public inquiry? Can you not investigate unofficially at first, until you can draw some conclusion as to the rightness of the verdict?"

Macdonald shook his head. "Whatever my own attitude is, and no matter how strong my anxiety to help you as a friend, I cannot investigate unofficially. From the point of view of my own job, it's impossible. Neither would it be desirable. I can only say this: The evidence relevant to your sister's death went through my hands. It was one of those cases which, while seeming obvious at first sight, are subjected to greater scrutiny than is generally realised. In some cases a Coroner's verdict has been reversed when fresh evidence has been procured. Sometimes a verdict has to stand even when it is considered unsatisfactory, because there is no evidence obtainable to enable the police to go forward. Since this case must be reopened, there is a possibility that I may be put in charge of it. There was some correspondence on the matter, and the county authorities would, I think, be glad of assistance in a difficult case."

Richard Surray stared. "Then the police were not satisfied—they allowed that verdict to go through...?" His voice broke, and Macdonald went on:

"I have said that there are cases when the findings at the inquest are reconsidered. It is all a matter of available evidence. Let us leave that for the moment, but believe me when I say that if there is any possible way in which I can help you, I will. I understand your feelings on the subject of publicity, and your anxiety to spare your parents further distress, but you—and they—will agree that a wrong verdict cannot be allowed to stand."

Richard Surray looked at the lean, clear-cut face of the Chief Inspector and met the glance of his observant grey eyes. When he had first talked to Macdonald he had liked him, liked his clear, straightforward intelligence, his humanity, and his anxiety to have a job done properly, without reference to his own personal prestige. Watching him now, Surray knew that there was an element of ruthlessness, too, in that clear mind. Macdonald was not the man to let sentiment interfere with his job. Humane he might be, but he would stop at nothing in the pursuit of justice, and to him justice could only be obtained by minute examination of the evidence—all the evidence, omitting nothing.

"That I admit," replied Richard; "yet if you consider the facts, admitting the validity of the will and the farewell message, can any other explanation than suicide be arrived at? You know who was staying in the house—four people, all of whom were devoted to Ruth. Montague—an old and trusted friend; Stanwood, whose gratitude to Ruth was unquestioned, and whose admiration for her was unbounded; Fellowes; and Mrs. Trant, the most normal, healthy people who ever lived. It's impossible to associate them with the idea of murder, more impossible still to credit them with a motive for such an action."

Richard broke off and stared at the Chief Inspector with a question written large all over his face.

"Can you imagine any of those four people inducing Ruth to write her will and a farewell message—she being in a perfectly normal and cheerful state of mind? Remember that your present hypothesis is that she did not kill herself or intend to kill herself. For reasons unknown, she was persuaded to write those documents; then a triple dose of thalmaine was administered, and finally the documents were placed at her bedside with nobody's fingerprints on them but her own. Does that sound reasonable to you?" Richard got up here and began to pace the room as though he could no longer bear to sit still. "The whole thing suggests the craziest solutions!" he cried. "Take it that Ruth *was* murdered. The obtaining of those documents which presupposed suicide can only be explained by the most extravagant and ludicrous suppositions. Do you imagine that she was put into a state of hypnosis, and in that state it was suggested to her that she re-write her will and take an overdose of thalmaine?"

"If that were possible, it is an explanation which would meet the facts," replied Macdonald. "I gather, from the manner in which you speak of it, that you are satisfied it is not possible?"

"That suggestions can be made to a subject while the latter is in a state of hypnosis seems established," replied Surray. "The hypnotic state can only be induced with the consent—more, with the co-operation, of the subject. The popular fallacy concerning hypnotic powers exercised against the active will of the subject has no foundation on fact; moreover, the power to induce an hypnotic state is limited to very few individuals. I do not believe for one moment that a course of action involving the writing of an elaborate and detailed document could be suggested under those conditions. Moreover, Ruth was not a person who would ever have consented to place herself in the hands of an hypnotist. I have discussed the matter with her, and she held that nothing is known with any certainty of the working of the mind in this way, and she would not have risked subjecting her will to another's, even for the most trivial experiment." He shook his head as he came to a halt by the fireplace, leaning back with his arms stretched against the mantel. "There is no reasonable explanation which meets the facts according to your murder hypothesis. The other—that Ruth did suffer some experience which changed her whole mental outlook, between the hours of half-past ten and three o'clock on the night she died—that I am willing to believe."

"When you first spoke to me this afternoon," went on Macdonald, "you admitted that you had observed certain reticences concerning her at the inquest. That is no longer possible. Whatever you know about her had better be told plainly—else the ensuing inquiry may result in the very publicity which you dread. From the police point of view, I can assure you that nothing will be published unnecessarily, but this conversation of ours will be valueless, and any help which I may try to render you made null if you cannot bring yourself to be quite frank."

He looked steadily at the other man. "You are afraid of something, Dr. Surray. Since you have trusted me so far, since you have shown me that letter greatly against your own wishes in certain respects, why not trust me with the rest of it? The most painful way of getting evidence—from the point of view of the witnesses' feelings—is extracting it by fractions."

"No. I'm not afraid of anything," began Richard, and he saw Macdonald's face alter.

"As you will. Then your simplest course is to report the arrival of this letter to your Coroner…"

Richard interrupted him with a sound that was half a cry, half a groan.

"Oh, damn you! I suppose you're right. Sit down again… This is just what I've been trying to avoid for the whole of the last four days…"

CHAPTER V

BY THE TIME THAT MACDONALD REACHED HIS OWN home again, after his long conversation with Richard Surray, the Chief Inspector knew exactly what was the line of thought which had caused the look of fear and horror which the psychologist had not been able to conceal from the acute eyes of the C.I.D. man. It was a curious situation, for both men were experts in the art of questioning, and both were accustomed to interpreting the exact shade of meaning which lay behind any hesitation or over-eagerness in answering their questions. Richard, once he had made up his mind to take Macdonald fully into his confidence, omitted nothing, and Macdonald was left with an intense feeling of sympathy for him.

Richard began by telling of his first realisation that there was any intimacy underlying the acquaintance between Ruth and Keith Brandon. Surray himself had been present at a dinner on the first Monday in July when his sister sat beside the explorer, but on that occasion there had been nothing in their manner to indicate anything but the intelligent association of two people who were thrown together on a social occasion, yet the following evening Richard had dined at Layo's—a quietly expensive restaurant off Berkeley Street—and had seen his sister and Brandon dining together there, and their attitude had been very different from that of the previous evening. Richard, sitting at a table a little behind the other two, had observed Brandon immediately and had seen the explorer's fair handsome head bent smilingly towards his companion; the latter was a woman, and Richard, knowing Brandon's habit of easy intimacy with women, had avoided making his presence obvious to the explorer. Brandon by himself was one thing, Brandon in company with a woman quite a different bag of tricks. It was not until nearly the end of his meal that Richard, who was dining with an American colleague, had turned right round to bow to an acquaintance farther down the room, and had seen that Brandon's vis-a-vis was Ruth herself. Richard saw her in profile, her beautiful dark head bent forward, her lips parted, her eyes fixed on her companion's face in a way which told him that she was oblivious to everything except the man whom she was watching. A sense of intense discomfort overcame Surray. He felt that he had intruded into a secret which he was not meant to share; that one glimpse of his sister's face had told him something which he would rather not have known. "Brandon is quite frankly a womaniser," he said to Macdonald, disgust on his weary face. "He enjoys that reputation and lives up to it. He's a right to his own notions of amusement and the women who have been associated with him have generally been of his own way of thinking, but to see Ruth, with that expression on her face, for a fellow like Keith Brandon—that was too much to swallow." In the pause which followed, Macdonald had asked if Surray had ever spoken to his sister on the subject, but the psychologist shook his head. Ruth, he said, was no child, but a woman of mature mind who needed no guidance in the ways of human beings. She lived among people who were in the habit of speaking their minds on any subject and her attitude to moral questions was one of cool impartiality. If she chose to have an affair with Brandon it was nobody's business but her own and she would certainly have resented any advice or interference from her brother. "I saw her face that evening," said Richard. "I thought that I knew her so well that I could picture her under any circumstances, but then I saw something which I had no power to imagine. To talk to a woman with that expression on her face and my own sister at that—no."

Richard went on to narrate that he learnt of Ruth's visit to the Downings; that visit, he was certain, was dictated by Brandon's presence there, for Ruth hated week-end visits as a rule. It was not until this juncture in his story that he mentioned Naomi and told Macdonald of the girl's infatuation for the same man who had been the first to light up Ruth's face with the passionate love of a woman for a man. "It was the sort of situation which fairly takes your breath away," he said to Macdonald. "Naomi knew that Ruth's feelings were involved, but she was in a queer, bitter, unreasoning mood. No one, man or woman, is quite sane when they are in love. You can't move them with facts or arguments; you've just got to wait until they recover some degree of sanity. I was in two minds. I could have said to Naomi, 'Do you realise what type of man this one is?'—and she would have replied, 'Tell that to

Ruth. I don't care—and I don't believe you. If the immaculate Ruth can be friends with him, that's a good enough testimonial to his value. You're only repeating smoking-room gossip, and in any case I don't care what you say.'"

Macdonald nodded; although he did not know any of the three people involved in the difficult triangle, he could see the difficulty of Surray's position.

"I thought it over," went on Richard, "and the only thing I could think of was to approach Brandon himself. I knew him pretty well at one time. In fact we were friends until he got himself in a mess and came to me to help him out of it. I needn't go into all that; I undertook to keep silent over it, and shall continue to do so, as other people besides Brandon are involved. It's enough to say that I was able to do him a service and in the process to lose any feelings of friendliness I once held towards him. When I left Upwood on the Monday evening—my mother's birthday—I found out that Brandon was in town and went to see him. Having told him that I had noticed his friendship with my sister, I went on to tell him that unless that friendship ceased I would take steps to make certain of his doings known in such a way that he would lose the backing he had been promised for his next expedition. In other words, I warned him off. It sounds as though it might have been a violent interview, with potentialities of shouting and bloody heads, but it was nothing of the kind. Brandon listened to me quite quietly, with a sort of amused smile, and finally gave me an undertaking not to speak to 'my sister' at any time if he could reasonably avoid it, and in any case to discontinue 'his friendship.' I could have shot him for that!" burst out Richard. "I'd got the undertaking I wanted and the obvious indifference with which he gave it made me see red. If I'd been capable of thrashing him, I'd have done it—great hefty animal, sitting there smiling! There's a cussedness in human nature; I'd got what I wanted, and the very ease of obtaining it made me more savage than if he'd told me to go to hell, or smashed my face in a blinding rage. His attitude was 'What do *I* care about your sister—or sisters? There's as good fish in the sea as ever came out of it.' My God!—I'd..."

For a man who, as Macdonald knew, was not given to swearing, Richard Surray produced some surprisingly original and telling invective, and the outburst did him good. A little colour returned to his haggard face and his eyes lost a little of their weariness as he resumed his story. "So far as I could see, I'd settled the situation where Brandon was concerned. He understood me perfectly well, and he wasn't intending to try conclusions with me. He's an ambitious beggar, but he's got no money of his own. In order to carry out this new Tibetan expedition he's got to have financial backing and old Griffin's putting up most of the money. Griffin would drop the chap like a hot coal if I told him a few facts. That was that. Now we come back to the main part of the story."

Surray went on to describe the conditions at home with Ruth and Naomi staying in the house, on the surface at any rate ignoring the bitterness which each felt. At last he came to the previous Sunday evening, and it was here that he hesitated and became confused, so that Macdonald had to make out the main thread of the other's apprehensions for himself. Thinking it over, the Chief Inspector was not surprised that Surray floundered miserably, contradicted himself and tried to cover up his own thoughts. Two ideas emerged from his troubled suppositions. The first being that Naomi, who said that she had driven over to Stow, had in reality met Brandon during the course of the evening; the second that Ruth had become aware of their meeting, or had even encountered them herself. In his arguments to and fro over the unhappy business, Richard suggested that Naomi had managed to get in touch with Brandon on the telephone and had urged him to the surreptitious meeting, and that Ruth coming upon them when she went to post her letter, had suffered just that emotional revulsion which had led her to take her life. It had seemed to Richard that there must be some reason why Ruth had cut out his own name as literary executor from her will, and it occurred to him that had there been a meeting between herself and Naomi and Brandon, his own name might have been mentioned between them, and his interference made plain.

Macdonald had begun to question him at this point, in order to get some coherence into the string of suppositions which Surray poured out.

"Your sister Naomi drove over to Stow after dinner and returned just after half-past ten. During that time, even supposing that she met Brandon, Ruth could not have seen them or become aware of their meeting. If Ruth *did* see them, it must have been later, when she went to the post."

"When Naomi came in," replied Richard miserably, "she asked if Ruth had gone to bed. Did she then go up to Ruth's room and tell her about her own meeting with Brandon—or even ask her to meet him to thresh the whole thing out? You may say that such a thing is beyond probability, but remember the type of women they are—given to controlling their feelings and to arriving at conclusions by discussion. Did

Naomi say with that misleading pedantry of hers, 'Let us discuss this thing like reasonable beings. Have we not sufficient self-control to settle our affairs rationally?' It may sound ludicrous to you, but it's not impossible as I see it." He broke off here, and said again, as he had kept on saying throughout the conversation, "What earthly good am I doing by going over all this? What object can be served by dragging out the whole wretched story? If those three did meet, and Ruth killed herself in consequence, am I to drag her name through the mud, and ensure that all the world knows how she lost her heart to a man like Brandon, and killed herself because he preferred her younger sister? Am I to be the instrument to break Naomi too, and involve her in a horror which will poison her life almost before it has begun? Aren't things bad enough already, without you and me digging over it all, like dogs over a buried bone?"

"Once again I remind you that you have no choice," Macdonald had replied. "When you admitted to that word 'if' in connection with your sister's death, you knew that you had to face these questions. You are losing sight of the main point. To my mind it is by no means certain that she did kill herself, and you cannot acquiesce in a verdict which may be unjust."

Yet Macdonald, who was a fair man, understood Richard Surray's fears and sympathised with him wholeheartedly. From the latter's point of view, and that of his family, it might have been better had Richard swallowed his own scruples and destroyed Ruth's letter without ever telling any one of its existence. Macdonald tried to place himself in the same predicament and imagine his own line of conduct. Could he have destroyed the letter—that voice from the dead, in which Ruth had said she was so "marvellously better," in order that such peace of mind as was left to the family might not be utterly destroyed?

It was a hard question to answer; hardest of all for Richard, whose real fear was that his youngest sister was responsible, directly or indirectly, for Ruth's death.

Macdonald had avoided questioning him too much about Naomi. Questions there would have to be eventually, but it was fairer—and less brutal—to ask them of Naomi directly than to ask Richard to supply evidence at second-hand and let him see the trend of the inquiry. It was towards the end of their interview that Richard had said, "It's a pretty bitter paradox. We used to be a byword—a synonym almost—amongst our friends, for our good fortune! People said we got everything that we wanted. One of us had only to sit an exam. or compete for a prize, and we got it. My mother's only complaint in the world was that none of us had ever failed an exam. We're inbred to brains—come of a family of scholars on either side. It doesn't pay. The brain that's overstrained breaks in contact with the coarseness of reality, among women more easily than among men. Brains! My God, have their minds helped Ruth and Naomi, their minds which were the finest imaginable?"

Macdonald, when he had finally left Surray, had undertaken the business of reopening the inquiry. The Coroner and the police of Upwood had to be acquainted with the fact of Ruth Surray's letter. Thereafter it was for them to decide what further steps were to be taken, but Macdonald held out no hope that the matter would be allowed to rest there.

The phrasing of the letter cut away the ground on which the verdict of suicide had rested and no police authorities would acquiesce in leaving things as they stood.

Carrying out his promise to Richard Surray, Macdonald did a thing he had never done before; he went to his own immediate chief—Colonel Wragley, the Assistant Commissioner—and asked that if the co-operation of the Yard were asked, he might have the handling of the case.

"It's a wretched business, sir, whichever way you look at it, but the more I consider it, the more I think it's possible that this is a case of murder, and an extraordinarily cunning case. It may not be possible to get any proof, but it's the sort of problem which calls for scrutiny at every turn. One can't afford to take anything, or any one, for granted."

"How do you fit that matter of the will and the farewell message into a theory of murder?" demanded Wragley. "Do you think the experts were mistaken and those papers were forged? You won't get much support on those lines. Jack and Willman, who examined the papers, were positive that deceased wrote them."

"I think she wrote them, too, but not to provide a verdict of suicide for herself," replied Macdonald. "My opinion's not worth having until I've looked into things more fully—I'd better wait and see if it's asked for."

"They'll probably be glad to have you," replied Wragley (referring to the County Police). "It's one of those problems which makes the average Super. wish he'd never been born. If the case comes our way, you can have it."

With which assurance, Macdonald went back to the copy of the evidence given at the inquest, on which his own opinion had already been sought. He had replied then that the verdict seemed to be consistent with the evidence, and since it seemed improbable that further evidence would be forthcoming, he had left it at that.

Brandon's name was not mentioned from first to last. All of those who had given evidence had attested in one way or another that Ruth Surray had been depressed and overwrought. Richard had confined himself to telling of his own conversation with Ruth and his observations upon it. He had been able to be strictly truthful and had not broken the letter of the law in any way, for Macdonald knew that Brandon's name had never been mentioned between Surray and the dead woman. Yet had the former told all that he knew or given the least hint of what he surmised, the inquiry might have proceeded on very different lines.

Macdonald went home in a very thoughtful mood. Officially he had, as yet, no standing in the case. It was not his business to set any inquiry on foot until he received instructions, but he felt unable to leave the matter alone and settle down to his own affairs as though Richard Surray had not called on him for help.

For that evening, at any rate, Macdonald found himself very much in the position of unofficial observer which Surray had suggested he might be able to maintain, and he determined to spend the evening in acquiring what facts he could. Obviously the first thing to be done was to fill in the gap in the evidence concerning the *dramatis personae* of the case. Brandon, through the medium of Surray's evidence, seemed to cast his shadow across the stage and yet had made no appearance on it, and it was on Brandon that Macdonald's attention fixed.

Just before dinner, the Chief Inspector rang up the explorer's rooms in Jermyn Street and gathered the information that Brandon was dining at "The Mountaineers," in Cork Street, and giving a private view of the film taken in his last expedition. It was, Macdonald gathered, an informal occasion, when only the members of the club would be present, not a "guest-night" or one of those occasions when "The Mountaineers" held a reception at which you might find most of the famous names in society.

Having got thus far, Macdonald sat and pondered for a while and then put through another call, this time to James Menzies, an elderly lawyer who had been a noted climber in his day. Macdonald was not a "Mountaineer," either in the sense of being a member of the famous club, or in that of being an Alpine enthusiast, but he was a fine rock climber, and had made Menzies' acquaintance in the Lake district, when the two men had met while negotiating peaks in the neighbourhood of Striding Edge. Menzies was a typical Scots lawyer, shrewd, learned, and discreet to the point of terseness, and Macdonald knew that he could trust him absolutely.

The Chief Inspector's luck was in. Menzies was just about to set out for "The Mountaineers," and Macdonald asked quite straightforwardly if it would be possible for himself to come to the club after dinner, either to see the film or to hear any of the discussion which might follow. The man at the other end of the line took his time over answering.

"I'm not saying it's impossible," he said at length, "but I should like to know this. Is it the film that interests you, or something else?"

"Something else," replied Macdonald. "Officially speaking,

I've no rights in the matter. I have been asked by a friend to help in a certain problem and it's possible that I may be put on to it officially later. For this evening it's my own pigeon."

"Is it Brandon who interests you?"

"Yes. I want a chance of observing him, and of talking to him if it comes my way. He may touch the case if the case materialises. I've nothing against him and no right to question him."

The other chuckled. "No official status. No case. Just a matter of human curiosity. Well…I'll warn you, Brandon's not the fellow to allow liberties, and he's not likely to forget a face once he's seen it. He's got weak points, but he's not altogether a fool… On your own head be it. Since it's not the film which interests you, it'd be better if you looked in later. Make it ten o'clock. Ask for me and I'll see what I can do."

Macdonald thanked him and rang off and then had his own dinner. With best part of two hours to spare he dressed and then went out into the fine summer evening and made his way to Jermyn Street. Here he found the constable on point duty, an elderly but eminently trustworthy fellow named Harris, whom Macdonald had known for some years. Warning the constable that his inquiries were confidential and must not be divulged, he inquired if Harris knew Brandon by sight and what make of car the latter drove. Harris not only knew Brandon to look at, but had had occasion to speak to him about "making an obstruction" by leaving his car standing beyond the permitted length of time. The car was a Humber saloon, number AXO 9876. Knowing the reliability of the trustworthy though slow-witted Harris, Macdonald determined to risk a further step.

"You know where he garages his car?"

"Yes, sir. At Broad's, just off Twist Street."

"Then go along to Broad's and see if you can find out if the Humber was in the garage on last Sunday night; you can say that you are investigating a complaint of a collision which took place about 11.30, and that you think the number of the Humber was similar to that given you by an eye-witness. You noticed the Humber coming out of the garage—and finally you've been mistaken over the whole thing. The number you want is really AXQ. Got that? Just casual inquiries, nothing important."

"Yes, sir. Report to you at the Yard?"

"No. I'll make a point of seeing you later. This is unofficial, remember. Just between you and me."

Harris nodded. He liked Macdonald, and their trust was mutual. The Chief Inspector never let his men down. "Very good, sir. I'll see to it, and see it goes no further."

Leaving Jermyn Street, Macdonald took a bus up to Fleet Street, where he had many useful acquaintances, and spent best part of an hour over the odd occupation of scanning files of one of the best-known "Society" dailies. Keith Brandon was being lionised, and when he was present at a function, reporters promptly noted it. On Sunday evening, July 28th, Mr. Brandon's name was "among those present" at the Stage Society's presentation of *Shadowy Heights*. Turning to a dramatic critique, Macdonald learnt with much satisfaction that the play centred around an Englishman who had become a Buddhist monk, and that one scene represented a lamaserie in Tibet. With his usual thoroughness, Macdonald sought out a reporter who was able to give him a good outline of the play, and who also produced a programme.

This accomplished, he hastened back to Jermyn Street, en route for Cork Street, and found that Harris had done his job and was able to report that the Humber had been taken out of the garage at seven o'clock on the evening of Sunday the 28th, and been returned in the early hours of Monday morning, the 29th, between four o'clock and five.

At ten o'clock Macdonald presented himself at "The Mountaineers" and asked for Mr. Menzies. After a few minutes of friendly conversation, during which the matter of the telephone call was not mentioned, Menzies got up and led the way into a comfortable smoking-room where a group of men were sitting yarning round the open window. Indicating a chair to Macdonald, his host said casually, "You know, Jarret, I expect?" as a large grizzled man pushed back his chair a little to make room for the newcomer. A nod was all that was necessary in reply, and Macdonald sat back in his chair and produced his pipe; nobody took any notice of him; in that easy circle of friendly experts, if old Menzies liked "to bring a chap in," they left the chap to find his own level, and the conversation went on blithely. Weights, heights, oxygen, endurance: less weight and less oxygen…the burden of the cylinders when every step was a supreme effort…a slow advance, a final effort unhampered by overmuch equipment… Macdonald had heard that sort of thing before, and settled down to listen, not anxious to obtrude himself.

Mr. Justice Hassocks was sitting in the far corner, and though the learned judge was reputed to be as blind as a bat Macdonald did not want to draw the glance of those near-sighted old eyes. Looking round through his cloud of pipe smoke, Macdonald recognised Tolling, the man who climbed Mount Mackinlay, and Hall, of Mount Kenya fame, before his eyes came to rest on Keith Brandon himself. The latter was sprawling across his chair, arguing good-humouredly with Hall. A very big fellow, unusually large for a climber, Brandon was beginning to put on weight after his summer among the fleshpots. He was fair-skinned, deeply tanned, with a fine shaped head well set on a long neck and sloping shoulders. There was a magnificent vitality about him, and he had a look of easy self-assurance and good temper, and a handsomeness of feature that it was difficult to carp over. His good looks were so eminently a matter of fine proportion, from the solid brow to the square cleft jaw, well-shaped ears, and magnificent teeth. This was no "matinée idol" type of good looks. Strip him of his fine clothes and set him to work sweating under a tropical sun in shorts and singlet and he would look his best, thought Macdonald, who admired physical fineness when he saw it. A magnificent animal, this one, with a reputation for dogged determination and the endurance of an Arctic wolf.

Macdonald, who could see a lot without appearing to watch, had turned his head away from Brandon and was looking at Tolling's lantern-jawed face when he became aware that Brandon was watching him. He turned his head again and met the stare of the surprisingly blue eyes. Macdonald was not a quick-tempered nor impulsive man, but something stirred within him at the calm appraising stare of the big man with the flushed fair face; it was as though the Scots blood in his veins moved to a challenge, and something inside him grew taut as he met that coolly insolent stare. It was then that Brandon unexpectedly gave him his opening.

"Haven't I seen you somewhere before?" he asked.

It was Mr. Justice Hassocks who replied, before Macdonald had time to speak.

"You've met him on a mountain somewhere, perhaps. He's a good man with a rope."

Macdonald caught the shrewd old eyes and knew that the judge had spotted him, myopic or not. He also knew that Hassocks would not go further than that grim piece of humour.

"No such luck," replied the C.I.D. man. "I only go rock scrambling—not your stuff. Weren't you at the Stage Society's show on Sunday? I wondered what you thought of that lamaserie scene. From the point of view of some one who knew the real thing, I suppose it was merely comic."

"Sunday?" said Brandon, and paused. ("Time reaction," thought Macdonald instantly, remembering Richard Surray). "Oh, that stuff," went on the other. "I was bored stiff. If I go to a show I like to be entertained. Sven Hedin's the chap who knows what the inside of a lamaserie looks like—dirt, decay, and childish posturings; their thoughts as rotten as their buildings, crumbling from the inertia of the occupants. I had an idea I'd seen you somewhere else."

"I first met him on Great Gable," put in Menzies with a chuckle, "and he showed me a new traverse. If he comes to you for a job any time, Brandon, I'll tell you he's worth his keep. By the way, are you really trying Kinchinjinga from the east?"

"Ever been in the Dolomites?" said a quiet voice at Macdonald's side. Fortunately he had, and, having a good memory and a considerable acquaintance with the literature of the region, he kept his end up. The conversation went on until Mr. Justice Hassocks got up to go. The dry, wizened old man had been a pioneer of some now famous Alpine routes in his day, and he couldn't help a friendly dig at Macdonald as he passed.

"If I were roped up with you in a climbing party I'd have you behind going up, and ahead coming down," he said. "You're said to be a safe chap. Good-night."

His going was a signal for the party to break up, and a moment later Macdonald found himself in the lounge with Keith Brandon beside him. The Chief Inspector was a tall man, more accustomed to looking down on his fellows than up to them, but he had to raise his eyes to meet the other's oddly-persistent stare.

"Can't think where I've seen you before," he said. "Somewhere or other. Can I give you a lift?"

"Thanks very much. No. I'm waiting for Menzies," replied Macdonald. "You didn't tell me what you thought of that show."

"I didn't go to it—so that won't wash," replied the other coolly, and turned away. Macdonald was a bit puzzled. He was certain that he had not seen Brandon before, and wondered if the other's preoccupation with himself could be caused by telepathy. There seemed no other explanation, for Macdonald had been much too cautious to study him overtly, though his mind had been intensely busy in registering impressions of him.

A few minutes later Menzies appeared, and he and Macdonald went out into the pleasant summer evening.

"I don't know if you've got what you wanted," he said, "but that chap's not going to forget you in a hurry. Is it a fact you've not tailed him before?"

"Never seen him in my life, and never had any dealings with him," replied Macdonald. "I'd like to meet him with a pair of gloves on—he'd take some pounding before he was laid out."

"Or you were laid out," chuckled the other. "I share your feeling, rather. He's a hefty great brute. Old Hassocks'll have me on the carpet over this, though. I didn't count on him being one of the party when you rang me up."

"A man's a man for a' that," replied Macdonald. "One's a right to one's own existence."

"But was it your own existence?" demanded Menzies, and the other replied:

"Yes. For this evening it was. I'm not on a job. Tell him so."

"Tell it to the horse marines! Hassocks has got eyes in his mind if not in his head. If ever I'm in quod it'll be your business to get me out, after this."

"I'll see to it," replied Macdonald.

CHAPTER VI

MACDONALD WAS STANDING IN THE SUNNY BEDROOM at Upwood House where Ruth Surray had been found asleep in the sleep that knows no awakening of mortal senses. He was on the job at last, officially, grappling with a problem that looked insoluble. The general opinion of the police was that the inquiry was at a dead end. Nobody knew anything, nobody had seen or heard anything, and those papers were foolproof evidence. Deceased had written them herself, and they could only mean one thing.

Beside Macdonald stood Mrs. Surray, quiet and dignified, controlled now to a point when she could talk to the C.I.D. man without flinching, but asking with her eyes the same question which Richard had asked: "How can this help? All the investigation in the world can't bring Ruth back!" It was in response to her general attitude and expression, rather than to any actual words, that Macdonald tried to explain his own attitude.

"The object of an inquiry like this is something in the matter of a safeguard. If any suspicion arises that a coroner's verdict may not be in accordance with the facts, it is due to deceased, in justice, that the evidence be re-examined. We—the police—have to be satisfied that there is no possibility of foul play."

Mrs. Surray looked at him steadily. "Is such a thing conceivable in this case, Inspector?"

"I don't know," replied Macdonald quietly, "but I can say this: if all the facts had been at the disposal of the investigators in the first place, the inquiry would have proceeded with that possibility in view. It is remote, but it exists."

Mrs. Surray said no more. Taking Macdonald up to Ruth's room, she had said, "As far as possible everything is as it was last Monday morning. The actual papers by the bedside have been removed, and Mr. Montague has taken some manuscripts from the writing desk. The letters and papers in it were examined by the police, but Mr. Montague is coming down to-day and will bring to you those which he removed in his capacity as literary executor."

"Thank you. First may I see the maid who came in to call your daughter? Gladys Rogers is her name, I think."

"I will send her up to you."

While he waited, Macdonald looked round the room. He knew quite well that he would find nothing to help him there. Far from being "as it was," every single object had been moved, cleaned, altered... He could only get an idea of the general arrangement, and the relation of this room to others.

The maid, Gladys, came in, looking white and frightened, a protest on her lips and in her eyes.

"I told the truth, and I told everything," she asserted, and Macdonald reassured her as best he could.

"You had a great shock, and very often in cases like that the shock of the important facts wipes out recollection of little things which may be helpful. What I want you to do is this: Come into this room with the tea tray and hot water just as you did on the Monday morning. With the same things in your hands it will be easier for you to carry out exactly the same actions."

After a little further expostulation the maid agreed. She went downstairs and came up again shortly with her tray. Macdonald had pulled the curtains across the windows, and he stood in the corner of the room.

"Don't take any notice of me," he had said to her. "Try to do exactly what you usually do in the morning when you call anybody."

Reassured by his quiet voice, the girl behaved sensibly. She came in, put down a can on the floor, closed the door, and carried the small tray to the bedside table, pushing back the papers and the small box of tablets. She then went to the window and drew back the curtains, fastening them in their sashes. Next, she went and picked up her can by the door and took it to the washstand, arranged it with a cover over it and set the china aright. Her face was set in a frown of concentration, and Macdonald could tell that she was trying hard to do as she had been asked. He saw her hand waver and hesitate, and then he asked:

"There was something else there which you moved?"

The girl turned white. "I'd forgotten. There was a coffee cup. I just took it down with me to the pantry, like I always should... I clean forgot."

"Never mind," said Macdonald. "I know one can forget

small things, especially when they are almost unconscious actions."

He went on with his inquiry, and the girl told him how she came into the room again and tried to wake Ruth. Finally he asked her about the other people in the house, and the second housemaid was called up, while Macdonald was shown the other bedrooms and told who had slept in them. The little room next to Ruth's was occupied by Naomi. Beyond that came Mrs. Trant's room. On the farther side of the staircase were Stanwood's and Montague's rooms—all these being at the back of the house. The front of the building contained Mrs. Surray's bedroom and sitting-room and the Professor's rooms. Fellowes had slept in a room above Ruth's on the second floor. Stanwood and Montague had both got up early, before the household was astir; the former had sat in the rose garden, writing, until breakfast time. The latter had gone for a walk. Fellowes had been fast asleep in his room when he was called.

Having got the disposition of the rooms into his head, Macdonald went downstairs and examined the ground floor of the house, particularly the conservatory which Richard had said his sister was in the habit of using as an exit if she went to the post late at night. The path leading from it to a small side gate ran through a shrubbery, and it seemed unlikely that any one walking along it would have been seen after dark from any of the bedroom windows. The only dog in the house was an old Sealyham which slept in a basket in the Professor's room.

Macdonald then asked Mrs. Surray about the coffee cup in Ruth's room, and he could see that she was puzzled about it. Ruth did not drink coffee after dinner. Mrs. Surray sent for

Gladys and questioned her. Was the cup one of those sent up for the after-dinner coffee? Eventually the parlourmaid was called in, since the cups were her province. That pointed out by Gladys, as similar to the one found in Ruth's room, was not one of the set used for after-dinner coffee. Following Mrs. Surray's instructions, a tray had been left in the dining-room, with an electric kettle, tea things, coffee things, glasses, and whisky. Mrs. Surray explained that she had on previous occasions found that guests who were writers often sat up late at night working (she knew that Montague, in particular, did this), and that they sometimes liked a cup of tea, or even coffee, while they were working. It was her custom to have a tray left out, so that if any one wanted a hot drink after the household had gone to bed, they could get it for themselves. Similarly, if anybody came down early they could make themselves a cup of tea if they wished. It had certainly not been a habit of Ruth's to make herself either tea or coffee before she went to bed; in the winter she occasionally drank hot milk at bedtime, but in the summer, never. "I can't explain it," she said to Macdonald unhappily.

The latter tried to determine from the parlourmaid if the teapot or coffee-making apparatus had been used, and if any of the cups had dregs in, but he could get no positive answer. The coffee had been made and was ready to heat up if anybody wanted it. The parlourmaid had been busy on the Monday morning, and had carried the things back to the pantry. Any china that had been used had been washed up while breakfast was in progress in the dining-room, together with the cups and teapots from the early morning trays. To the best of the girl's recollection, nothing had been used on the trays in the dining-room, but she could not be certain.

In reply to Mrs. Surray's question, Macdonald replied that it looked as though Richard's theory were right. Ruth had written her letter and come downstairs again, and had made herself a cup of coffee either before or after she went to the post. He did not add the remainder of his theory—that she had had a conversation with somebody during that interval which had induced her to remake her will. Neither Mrs. Surray nor the Professor had heard anything after they went to bed which led them to suppose that anybody was astir in the house after eleven o'clock but as both were sound sleep-ers, nothing much could be argued from that. The maids, who slept on the top floor, were all agreed that they had heard nothing.

Shortly after mid-day, Vernon Montague appeared, bring-ing with him the papers he had taken from Ruth's writing desk. He came into Macdonald in the Professor's study, which room had been offered to the former for his use during his investigation, and Macdonald looked up as the tall round-shouldered man came across the room with a dispatch case in his hand. Montague put forward the inevitable question.

"Is this added inquisition justifiable? Aren't things bad enough already?"

With him the Chief Inspector was curt and to the point.

"Somebody in this case is refraining from giving evi-dence, or else somebody has been telling lies. Whichever it is, it has got to be cleared up. The facts point to the conclu-sion that deceased had some conversation with an unknown person after she was supposed to have gone to bed. It is necessary to find out who that person was, and why they have not come forward."

"Police point of view—nobody has a right to call their souls their own," said Montague in his clipped, staccato way. "If Ruth Surray confided a secret to some one, they may prefer to keep their faith with her, rather than be regarded as a sound witness by Scotland Yard. I don't give a damn what you think of my principles—if I'd been Richard I'd have burned that letter. Here are the papers I took from her desk. I haven't destroyed any of them yet, though there's nothing here which can be of any concern to you."

"I'll go through them later," replied Macdonald. "It will be a pity if you determine to be hostile at the outset. You regard Miss Surray's death as suicide, presumably. I am disposed to regard it as murder. It makes a difference to one's outlook."

Montague's jaw dropped, and he stared incredulously at Macdonald, pulling off his glasses and fidgeting with them unconsciously in his astonishment.

"Don't believe it. No one would… By God, it's unbelievable. Her will—that message… Not forged. Couldn't be. You chaps—get murder on the brain…"

"You're obsessed by one idea, perhaps I'm obsessed by another," replied Macdonald, "but it's my business to prove which of us is right if proof be possible. I want you to answer some questions. Had you any idea that Miss Surray intended to appoint you as her literary executor?"

"None. She never mentioned such a thing. Stands to reason. I'm years older than she was. In the nature of things I ought not to have survived her. The fact that she appointed me goes to show she knew what she was going to do."

"Had you ever had any conversation with her on the topic—in reference to anybody else's posthumous publications?"

Montague's limbs jerked in the odd way that betokened surprise. "No. Not directly. I acted for poor Weathering… Didn't discuss it with Miss Surray, though I heard she approved of what I did. Had to decide whether to publish an unfinished work—not a coherent narrative like Conrad's 'Suspense.' No kindness to a man to publish stuff he'd only roughed out—but I never discussed it with her directly."

"Does the same problem arise with regard to any MSS. of Miss Surray's? Is there anything unfinished over which you will have to exercise your own judgment?"

"Problem doesn't arise. Clear instructions as to what I'm to do. There's one completed MS.—a short novel. I'm to publish that. Nothing else. Most of her work—note-books, sketches, outlines, verse, and short stories—are to be destroyed."

"Doesn't it occur to you that her will was curiously explicit, considering the circumstances under which you supposed it to have been written?" went on Macdonald. "In cases of suicide, the mind is generally too preoccupied with its main intention to concentrate on practical details."

"Miss Surray was an unusual woman; very businesslike over practical details. No use arguing about it. She wrote that will on the Sunday night, clearly dated. She didn't do it without a reason."

"No. I'm quite sure she didn't. My own idea is this. She was intending to go abroad for a holiday shortly. Perhaps she thought it would be desirable to re-write her will before she left. Accidents may happen to any of us."

Macdonald was careful not to develop his idea on this subject to its full extent; he wanted to see if Montague would respond to the suggestion. The man was known to have an acute mind—but in this interview he did not seem to be exercising it. Montague twisted his lower lip between his fingers, his forehead corrugated in a frown that was almost a scowl.

"Doesn't make sense. She was used to travelling; going abroad was no more portentous to her than going to Brighton would be to you. Not given to nerve attacks over railway smashes or disasters at sea."

"Does any of the evidence make sense—or are you making sense of your argument?" replied Macdonald. "Along one line of thought you can reason thus: deceased was in a normal state of mind; she wrote to her brother happily and sensibly; therefore one has to look for a normal explanation of her actions. She wrote a coherent, businesslike document for reasons which may be adduced as sensible—no nervous premonitions of disaster. On the other hand, you can assume that she was in such a state of nervous instability that her mental processes were not predictable. Either point of view is tenable, but not a mixture of both." He paused here, to see if Montague would reply, but, receiving no answer, he went on: "Your evidence at the inquest was to the effect that deceased had been in a state of nervous depression. Can you account for that in any way? Have you any knowledge of her private life which would account for that depression?"

Montague answered promptly here.

"None whatever. Her state was due to brainfag—insomnia, too. Evidence of her brother and her medical man brought that out clearly enough. Insomnia's the devil."

"Undoubtedly. You suffer from it yourself?"

"On and off. Seldom sleep till the small hours."

"On the night of Miss Surray's death you went to bed early?"

"Yes. We all turned in early. I went to bed about eleven."

"But not to sleep?"

Montague was fiddling with a propelling pencil which he had picked up from the desk; he seemed unable to keep his hands still for a moment.

"No, not immediately," he replied.

"Not until the small hours, I take it," said Macdonald. "Did you come downstairs again—to make tea or coffee in the dining-room?"

"Good God, no! Coffee—when you want to go to sleep! I was reading in bed for an hour or two, but I didn't leave my room until I got up."

"You got up very early and went into the garden?"

"Yes. The birds woke me up—always a row in the country." He threw the pencil down on the table. "If you're arguing that I went and talked to Miss Surray, persuaded her to write a will giving me power over her MSS., and then induced her to take an overdose of thalmaine, you're an even bigger fool than you're assuming to be. Motive, profits as a publisher. That it? If so, say so."

"I can't say it sounds convincing," replied Macdonald. "You're not deaf by any chance?"

"Not to my knowledge."

"Yet, lying awake, you did not hear a sound to suggest that any one was moving about in the house, or talking? So far as we can gather, Miss Surray must have posted that letter to her brother herself. She also went into the dining-room and took a cup of coffee up to her room; at least, that's the presumption. A coffee cup with dregs in it was taken from the washstand in her room on Monday morning. Once again, I say that it's hard to make sense of all this evidence."

For the first time during the interview Montague sat curiously still; far from being relaxed, his limbs were tense and his long fingers seemed to have become rigid, stretched out in ungainly fashion along the arms of his chair. His voice, too, was different in quality when he spoke again:

"I give you my word that I heard nothing—no movement and no voices after I went to bed. I'm not keeping back a single fact. As to whether I can make out a line of thought which rationalises the evidence, that's my own affair. It's between me and my own conscience. I believe that Ruth took her own life deliberately, and I believe that this inquiry of yours is a thrice-damned thing—its only object to publish the distress which drove a woman to death. It's no use asking me to confide my thoughts to you, or to anybody else. My suppositions may be entirely wrong, and I'm not going to make a present of them to the police or to the public. This conversation is held without witnesses, and you needn't hope that I shall repeat what I'm now saying in the witness-box. I shan't. But I put it to you, as a man and not as a policeman—let her rest in peace. It would be less ghoulish to dig up a corpse and exhibit it to the public view than to do what you're doing."

Macdonald felt the tensity of emotion in the speaker's voice, and he replied very quietly: "So long as there is a possibility that the Coroner's verdict was at fault, this inquiry must go on. One successful murder begets others; we know that only too well. Suppression of evidence—or even of ideas— may mean that a murderer will not only escape, but may repeat the crime later."

Montague got up from his chair. "I've nothing more to say. I've said too much already, but on another occasion I shall hold my tongue. You've got my sworn evidence in the Coroner's court, and I have brought you the papers you asked for. Not a scrap has been destroyed, either of the papers found here or those in her London rooms."

He walked to the door, and Macdonald made no effort to stop him.

Drawing the dispatch case towards him, the Chief Inspector began to go through the contents. The papers were enclosed in some large sheets of blotting paper, evidently taken from the blotter on Ruth Surray's desk, and at first sight it appeared that Montague's statement "nothing has been destroyed" was fully true. Letters and envelopes, one or two scribbled notes concerning purchases and bills, telephone numbers and addresses were included, also the remains of two writing blocks. Both of these were the same quality of paper—thin, tough, smooth sheets, very easy to write upon. One was a large size, ten inches by seven-and-a-half, the other considerably smaller. The larger appeared to have been used for manuscript paper, the smaller for writing informal letters; it was on this paper that Ruth had written her brother's letter. Putting aside the blocks, Macdonald began to examine the written papers; it was not an easy task, for Ruth Surray had frequently used a sort of private shorthand, whose symbols and abbreviations conveyed nothing to Macdonald at first sight. So far as he could make out, several of the sheets were covered with notes concerning future books and essays, experiments rather than a settled scheme, and there was a series of comments on recently published books. These latter were sufficiently legible to be read without difficulty, and Macdonald put one aside for further consideration. He knew something of the book dealt with—a collection of essays, notes, and short stories published after the writer's death. The manuscript which interested him most was an unfinished short story, describing an incident in the life of a newly-married girl. The theme was simple and commonplace enough—the reactions of the young wife to the discovery of her husband's previous liaison with a married woman old enough to be the bride's mother; it was the writing which made the narrative memorable, so beautiful was the simple phrasing, so complete the understanding of the theme. Macdonald could have sworn that the husband in the story was a portrait of Keith Brandon. While studying the latter at The Mountaineers, Macdonald had noticed Brandon's long flexible hands, with powerful yet supple fingers, loosely webbed so that their span was remarkable in length, spatulate of tip, with flat strong nails. He read on, getting more and more interested until he was brought to an abrupt end where the manuscript broke off at the bottom of a page. He searched through the remaining papers, but could find no continuation, nor were there any notes to give a hint of how the story should have ended.

Putting aside the manuscript, he examined the blotting paper which had been folded round the sheets. He carried it to the light and studied the reverse side; then, turning up the reading lamp, with the aid of a mirror and a reading glass, he continued his scrutiny. Finally he felt satisfied that his case was clear. The manuscript of the story which had interested him broke off at page twelve. On the blotting paper was a faint reproduction of the top of another page, numbered sixteen, and the first line beneath the number showed that there had been more of the story written than was contained in the dispatch case. The name of the girl wife had been Hilary Fielding, and the letters of the Christian name showed clearly enough on the blotting paper. Macdonald took out the sheet on which was written Ruth Surray's farewell message, and compared it with the sheets of the story. The former had been written, apparently, on a sheet torn from the smaller block, but Ruth Surray, when she wrote her manuscripts, had been in the habit of leaving a wide margin on either side of the page. In this margin she wrote corrections and suggestions, as a reader does in correcting the galley slips of a book in proof, and her neat, tiny writing made a surprisingly compact regular block down the page. The numbering was in the top right-hand corner of each page. Macdonald now believed that the farewell message had been written as the conclusion to the story of Hilary Fielding, and that the page containing these lines had been cut down to the size of the smaller sheets which she used for letter writing. The necessity of the cutting down was obvious if his theory were true. It was necessary to get rid of the numbering at the top of the page, and since it would have been obvious immediately if the page did not conform in size to the other large sheets, the whole had been cut to the size and shape of the smaller block on which Ruth Surray had often written breadthwise. If this were not the explanation, Macdonald believed that he would have found the remaining pages of the story; that they had been written, the blotting paper proved, and Ruth Surray had obviously not destroyed any of the papers in her writing desk; all her odd notes were there, as well as the compact manuscript of the main part of the story.

Macdonald then went back to his theory about the will. Ruth had written a notice of "Last Leaves," a volume published by the author's wife after the former's death, and she had expressed very strongly the view put into words by Montague: "No kindness to a man to publish stuff he'd only roughed out." Ruth, writing with strong feeling because she had been a great admirer of the author's earlier work, had developed Montague's sentiment with trenchant energy. There had been too much of this sort of thing of recent years, she had written. It was mistaken sentiment to give to the world the experiments and trivial scraps of narrative which the living author would have consigned to the waste-paper basket had he lived to do so. Neither were those who had been nearest to the author during his life, nor those who had loved him the most devotedly, the best judges of what should be published among the mass of work which every author leaves behind him. Literature should be judged on its merits alone, and to believe it to be a pious duty to publish all the trifles which a great writer might leave behind him was a disservice to his memory.

Macdonald put down the sheets of this review with a clear purpose in his mind. He meant to find out if this work had been commissioned or were intended for publication, and if the book in question had been sent to Ruth Surray to review. In his own mind he believed that the book had been given to her by one who was preparing the way for murder. "How should I like to have all my papers published after my death, to suffer the same treatment meted out to other writers in like circumstances?" Had that suggestion been made to her, so that Ruth, impulsive in the sense of acting quickly after a decision had been made, had re-written her own will to safeguard herself in the contingency of her death?

Macdonald went back to the story of Hilary Fielding. At the top right-hand corner of the page was a date in minute Roman numerals: "xv. vii. M°DCCCC°XXXV°." Apparently it was the writer's custom to date her work in this way—a touch of pedantry which seemed to conform to the scholarly writing and meticulous neatness of the completed pages. July 15th. Ruth Surray had been staying at the Downings on that date, and Keith Brandon had been there, too. Had he read the story of Hilary Fielding, and recognised the description of some of his own physical attributes, hidden under a portrait sketch which, in the main, resembled him not at all?

From the short story, Macdonald turned to the will. The date on this was also written in Roman numerals, but the word "Sunday" was clear enough in the characteristic writing which the experts had declared to be valid. Could the date have been altered in any way? He traced out the figures and came to the conclusion that it could have been done very easily. "xxix. vii."—the 29th day of the seventh month. The mere addition or deletion of a stroke would make all the difference in the world.

At this stage Macdonald put down the papers and began to fill his pipe. He was in danger of theorising too much. How far would any of these ideas go in convincing other people that Ruth Surray's death was not the result of suicide? Montague had said: "You're obsessed with the thought of murder." Other people would say the same thing. What concrete evidence was there to support his theory? That certain sheets of the short story had been destroyed was no proof of anything; authors habitually destroyed portions of their work when it did not satisfy them. Was it possible to prove that one sheet had been cut down? If that point were established, there could be no argument about the likelihood of foul play, it would then be a certainty. Examining the edges of the sheet under his lens, Macdonald felt sceptical of the result. If it *had* been cut, it had been done with great skill; a razor blade must have been used, guided by an accurate straight-edge—a metal or ivory ruler which was absolutely true. Fitting the sheet over one of the pages of the smaller block, Macdonald saw the manner in which the two coincided, and he knew how difficult it was to cut a sheet to that degree of exactness. He put it aside: this was no job for mere visual comparison. A high-power magnification would tell if the cut were made by hand or by machine.

Apart from that, what other evidence could he hope for? There was the fact of the used coffee cup on the washstand, but no hope of evidence to show what it had contained or how it had come to be there. He might theorise as much as he liked, but against the persistent ignorance of those in the house, how could he hope for fresh facts? Vernon Montague, for instance, lying awake in bed, reading; rising at dawn, woken by bird song, denying that he had heard or seen anything. Macdonald looked down at that sheet of paper with the Spenser couplet on it:

"Sleep after toyle, port after stormie seas…"

If the microscope proved his present theory, and the fact of murder was established, would the "reticence" of these witnesses break down?

Packing the papers carefully away in his own case and locking it, Macdonald rang the bell and asked for Mrs. Surray. He asked her if she would take him round the house, adding that he wished after that to carry out some experiments regarding the sound-carrying properties of some of the rooms. Mrs. Surray acquiesced at once, saying that she would go round with him herself, and after that he could carry out any experiments he wished.

She was a very thorough guide. Beginning with the kitchens, she opened each door with a word of explanation; cellars, cold storage, furnace-room, electric pump, "fruit-room" (where fruit and vegetables from the garden were stored in winter), "jumble-room," where old oddments were housed before they were disposed of for charitable purposes. As she was about to close the door of this tiny room Macdonald made his first inquiry.

"All the waste paper—from paper-baskets and so on—is put into sacks and sent away?"

Mrs. Surray nodded. "Yes: we seem to amass an enormous amount of it in this house—my husband writes, of course, and the whole family seem to take after him in that respect; then there are papers and reviews—an endless supply! It was rather a problem to dispose of it until we made an arrangement with Hills. They collect the sacks about four times a year."

"Can you remember when they collected last?"

"Early in June, I think—about then, anyway."

"Then I shall have to examine the sacks. Could you have this door locked until I have done so?"

"Certainly. The key is there. You can take charge of it."

She made no other comment, and Macdonald locked the

door and put the key in his pocket. There was no window to the little room, only a skylight.

He turned again to the grey-haired lady who stood beside him, saying, "Thank you," and then added, "I am very sorry that I have to bother you about all this."

"Of course you have to do what you consider necessary," she replied, and Macdonald was unhappily aware of the antagonism which lay behind her courteous and dignified bearing. Mrs. Surray was finding it hard to put up with this domestic inquisition, and she visited her feelings on Macdonald. "There are the three back entrances, as you see," she explained carefully. "One in the passage, one in the scullery, and one by the servants' sitting-room. They are having their lunch in there just now, so perhaps later would do? There is only one room in this part of the house which we use ourselves; we call it the workroom—it used to be the children's playroom."

The door she opened this time opened into a very large stone-flagged room, containing trestle tables and a carpenter's bench. Macdonald went right in and stood looking at various pieces of apparatus.

"Some one does bookbinding?" he queried, recognising a sewing frame standing against the wall.

"Yes. My youngest daughter does; my husband works at tooling the bindings occasionally. That" (pointing to a large, shrouded object on a pair of trestles) "is my own embroidery frame. My son Robert is fond of carpentry, and Mrs. Beech, my married daughter, used to do woodcuts. That is her press. The room is not often used now."

Macdonald felt increasingly uncomfortable as she talked; in just such a tone of serene impersonal courtesy Mrs. Surray might have talked to a dealer who had come in to value her furniture. She did not display any feeling, just that cold, detailed deliberation, as of one who says, "This man has his work to do; let us get it over as soon as possible, but let us be thorough over it."

"You would perhaps like the key of this room, too?" she ended up, seeing Macdonald studying the benches.

"No, thank you," he replied quietly. "I have seen all that is necessary in here."

They went on, Mrs. Surray mentioning the use of each room.

"The drawing-room, the morning-room, the men's cloak-room, the telephone-room... Letters to be posted are left here, on the chest. No. We have no post-bag. The dining-room, the study. This is all on the ground floor." She completed the round of the house with him, adding as they came downstairs, "Luncheon is at half-past one. It will be served for you in the morning-room. Would you like the other detective to lunch with you, or would it be more correct for him to have another room? I am so sorry; I feel I ought to know—but it shall be just as you wish."

Macdonald felt his face grow a little hot. This quiet-voiced lady was not being easy to deal with, but he replied with a calm equal to her own.

"Thank you very much. It was kind of you to think of it, but it would be more correct if Detective Reeves and I had our lunch in the village. I shall not be bothering you again for the time being, I hope, but I should like to see Mr. Montague after he has had lunch. Mr. Stanwood and Mr. Fellowes are both coming here this afternoon, I understand.

It would be convenient if I could see them here before I return to town."

She looked at him as though she were uncertain whether to reply or not, and suddenly Macdonald determined to say a word more. "I have already told you that I am sorry that you should be distressed by this additional inquiry, Mrs. Surray. I, personally, am no more able to prevent it than are you yourself. The inquiry is inevitable, and rightly so, but after to-day I hope that my department will not have to trouble you personally with our inquiries."

Mrs. Surray looked at the tall man with the quiet voice; he stood easily, looking no more like a policeman in dress, or face, or manner, than did her own sons. When she replied there was a trace more of feeling in her voice.

"I am grateful to you for your sympathy, Inspector. I know that my son was glad that you were able to undertake this matter, and you have been very considerate to us all. I won't try to explain to you my own feelings about it. I may be illogical, but that is a failing of mothers with regard to their children." She flushed a little as she added, "I am sorry that you will not accept our hospitality. I intended no discourtesy to you when I mentioned it. I hope that you will change your mind."

"Thank you. I think it will be better if we adhere to my original plan, as we have some business in the village," he replied. "Meantime, many thanks for acting as my guide."

He bowed as he turned away, and Mrs. Surray was left in the hall with her eyes pricking with unshed tears. She knew enough of mankind to recognise when "she had put a man's back up." She had resented the Chief Inspector's presence and the reiteration of those questions which she had answered already, and she resented the implication of his presence that there was more to be told than had been told. Trying to keep a firm hand on nerves that were beginning to torture her, she admitted that Macdonald was considerate and courteous and capable—and in spite of it she hated him, and unfortunately she had let him see it.

CHAPTER VII

MACDONALD STOOD AT THE FRONT DOOR OF THE KING'S
Arms, and looked at the pleasant cottages across the way, himself looking the most placid of visitors, waiting for the lunch
he had just ordered, while Detective Reeves made friends
with a liver-and-white spaniel in the garden. Far from feeling
as contented as he looked, the Chief Inspector was troubled
in mind; he felt baffled at this moment, not from inability
to present a logical case, but because all the evidence he had
collected was capable of different interpretations.

The experiments he had carried out with the assistance
of Reeves, in which he had hoped to ascertain the probabilities of the passage of sound from room to room and floor to
floor in the Surrays' big house had been quite inconclusive
in result. Owing to the excellence of the thick walls and the
quality of the deep carpets, it was obviously quite possible
for anybody in Ruth Surray's room to move about and to go
downstairs and to let themselves out of the house without
making enough sound to attract the attention of anybody

else in the house. A conversation in Ruth's bedroom would be faintly audible to any one sleeping in Naomi's room next door, but would not be heard by the occupants of Montague's or Stanwood's rooms, which were divided from Ruth's by the wide stairway. Similarly with sounds from below; a conversation in the dining-room should have been heard to some extent in Montague's room—the sound of voices and movements seemed to come up the chimney space. Similar sounds from the window end of the drawing-room were audible in Stanwood's bedroom, and those of the morning-room in the Professor's bedroom. On the other hand, no sounds from the study could be heard upstairs at all.

While Macdonald was chewing over these reflections, a car pulled up just opposite the front door and the driver alighted. As the latter turned to enter the inn, he stopped and stared at the Chief Inspector, and the latter returned the look with interest, for the driver was Keith Brandon.

"Rather odd the way we butt into one another," said Brandon. "I haven't remembered yet where I first saw you. Are you staying here? They do you rather well; it's one of the best pubs I know in a small way."

"I'm having lunch here," replied Macdonald. "It is a bit odd—you're the very man I wanted to see."

"Thinking of scrounging a job in my next show, as Menzies suggested?"

"No. I'm ten years too old, and definitely occupied otherwise. It's something quite different." Macdonald drew a card out of his pocket and handed it to Brandon. "That's my job. Will you come into the garden and talk to me for a few minutes?"

Brandon studied the card, and then his eyes rested on Macdonald's face with the cool appraising stare that had a quality of insolence in it.

"So that's it... Wait a minute... You were the chap who gave evidence for the police in that forgery case... Old Hassocks tried it. Good God! The old blighter! 'A good man with a rope!' I remember. I heard part of that case. I've a good memory for faces and a rotten one for placing the circumstances in which I saw them. Since when have they made the C.I.D. free of The Mountaineers? If you want to talk to me I'll give you ten minutes after I've ordered my lunch and bunged the car into the yard; but if you want to pump me, I'll tell you straight the answer's a lemon."

A few minutes later the explorer came into the garden, sat down at the little table where Macdonald was awaiting him, saying, "What about it?" as he lighted a cigarette.

"I am down here in connection with the death of Miss Ruth Surray," said Macdonald, his eyes on the other's face. He saw the muscles of Brandon's jaw contract, and there was a pause before the latter answered:

"I thought that case was over. The Coroner gave a straight verdict—no fencing about it."

"Other evidence has been brought forward which has caused the inquiry to be reopened."

"What has that to do with me?"

"I believe that you knew Miss Surray. I thought it possible that you could tell something of her state of mind."

"Good Lord! Why the devil—? I barely knew her. Let's think. I met her at some function at Grosvenor House, and then again at the Downings' place one week-end. Not in my line. Too precious. The word high-brow affronted her good taste—but there you have it."

Macdonald met the other's eyes squarely.

"That's rather curious. I thought you must have known her rather well."

"Then you thought wrong. Whence these deductions, might I ask?"

"I have been reading some manuscripts she left in the hope of getting a lead in a difficult case. In a short story there was a very good description of yourself—so detailed in some ways that it seemed as though she must have had opportunities of observing you pretty closely."

There was no doubt that this sentence got home. Brandon's face flushed, as some fair faces do flush, until his ears were scarlet.

"Since Miss Surray is dead, I won't use the expressions I might have done. There's no end to the impertinences of these best sellers; journalism's mild in comparison with them. If that manuscript's published, I'll take action against the publishers in double-quick time. As a guardian of law and order you might like to tell them so in advance."

"Why?" queried Macdonald. "I didn't say that the story was libellous. I only suggested that the writer seemed to have had opportunities of observing you."

Brandon was beginning to recover from the shock of hearing about the short story.

"And how were you able to recognise a description of my own peculiarities? Hell! Anybody might think you'd had me through the Bertillon business. You'd better watch your own step a little."

"It's my business to observe people's peculiarities," replied Macdonald. "It will save time if I tell you that you are fencing. You have met Miss Surray on more than the two occasions you mention."

If Brandon had got up and told him to go to hell at this juncture Macdonald would have regarded him with a much more sympathetic eye. It seemed so out of character for this huge, quick-tempered fellow to sit there trying to swallow his all-too-obvious wrath unless he had some motive to do so.

"I don't pretend to know what you're driving at," went on Brandon, "but your insinuations seem on a par with the mentality of the plainclothes men who go muck-raking in Hyde Park. Miss Surray may have been an acquaintance of mine, but that's all there was to it, and if you're suggesting anything else you're asking for the hell of a kick in the pants— and you'll get it."

"I'll take my chance of that," returned Macdonald. "There is no insinuation about the following question—it's a perfectly plain one: What were you doing on Sunday evening, July 29th?"

Brandon's bright blue eyes flickered curiously, as though a light shone behind them for a split second; then the pupils contracted to mere pin points. Macdonald had often observed that nervous stress causes the muscles of the eyes to react oddly, in the same manner that the hands and jaw may be clenched and unclenched unconsciously during a period of intense excitement. Ruth Surray, too, had set on record that curious dilation and expansion of a man's eyes.

"July 29th?" queried the other, with a snort which might

have been laughter or contempt. "You know the answer to that already. It was the evening you saw me at *Shadowy Heights*."

"I asked you if you were there," corrected Macdonald, "and subsequently you told me that you were not there."

"That won't wash," retorted Brandon, coolly using the same phrase which he had used when he said at the door of The Mountaineers that he had not seen *Shadowy Heights*. "You asked me about the play in the presence of witnesses—old Hassocks was one. I told you that I'd been bored stiff by it."

"Later you told me that you had not seen it."

"Bunkum! You're using your imagination to indulge your own beastly reasoning. If you want evidence go and look in the files of the *Mayfair Messenger*. It's a low rag—doubtless you know it. However, its photographs are good. You'll find a photograph of people in the lobby at the Duchess of Kent's Theatre at the production of *Shadowy Heights* that Sunday night, among whom is myself."

"Thanks," replied Macdonald. "That seems indisputable. One can assume, however, that you didn't sit the play through, since you have admitted that you were bored stiff by it. Your car returned to the garage about five o'clock in the morning. I should be very glad if you would tell me what you were doing between the time you left the theatre and the time you returned your car to its garage. Let me make this quite clear: I only ask these questions in order to eliminate you from the complications which have arisen in this case."

"I'm not disposed to advertise my whereabouts during that period," said Brandon slowly. "The answer would involve other people besides myself, and I'm not inclined to give you the chance of throwing mud at my friends. It seems to be a favourite pastime of yours."

"It might save you a lot of trouble eventually if you answered that question frankly," said Macdonald. "However, that's for you to decide."

"And now you can damn well tell me what right you have to dog my movements and ask me infernally insolent questions," said Brandon heatedly. "There's been trouble for you damned Bobbies over smaller things than that. If you've been exceeding your authority—"

"Far from exceeding it, I've hardly begun to use it," interpolated Macdonald. "It's the business of every member of the public to answer questions asked them by an accredited member of the police force. So far as my right to ask questions is concerned, it's only limited by the Judge's rules. Presumably you're not suggesting that these should apply to you."

"Don't know what you're talking about," retorted Brandon, and got up. "I'd intended to have my lunch here, but I wasn't counting on the company of your department. Enough to spoil a man's appetite to see you snooping around."

Macdonald looked after the big fellow as he swung away and resolutely put out of his mind the feeling that if Brandon were hit hard enough and long enough somewhere in the region of his wind, things would look more satisfactory all round. Finding Reeves just inside the inn, Macdonald said to him:

"I'm sorry for you, because there's a good meal waiting to be eaten, and you're not going to eat it. Get your motor-bike out and see if you can tail that chap in the Humber without his spotting you. If he goes to another pub for a meal you can get one, too, but try not to let him see you. I want to know if he goes to any place in this district. I shall be at Upwood House this afternoon and back in town this evening. Report when and as you can."

Reeves did not complain over his lost meal; he was being given the sort of job he liked; and, with a "Very good, sir," he made for the stable, where his motor-cycle was standing, and a few minutes later Macdonald heard him start up the engine and knew that a good man was on the trail.

He himself went in and settled to his meal and thought over that interview with Brandon. The latter had lied about the nature of his friendship with Ruth Surray, and, much though Macdonald disliked him, he was fair-minded enough to admit that many men would have lied under like circumstances, and counted their lie for righteousness. From Brandon's point of view it would have been mere caddishness to claim intimacy with the dead woman. Next came his reaction to the matter of the short story; he had assumed at once that it contained something damaging to himself. That looked as though he and Ruth must have quarrelled—or at least as though she had grounds for resentment towards him. Quite probable, if he had wearied of her and then displayed an interest in her sister. Finally came the point about the Sunday evening. Brandon had expected that question; he had been ready for it, and the fact that Macdonald had stolen a march on him and found out that the Humber had not been returned to the garage until the early morning had infuriated him. If the explorer were implicated in the case, mused Macdonald, it was probable that he would take immediate steps to reinforce his alibi for the Sunday evening—in which case Reeves should be able to do some useful work. The other question that arose was concerning Brandon's presence here at The King's Arms. He had evidently been here before, had admitted as much himself. To that question Macdonald got an early answer.

Mrs. Shaw, the wife of the innkeeper, came into the room with a pair of driving gloves.

"Some people don't seem to know their own minds," she complained. "First it's two for dinner, then it's three for dinner, and when it comes to the point it's only one for dinner. If Mr. Keith's a friend of yours, maybe you'd like to give him back his gloves. Left them here last time he came, and then says he's come to fetch them, and after all that goes tearing off without waiting for them. I do my best, but a woman can't make a meal cook faster than's natural. Hurry, hurry, hurry it is these days, and then no one's satisfied."

"Well, I'm satisfied for one," replied Macdonald. "I've never eaten a better duck than that one, or better green peas either. I'll take charge of the gloves, if you like, and see that they're returned to their owner. He's one of these impatient fellows. However, he took the trouble to tell me how comfortable he'd been when he stayed here, and what a good cook you are, into the bargain."

"Well, why didn't he stop for his dinner, then?" retorted Mrs. Shaw. "He stayed a night here a fortnight or so ago—the week before last it was, and said he was that comfortable. I've looked after his gloves for him, thinking he might drop in for them—they're a good pair, too—and then he goes tearing off like a lunatic, forgetting all about them again. There's a raspberry tart coming, sir, and some very good Stilton we've got."

"Then you've got all the things I like best," replied

Macdonald. "I should like to come and stay here some time. Good cooking's all too rare nowadays."

"Just a matter of taking trouble, that's what I say," replied Mrs. Shaw. "We had a lot of visitors last week—for the inquest, it was. You'll have read about it?"

Macdonald nodded. "Yes. A sad business."

"Sad? I should say it was. I'd known her from a child. As nice a family as there is in this world. Too much learning, that's what I say. Now if Miss Ruth'd got married and had a few babies to think about, that'd never have happened. I can't think what came over her. You don't know the family by any chance, sir?"

"Slightly," replied Macdonald, "though I never met Miss Ruth Surray. I've read some of her books, though."

"Ah, I thought that might be it," replied Mrs. Shaw placidly, taking the tart from the girl who had just brought it in and setting it before Macdonald. "I hope you'll enjoy my pastry, sir. I'm a rare one for pastry—good butter's the secret. We see a lot of the writing gentlemen they have up at the house, and when I saw you I said to myself, 'That'll be a writing gentleman, that will.' Now Mr. Keith, he's quite different, more impatient like, if you take me. He's one of Miss Naomi's friends, I'm thinking."

"What makes you think that?" inquired Macdonald. (The tart was very good indeed, and he felt more than ever sorry for Reeves.)

"Well, it was just an idea that came into my head," said Mrs. Shaw. "I told you he stayed here, and he was talking to me about the Surrays. I told him Miss Surray might look in that morning, and he asked, hopeful-like, 'Miss Naomi?'

and looked as downcast as you please when I said, 'No. Miss Ruth.' Not that I'm one to gossip."

"But you're one to cook—and one in a thousand," said Macdonald. "A good tart takes some beating, and this one's a marvel. I'm sorry to be in a hurry, but could you let me have my bill—for two, of course? I'm sorry that my man couldn't stay to enjoy this."

"Well, things happen like that sometimes," replied the stout lady, and there was a look in her shrewd eyes which made Macdonald wonder whether she was good at seeing through mental hedges as well as hearing through actual ones.

During part of the time that the Chief Inspector had been cogitating over the papers collected from Ruth Surray's writing desk that morning, two men had been discussing the reopening of the inquiry into her death while they travelled to Upwood on the Great Western Railway. These were Geoffrey Stanwood and Charlton Fellowes, seated opposite to one another in an otherwise empty compartment. Fellowes had seen Stanwood sitting in a corner seat, absorbed in a chess problem. He had a little folding case, into which the pictured pieces could be slipped in and out of the slotted squares, and his face had that look of intense concentration common to chess players when intent on their game. Fellowes, after a moment of hesitation, got in and sat down opposite to the other man and bade him good-morning. Stanwood looked up with an expression which said, "Damn the fellow—interrupting my game," and then his face relaxed as he saw who greeted him.

"Good-morning." He closed his little case carefully, adding,

"King to move and mate in umpteen moves—we being the pawns. Richard Surray seems to have changed his mind."

Fellowes lighted a cigarette. "Yes—though I don't see how he could have acted otherwise. It's a hellish problem. What's your opinion about it all?"

Stanwood studied the younger man's face. Fellowes looked out of form—heavy-eyed, patchy in colour, queer about the eyes.

"Difficult to have an opinion without knowing the facts," Stanwood replied, and his searching look made Fellowes squirm irritably.

"What's Surray getting at? He wouldn't have reopened the case just to have the suicide verdict re-established."

"Presumably not. I don't know him well enough to read his mind. He was in a state of nerves when I met him. Curious thing. The Professor and his wife seemed as placid a pair as you could meet, their family all the reverse. Don't know if you react to other people's nerves. Struck me that Miss Surray and her sister were all strung up about something, and the psychologist wallah looked as though he hadn't slept for a month. Anything may happen when you get minds of that calibre stretched to breaking point. Something did happen."

"What? That's the point." Fellowes' voice reflected the agitation of his mind. "If I could only make up my own mind about it, one way or another, I'd follow my own judgment and see Scotland Yard at hell before I dished out anything but a lemon."

"Look here," said Stanwood, "you'd better make up your own mind before you start talking to me or anybody else. I don't want to be involved in your mental difficulties."

Fellowes leant forward towards his companion. The train

had started, and the two men were alone together in that curious intimacy of a railway compartment, in which there is no possibility of eavesdropping or observation from without.

"I've got to the state when I must talk to somebody. Not to the Surrays—that's impossible. Not to Montague—he'd be worse. Mrs. Trant won't utter a word. You were there. You know the evidence that was given."

"Yes. Every one saying what they thought best under the circumstances," said Stanwood, taking his chess wallet out of his pocket again. "No use asking advice from me. The best thing in present circumstances is to follow the psalmist's dictum. Psalm 39; verses 1 and 2. Look it up."

Fellowes refused to take the suggestion implicit in the other man's action, and references to the psalms were wasted on him. He flung his newspaper violently on the other seat and went on:

"The verdict of suicide seemed a foregone conclusion. Admitting that, the best thing to do was to get the whole thing over without stirring up mud. Surray knew that. Although he was so circumspect, you could see that his one idea was to—well, was to..."

"Was to say no more than had to be said in order to convince the Coroner that Ruth Surray deliberately took an overdose of thalmaine? Yes. If the inquest had been held on your sister, what attitude would you have taken? Raked up every pro and con for the journalists to pick out the plums?"

Fellowes squirmed in his place. "I don't know how much you know," he began.

"Then take it for granted that I don't know anything," replied Stanwood dryly.

"I can't understand Surray's motive in starting the thing all over again, unless he thinks there's a suspicion of foul play," said Fellowes. "If that's his point—my God! it's a ghastly business."

"You might as well use plain English. If Ruth Surray didn't commit suicide, then she was murdered," said Stanwood, "and the murderer—or murderess—must have been in the house that night. To me the suggestion's ludicrous—unless you're going to apply the description 'temporarily insane' to one member of the household that night."

Fellowes threw himself back in his place and rubbed up his hair wildly. "That night—did you go to sleep early?"

"So so." Stanwood's face was a mask, perfectly steady.

"I didn't. I lay awake. I couldn't sleep. I heard Ruth go downstairs. She was talking to some one—for ages."

Stanwood's steady gaze never flickered.

"Look here. You'd better use your wits a little. At the inquest you swore that you heard nothing during the course of the night—after you'd gone to bed. Before you produce a statement which proves you to have committed perjury, you'd better think out the implications—for yourself and other people."

"I've been thinking," said Fellowes slowly. "I knew Ruth was wretched. I knew she wasn't herself. Hadn't been—for weeks. She *was* desperate. She went downstairs that night—I don't know why—I've been trying to reason it out. She and Montague were talking. He's adored her for years. I know. Perhaps she thought she could make one man happier before... God, I don't know! I dare not think. How could I tell that about her to that hard-boiled Coroner and the cod-faced Inspector? I tell you I couldn't."

His incoherent voice broke off, and Stanwood asked in his clear incisive voice, "Montague? Are you certain?"

The other nodded. "I heard that queer little cough of his. I knew it was Montague. Yet he swore that he didn't go out of his room. Montague's a decent chap. He had a reason for saying what he did."

"Did you tell him that you heard him talking to her?"

"No. He'd already told me that he hadn't seen Ruth, or heard a sound of her, after she went upstairs."

"Do you imagine that Montague killed her?" The quiet voice had a note of impatience in it now, and Fellowes shouted back:

"No, you damned fool, you. I was certain she killed herself... But now... God knows..."

Stanwood heaved a large sigh. "You and Richard Surray are alike in this respect. You make up your minds, and then unmake them. You can't be consistent. First you argue out a case for yourself—some crazy theory about Ruth Surray repaying Montague for the devotion of years. I won't argue about that; every man's a right to his own interpretation of things. Having made your own theory, you decide to act on it to the extent of suppressing evidence so that the Coroner may not ask questions about how Ruth Surray *did* spend her last night in this world. I can understand that to some extent. The interference of the police has an element of the indecent. But, having made up your mind, why in God's name can't you stick to it? Why blurt out to me the very facts you were at pains to hide?"

"Because you're the only person I can talk to," groaned Fellowes. "You understand. You knew her."

Stanwood cried out for the first time in sheer impatience.

"Don't go dragging me and my feelings into your sickening arguments. Whatever I felt about it isn't your business, damn you! Try to think clearly for a change. You're debating with yourself whether to give the journalists their headlines. What are the police going to say when you tell them you've changed your mind and have another story to tell them?"

"Blast the police! I don't care a tuppenny damn for them!"

"They'll care more than a tuppenny damn for you," replied Stanwood dryly. "Remember again that if the suicide verdict is upset, the alternative is murder. It's your word against Montague's."

"I tell you I don't care. The only person I cared about was Ruth. I'm trying to think this out from her point of view. Stanwood, is it true that you didn't hear anything?"

The other frowned. "You're trying to shift the responsibility on to me. That's no use. I'm not one of the shilly-shallying kind. I gave my evidence, and I stick to it—and I'll tell you this for what it's worth: If I believed what you believe, I should stick tighter than ever to what I'd sworn. I'm quite clear about my own point of view. Ruth Surray killed herself, and all the post-mortems in the world can't alter the fact."

"If I were only certain," groaned Fellowes, and Stanwood seemed suddenly to take pity for the younger man's obvious misery.

"My dear chap, you've been going through hell, tearing your nerves to tatters over an insoluble problem. I've been through it, too, but I'm old enough to realise the uselessness of inflicting suffering on yourself by the sort of self-searching you're doing. The only way to get any peace of mind is to try to rationalise the thing—think it out as though it were a chess problem." Fellowes swore under his breath, but Stanwood went on, "Face your problem squarely and put your pieces in order. The question is: murder or suicide. It's only the first alternative that need come into the scope of this argument, because the second is not our business. If Miss Surray were murdered, the murderer was either staying in the house or was well acquainted with the house; in either case he must have known her well. Now whom can one rule out from the range of suspicion? First, our two selves. Remember, I'm stating this argument as from your point of view or my own. I know I didn't do it, and I can't see by what means you could have induced her to leave those documents. If this is a case of murder, you've got to explain how the murderer obtained those papers."

"Forgery?" Fellowes shot out the word vindictively, but Stanwood shook his head. "No. The experts passed them. She wrote them herself."

"There's another explanation besides forgery," said Fellowes slowly, "but it's so fantastic that it passes belief."

"Never mind that. Put it into words and let's consider it."

"Think for yourself. Who knew that Ruth Surray took sleeping tablets? Who knew that she had made an earlier will leaving Richard Surray as executor? Who in this case has studied and developed powers of hypnotic suggestion—as all practising psychologists do?"

Stanwood stared at the other with amazement in his eyes.

"Good God, man! The idea's so far-fetched that it's ludicrous! What are you getting at?"

"This: If Ruth *were* murdered, there's one person against

whom a far-fetched case can be made out, and that is Richard Surray himself. Remember it's been proved that Ruth wrote those papers—proved. If she did not write that farewell message of her own volition, and with the intention of committing suicide when she had written it, then Ruth Surray must have written it under hypnotic control. There's no other explanation, since it's established beyond cavil that the message was in her own handwriting."

"Far-fetched is a mild way of expressing it," said Stanwood dryly. "If there's any possibility that you're right, you've got to accept the fact that Richard Surray is mad. You might as well suggest that I'm mad—or you're mad."

Fellowes nodded his head miserably. "Agreed—but neither you nor I nor Montague have any knowledge of hypnotic control—at least, I'm assuming that. Don't imagine that I believe in my own argument," he added. "It's just that you urged me to think out all the possibilities, and that one did occur to me. After all, isn't it true to say that Richard Surray did his best to obtain a verdict of suicide?"

Stanwood nodded his head in agreement, his face as calm as Fellowes's was agitated. "Quite, and so would you or I have tried to get it over with as little publicity as we could. But how do you fit in Montague with this last theory of yours? You're not supposing that he and Surray aided and abetted one another in this horror?"

"My God! I don't know. The whole thing is driving me crazy! Perhaps I'm mad, too…"

"Steady on, steady on," put in Stanwood quietly. "I told you to try to use your mind, and to control your emotional bias. The only way I could get any peace was to treat the whole thing as an intellectual problem, using the only facts at my disposal. What about the additional factor you had up your sleeve?" He looked steadily at Fellowes. "You say that Montague was downstairs, talking to her. How can you be certain that it *was* Montague? Did you, for instance, hear a single sentence of the conversation?"

"No. Of course I didn't. I got up some time after midnight. I'd been asleep for a bit, and I woke up—Lord knows why—and I opened the door of my room. It was a hot night and I was restless. I heard somebody moving downstairs and knew it was Montague, because I heard him cough. Then a door opened somewhere—down in the hall. I heard Ruth's voice—just faintly, and a door shut. Then just an occasional murmur, enough to tell me they were talking. I shut my own door at last."

"Then why, in the name of common sense, didn't you tell Richard Surray what you'd heard when he asked you—or even ask Montague about it? I can understand any one fighting shy of the police, but to say nothing—"

"It would have been like eavesdropping, and then telling," mumbled Fellowes. "If Ruth talked to Montague like that—after saying good-night to him in front of all of us—it was because she didn't want us to know. If Montague had thought the police should know, he'd have told them."

Stanwood shrugged his shoulders as though the other man's argument passed his comprehension.

"It's difficult for me to judge," he said slowly. "You and Montague both knew her well—knew that there was something to hide, it seems—but common sense tells me this: If you go to the police with your new version of that night's doings you're asking for suspicion of yourself as strongly as of Montague. It's obvious that any of us could start a hare. I *might* say that I heard Richard Surray's voice downstairs that night. I'm not saying it, though."

"D'you mean that you did hear him—or that you think I'm lying for reasons of my own?"

"In answer to one: No. I did not hear him or anybody else. In answer to two: I don't think you're lying, but it's possible you were mistaken. Think it over again before you make an admission of perjury. You may not be believed, but if you are believed, are you going to do any good?"

He took his chess case firmly out of his pocket and began to study it, while Fellowes, for the first time since he was a small boy, sat and chewed his finger-nails in a state of miserable indecision.

CHAPTER VIII

"Admittedly the problem is a difficult one, Mr. Stanwood; conceivably we shall not be able to do more than assess the probabilities, but every fraction of evidence is important."

Macdonald had returned from his lunch at The King's Arms to interview Stanwood and Fellowes at Upwood House. The former, whom he was tackling first, came rather as a surprise to the Chief Inspector; there was a look of patient pessimism about the lean, tired-eyed man, and nothing at all to denote the successful author whose name was now familiar enough from the publishers' advertisements, and those on the bookstalls.

"It struck me that all of you who were visitors here agreed that Miss Surray had seemed depressed and out of sorts," went on Macdonald. "You knew her pretty well, I take it?"

"I had only met her twice before," replied Stanwood. "On the first occasion we met at Mrs. Trant's studio; there was a number of other writers present, but I had a long conversation with Miss Surray purely on literary subjects. On the second occasion I had lunch with her at her flat, and at her invitation stayed on after her other visitors had gone. As writers will, we talked about our work, discussing, I remember, the technique of the short story."

Macdonald interrupted here. "Can you tell me the date of that meeting?"

"The first Tuesday in July."

"Thanks. I had a reason for asking. Did you have any further conversation with her, except that dealing with her work?"

Stanwood shrugged his shoulders slightly. "A writer's work is the outcome of a philosophy of life, if you will accept a wide and general phrase. Miss Surray had reached a stage when she no longer regarded the 'happy ending' as characteristic of life as she saw it. I wouldn't go so far as to say that she was unhappy in herself—I didn't know enough of her to risk guesses which would be impertinences—but I did find that she was preoccupied with the question of human suffering. From my own experience, I should say that a person has to suffer themselves before they have anything worth while to utter on that subject."

"So far as you could tell, was she in a normal state of mind during the week-end preceding her death?"

Again that slight shrug and a lift of the dark brows.

"How can I answer that? I had not had enough experience of her to judge what was her normal state. I saw no traces of hysteria or nervous excitability. She was calm and cheerful, most thoughtful for the welfare of her guests, more than thoughtful for my own particular welfare. I owed her a great deal—something which I can never repay." He broke off here, as though mistrusting his own voice. "This is all particularly horrible," he went on after a moment's pause. "All of us have reticences; we do our utmost to conceal our own emotional instabilities, and at the very moment when life proves too great a burden and its thread is cut short, a searchlight of inquiry is directed on the things which we strove to keep secret." He stopped suddenly as though aware of his own incoherence. "I am talking nonsense, but I do feel very deeply that this delving for motives of suicide is indecent."

"If it were certain that Miss Surray's death were due to suicide, you might justify that attitude to yourself," said Macdonald; "but that is not the point at issue. However, you would give it as your opinion that her mind was distressed during the period when you were able to observe her?"

"So far as I could tell, yes, but I did not know her long enough for my opinion to have any value."

"Did you gather at all the nature of her distress?"

"No."

"Returning to the subject of the Sunday evening when she died, can you remember if she took a book up with her when she left the drawing-room?"

Stanwood pondered. "Not to my recollection, but I can't be certain."

"She had been discussing *The Willoughby Memoirs* earlier in the evening, I am told, and had said that she intended to finish the book when she went to bed. It was found in the morning-room the next day. It occurred to me that she might have come down to fetch it."

"I don't know. The point's immaterial, isn't it? Aren't you assuming that she went out to post her brother's letter?"

"Presumably, yes. Can you remember if Miss Surray took any coffee after dinner?"

"No. She did not. She never drank after-dinner coffee—or so she said."

"After you said good-night to the Professor on the terrace, did you go into the dining-room?"

"No. I went straight to bed."

"Did you fall asleep quickly?"

"Reasonably quickly."

"You sleep well?"

"Very well."

"These must seem very futile questions to you, Mr. Stanwood, but there is a modicum of sense in them."

"I'm quite willing to assume that there is, even though I can't see the drift."

"After you went to sleep, did you wake again before morning?"

"No. I woke first about six o'clock when the servants began to move about downstairs. I was awake for an hour or so, and then fell asleep again."

"Did you hear anything whatever during the course of the night which may have indicated any movement or activity either inside or outside the house?"

"Nothing. I remember thinking how intensely quiet the country seemed. I live in a flat in London, and I am used to the traffic and the noises made by other tenants in the building, and the silence here was noticeable to me on that account."

"Then you can tell me nothing whatever which can throw any light on Miss Surray's death?"

"Nothing. I came down here to-day at Dr. Surray's

request, but I knew beforehand that I could be of no assistance. I am sorry."

"There's one other point," said Macdonald. "When you were discussing writing with her, did she mention any of her current work, or show you any manuscript which she had recently written?"

"No; that is to say she showed me no manuscript. She mentioned one short story that she was working out, concerning the psychology of a judge who was hag-ridden in his old age by the recollection of death sentences he had uttered."

"An unusually grim topic for one of her philosophic trend."

"Philosophy is concerned with truth. So presumably was the judge."

"And so are we, in this inquiry," replied Macdonald. "Thank you, Mr. Stanwood. I have your address. I may be glad of your help later in considering a fragment of one of Miss Surray's manuscripts which puzzles me. As a writer whose method of work has been compared to hers, your opinion may be valuable."

Stanwood frowned. "That comparison has no justification. My own work has never reached the standard of Miss Surray's, and no one knows it better than I do. I am, however, at your service, though I admit that the prolonging of this inquiry seems to me to be as useless as it is painful."

Just as Stanwood was crossing the study to leave Macdonald, Montague's figure came hurrying up to the closed window and the big man gesticulated to the Chief Inspector through the glass. As the latter opened the French window Montague burst out: "Do, for God's sake, come; looks to me as though the chap's broken his neck. Don't want to alarm the Surrays—they've had enough to put up with. In the rose garden, by the pool. He tripped and fell in. I don't know what I ought to have done. Didn't like to leave him like that; had to get help somehow. No good at doctoring myself."

As he spoke he hurried forward again, and Macdonald, not knowing in the least whom Montague was talking about, hastened beside him. Stanwood, who had only caught the first few words of the hurried speech, followed them. They had to cross the full length of the house, past the terrace, and then Montague plunged over one of the borders without heeding the flowers he trampled down, and as they went through the archway Macdonald saw a prone figure lying in the sunshine.

"Who is he?" he asked, as he knelt down on the grass.

"Fellowes. He was talking to me, stepped backwards, tripped over the edge, and came a smashing whack against that bronze figure. All in a second."

Macdonald lifted one of the slack hands and felt for the pulse. "He's stunned—certainly not dead. Try to keep the sun off him for a minute." He undid the tie and collar and felt round the neck, adding, "Neither's his neck broken, so far as I can tell. Go and telephone for a doctor; it's impossible for any of us to tell how much he's damaged. He fell sideways, it seems, and his skull may be smashed. Quickly!"

He spoke sharply to Montague, whose wits seemed to be wool-gathering, and added: "Ask the doctor about sending an ambulance; he'll have to be moved carefully. Hurry up."

Stanwood put a word in while Macdonald was still examining Fellowes's head. "We'd better rig up something to keep the sun off him. If he's badly hurt it'd be safer not to move him ourselves. We might finish him off if we jarred him. What d'you make of him?"

"He's alive. That's all I'd care to say. A 'smashing whack' about describes it. He's not bleeding much, not externally, anyway. If you move those chairs and we put our coats across them that'll keep the sun off him."

When they had made a shelter, so that Fellowes now lay in the shade, Macdonald added: "I'll stay here. Go into the house and tell Mrs. Surray there's been an accident. Get some cold water and swabs and boracic, if you can. I shan't risk bandaging, but a wet compress can't do any harm. If he's been head first in the pool that won't improve things. The water's septic, of course."

Stanwood hurried off. Macdonald could see that he was cool and level-headed, and guessed that he would do what he could. The Chief Inspector was loath to leave the wounded man; this might be an accident or it might not; and, since Fellowes was still alive, Macdonald intended to keep him alive if he could, and he guessed that a very little would be enough to kill him. When Stanwood hurried off, Macdonald stood and looked at the pool and measured the distance with his eye from the parapet to the bronze figure. A man, standing with his back to the pool, might trip over the edge if he stepped back against it suddenly, but it seemed odd that he couldn't have saved himself by side-stepping. On the other hand, if he had been deliberately tripped up, or thrown backwards, the accident might have resulted in the 'smashing whack.' Moreover, a blow from behind with a loaded stick would have had the same result. All around the fragrant pergolas shut the place in from observation—a safe spot to stage an accident.

In a very few minutes Mrs. Surray came through the archway, carrying a first-aid box, and followed by Stanwood with
a bowl of water.

"You think it would be dangerous to move him?" she asked
quietly, and Macdonald replied:

"I don't like to risk it. He's badly hurt, and moving is a
skilled job. I'll make a compress for his head, and he wants
covering up. His clothes are soaked. How long will it be before
the doctor can get here?"

"A very few minutes. He's coming up now, and the ambulance will be here from the cottage hospital quite soon. You
can manage the swab? I'm sending a screen down, and I'll get
some rugs. Poor boy..."

Macdonald was still kneeling by Fellowes, adjusting swabs
as best he could when Doctor Saunders arrived. After a brief
examination he, together with Macdonald and the ambulance
man, got Fellowes on to a stretcher and had it carried to the
ambulance. To Macdonald's satisfaction, the doctor insisted
on having the injured man taken direct to the hospital, saying
that he would need to X-ray his head to ascertain the extent
of the damage.

"May be all right, but it may be all wrong," he said. "If his
skull's splintered, we may have to operate. He must have come
the devil of a cropper to have damaged himself like that."

Before the doctor left, Macdonald contrived to get a few
words with him alone. "When you examine him, will you
ascertain that there are no marks other than those accounted
for by the fall?"

Saunders stared at him, and Macdonald realised that the
doctor had no knowledge of the man who was making this

somewhat sinister suggestion. Producing a card, Macdonald continued, "I am here officially, making some additional inquiries into Miss Surray's death. For the sake of her family I don't want to advertise the fact needlessly."

Saunders studied the card with a frowning face. "I see," he replied, and his voice and face expressed a lot which he refrained from putting into words. With a gesture towards the ambulance he continued: "All right. I'll let you know."

Going back to the house, Macdonald saw Stanwood, and the latter came towards him, saying, "From the point of view of elucidating things, our visit doesn't seem to have been a success. If you don't want to ask me any further questions I shall be glad to clear out. The Surrays have enough to put up with. Additional visitors are a gratuitous horror."

"Did you travel down with Mr. Fellowes this morning?"

"Yes. We both came by the 11.30 from Paddington—not by mutual arrangement. He saw me when he was on the platform and got in with me."

"It did not occur to me to ask you this before, because I expected to talk to Mr. Fellowes himself; but now I must ask you: Did you discuss the case with him?"

"Naturally, we discussed the implications of this fresh inquiry. One hazards a lot of wild suppositions which have no contact with reality over such a matter. It will be simplest if I say straight away that I shall not repeat any of Fellowes's notions. He, like myself, had already given evidence at the inquest, in which he told everything germane to the case."

"The circumstances are no longer the same."

"No fresh circumstances can alter past facts. Now that the man is laid out and unable to speak for himself, it would be grossly unfair if I repeated any of the foolishness he voiced under stress of strong feeling. For him to air suppositions to me was natural enough; for me to repeat them when he is unable to deny them or defend himself is unthinkable. I might give you an entirely wrong impression of his meaning. You've got his evidence—that's what was important. His opinions—and mine—aren't evidence."

"Did he mention Mr. Montague's name?"

"Obviously, in discussing the events of the week-end, the name of everybody in the house was mentioned. At any rate, I can say this: Fellowes was convinced that Ruth Surray took her own life. Any suppositions which he made as to her reason for doing so are not in the nature of evidence."

Macdonald went no further along this line. He merely said, "I think it would be better if you waited for an hour or two before you leave. I have to see Mr. Montague to get at the facts of this accident. After that I should like to talk to you again."

"As you will. I don't know if it's worth while my saying so, but Fellowes did express a strong feeling of respect and regard for Montague."

"Thanks. I shall find you here later?"

"Since you make a point of it. I will wait in the garden."

With Montague, Macdonald was terse and to the point.

"I want you to come into the rose garden and to show me exactly how the accident happened."

The publisher looked distinctly unhappy—as well he might. He was far from devoid of imagination, and he had not been slow in grasping all the implications of Macdonald's conversation that morning.

"Look here," he began. "If you believe I chucked Fellowes

into that pool with the intention of drowning him, you've got hold of the wrong end of the stick. You're out to prove that we're all raving lunatics, or that I'm a raving lunatic."

"All that I'm asking of you is a straightforward explanation," said Macdonald, studying Montague's frowning face. He saw the queer nervous action of the long jaw, which gave an almost humorous effect of the chin being dislocated. It was as though Montague were arguing with himself, showing his own perplexity in a way that was obvious to the beholder. "If you refuse any explanation of how this accident came about, the inference is obvious, but I can't believe that you would be so foolish. Matters are difficult enough without you making additional mysteries. If this was a simple accident, I take it that you can explain exactly how it happened—your relative positions, and so forth?"

"By all means," Montague replied to the Chief Inspector. "I'll do my best to make it clear, only I'm not sure myself how it did happen. Accidents are like that—take you by surprise. All happened in a second or two. Never rains but it pours. D'you think he's in any real danger? Seems as though the devil goes on the loose sometimes."

When they reached the rose garden again, Montague proved himself to be singularly useless at reconstructing events. He could not remember which way he was facing, nor exactly where he was standing when Fellowes tripped. "About here—or perhaps there," he said vaguely. "We were talking, and he was standing with his back to the pool; he took a step back and simply lost his balance. I was a yard or so away from him—couldn't save him, of course."

"I see," said Macdonald. "What happened in the moments preceding the accident? You came in by the archway?"

"I suppose we did," said Montague. "That's the way one would come from the terrace, isn't it? Honestly, I don't remember. I wasn't thinking of where I was at the moment. Curious thing, I've no recollection of crossing the terrace, even. Mind didn't register anything. Like that sometimes. I've found myself in a tube train without any recollection of how I'd got there."

"You were talking to Mr. Fellowes as you strolled along?"

"He was talking to me—same thing."

"Not quite. I take it your mind registered something of the conversation?"

"Something, yes: all pretty useless from your point of view. We were debating what the devil was the good of it all—you and your everlasting questions. Not helping anybody. Going over the same ground twice—pretty maddening."

"And at one stage in your conversation you left off strolling and stood still and faced one another, Mr. Fellowes with his back to the pool, you facing him about a yard away. What were you saying at the moment he stepped back?"

"God knows, I don't," replied Montague helplessly. However good he was at writing, he was definitely bad at improvising verbally, and he had not thought his subject matter out because he had not had time to do so. "I believe he was wishing you at the devil," he ended feebly.

"Look here, Mr. Montague, this isn't good enough," said Macdonald. "A man may forget where he is standing and take a step backwards if he is startled or bewildered. Similarly he might do so if anybody threatened him, threw anything at him, or even advanced upon him suddenly as though to snatch something, but in a desultory conversation a man doesn't forget where he's standing and trip backwards into a pool with whose position he's perfectly familiar. The only condition which would make your description of an accident convincing is that Mr. Fellowes, already in a state of nervous excitement and oblivious of his surroundings, was suddenly startled by a speech or movement which made him recoil."

"Look here, Mr. Chief Inspector, this isn't good enough," retorted Montague, whose wits were stimulated by a direct attack. "You've asked me questions and I've answered them. If you don't believe what I tell you, that's your own affair. I don't care a cuss what you believe, but if you think I'm going to stand here and listen to you lecturing on cause and effect in order to prove that I'm a sanguinary liar, then you're mistaken."

"My beliefs are immaterial," replied Macdonald. "I want an explanation of an accident, realising that a man may have lost his life through that accident. You have no explanation to offer. We'll leave it at that and go on to a different point. Do you know Keith Brandon?"

Macdonald shot out the question, hoping that Montague's expressive face would show if the name were of any import to him, and there was no question that the shot reached its mark. Montague's jaw dropped and his mouth opened as though to make a swift reply, but shut again before the words were framed. Then, with elaborate unconcern, he bent towards the stonework bordering the pool. "You can see where the poor chap caught his heel against the stone," he said—"all a matter of balance, his weight went back before he realised he'd no footing. What's that you asked? Brandon? What the dickens has he got to do with it?"

"He was a friend of Miss Surray's, I understand."

"Indeed? I wasn't aware of it. I've met him once or twice. We're doing a book for him—mostly devilled. He's got the facts, but he writes like a prep. schoolboy. Have you finished your inquiries at this particular spot? Not doing any good here that I can see."

"Perhaps not, so I won't keep you any longer for the moment," replied Macdonald, and Montague strode off with a frown corrugating his lofty forehead.

After Montague had left him, Macdonald spent some time in the study making notes of ideas which had occurred to him during the day's happenings. The door opened and he saw Stanwood looking at him with an inquiring face.

"If you haven't any more questions to ask, I should be glad to get away and save the Surrays the infliction of my presence," said the latter. "They must regard the three of us as crows of ill omen. We seem to congregate with trouble in our midst. I've been hanging about in the garden trying to avoid everybody."

"I'm sorry," replied Macdonald. "Quite honestly I'd forgotten all about you. I won't keep you now, save for two brief questions. Do you know anything about a book called *Last Leaves*?"

"Nothing. What is it—verse?"

"No. Essays. The second question is this: When you lunched with Miss Surray early in July did you get the definite impression that she was depressed and unhappy? I'm trying to correlate ideas of her mental state previous to her death."

"Changing your mind again and reverting to the Coroner's verdict? For what my opinion is worth, I should say that she was pretty miserable on that occasion—but that is merely an impression."

"I'm sorry to have kept you so long for so little reason," said Macdonald. "You will be at your London address if I want to consult you again?"

"Yes. I'm not going away until September. I hope that if there's anything to discover you'll soon get on to it. This dragging-out business is horrible for every one concerned."

"It is—but that can't be helped."

Stanwood shrugged his shoulders and nodded a sort of pessimistic farewell.

CHAPTER IX

MACDONALD DID NOT RETURN TO LONDON ON THE Monday night as he had originally intended to do; he had an idea which he wanted to try out, and the report which he received from Detective Reeves seemed to indicate that Upwood, rather than London, was the strategic point for the time being. Reeves had been very successful in "tailing" Brandon, and had run the latter to earth near Moreton-in-the-Marsh. In a wooded lane, about half a mile from the village, stood a small stone cottage belonging to a painter named Flemming, and Reeves had followed Brandon until the latter stopped outside the cottage and had admitted himself with a key.

After a guarded inspection of the cottage from without, Reeves had proceeded to find the nearest neighbours, and by dint of pretending that he was looking for a small house in the neighbourhood ("Something with a nice bit of ground, large enough for chickens," explained Reeves) the detective had learnt the name of the owner, and the fact that Mr. Flemming often lent his cottage to friends, but it was no use hoping he'd let it or sell it.

"What about the bloke who's there now?" inquired Reeves. "I didn't like to stop him and ask him questions. Big fair fellow, looks a nob, and got a car that's too big for the lane."

"Mr. Keith that'd be. My girl's been doing for him. He stops a night or so occasionally." Reeves's informant—a farmer in a very small way—looked knowingly at his questioner. "Big fair chap, as you say. Struck me and my missis that he'd a look of some one who'd been in the papers lately. Not the same name, though."

"Funny you should say that," said Reeves. "Same thing struck me. Relative, perhaps."

"Perhaps," said the farmer. "He's thinking of joining the Hunt, maybe. Got a bit of a hunter's eye."

He chuckled wheezily, and Reeves joined in with a snigger and then added: "I reckon you're a sportsman. Like to take a bet—five to one in shillings? Easy enough to find out if you're right about who the bloke is. In my own opinion it's not the same one. Matter of likeness, that's all."

"Tell that to the marines. But how'll you settle it?"

"Like this: D'you know which night the chap stayed down here? A man can't be in two places at once if you take me. The other one's always in the papers."

"Um…lemme think. To-day's Monday. He wasn't down here last week; it'd be the week before. Market day—Thursday—that was it."

"Not since then?" asked Reeves, and the farmer went on:

"Not to stay at the cottage. Leastways, he's not had any cleaning nor cooking done; but our Jack saw his car out

Upwood way on last Sunday evening, late. That's a very handsome car he's got, that is."

"It is—striking, as you might say," replied Reeves. "I'll look into it. Sunday evening, you said—that'd be a week ago yesterday, the 29th?"

"That'd be it."

"Well, if I find out that the party you thinks he might be was in London that Sunday night, that'll be a bob for me, and if I find out that the same party drives a car like that one—"

"—That'll be five bob for me," chuckled the farmer. "That's easy money, that is—not that I expecks to get it. You'll just give this turning a miss next time you're hereabouts."

"No, I shan't. Nothing of that sort about me," replied Reeves. "So long. See you later."

The relevant part of this information was telephoned to Macdonald during the afternoon, and Reeves was told to return to the cottage and "see what he could see without being spotted himself. Any information about Mr. Keith's visits or visitors might be of value."

When Macdonald left Upwood House, Stanwood had been driven to the station to catch a London train, Fellowes was in bed in the cottage hospital, the surgeon there in consultation with Dr. Saunders having issued a hopeful, though guarded, account of his state, and Montague had taken himself off "for a walk." He was staying the night in Upwood House, and Richard Surray was coming down to dinner there.

Macdonald had had a talk with the Professor, and had found his straightforward friendliness and simplicity of bearing much more embarrassing than Mrs. Surray's barely-concealed dislike and resentment.

"Certain allowances have to be made for the fact that we have all been living in a state of tension," said the Professor. "Montague, for instance, and Fellowes—they were totally unlike themselves; my wife, as you can tell, is finding life very hard. I know that Richard was grateful to you for undertaking this inquiry, and I don't want you to think that we are in any way inimical." He made a little gesture with his hands as though to convey the thoughts which it was difficult to put into words. "My son will be staying the night here. I know that he will be anxious to talk to you. Can't we put you up and give you dinner? My wife is distressed that she should have appeared churlish."

"Please don't let her think that," said Macdonald quickly, "and thank you very much for your offer of hospitality; I'm sure that both you and Mrs. Surray will understand me when I say that it is better for me to remain quite a free agent. My comings and goings are of necessity erratic, and I don't want to bother you with my presence here."

"Just as you like. The whole thing is so difficult, it's hard to see light anywhere. Richard had to do what he did over that letter—but it's a wretched business for my wife."

"I know. I do realise that fully," replied Macdonald quickly, "and the knowledge that I am here only makes it worse for her."

Macdonald did not go up to the house again to talk to Richard Surray after dinner. At this stage in the case the Chief Inspector felt that he could not afford to be frank with anybody—except the Assistant Commissioner, to whom he would have to report. He could imagine Colonel Wragley's brisk voice saying, "What *tangible* evidence have you got to prove that the Coroner's verdict was mistaken? Suppositions, I grant you, but pretty contradictory at that."

The matter of Brandon's presence in the neighbourhood gave Macdonald employment after he had dined at The King's Arms. He wanted to get a clear idea of the roads between Moreton and Upwood, and while he was near at hand he determined to call in at Stow to make inquiries about Naomi's visit there on the Sunday evening. The problem of Naomi was looming ahead and would have to be faced. Richard had undertaken to bring her down from the Hebrides if Macdonald considered it necessary to interrogate her, and while Macdonald saw the necessity facing him, he did not want to involve Richard in this aspect of the matter more than he could help. There was something very grim in the thought that one sister might be involved in the death of another sister, and that the brother to both might be the means of proving it.

There was also something grim in the thought that all Macdonald's suspicions might be wrong, and that the only result of his inquiry would be to add to the distress which the Surrays had already endured. If Macdonald were not very circumspect in his line of approach the inevitable rumours would begin to spread, and if he were eventually unable to arrive at the truth, he would have no means of scotching them.

Thinking things over, the Chief Inspector went to see Dr. Saunders, and to him expressed some of the immediate difficulties.

"I've got to get the facts established as fully as possible, but I don't want every scandalmonger for miles round saying that Scotland Yard's asking questions about Naomi Surray. Yet I can't very well go and call on these people at Stow—the

Langs—with a cooked-up story. Can you tell me if they're trustworthy people—by that, I mean capable of keeping their own counsel?"

"I should say that Mrs. Lang is eminently reliable in that respect; she's a shrewd, kind-hearted, clear-headed body. The husband hasn't half her common sense. He wouldn't let a thing out from malice, but he might from stupidity. There are two daughters, and a son who's at Cambridge. I don't know them well, but I'd say you'd do best to ask to see Mrs. Lang by herself, explain who you are without any beating about the bush, and ask her to hold her tongue." Dr. Saunders paused here and looked up at Macdonald. "About the other business—young Fellowes. He ought to recover all right; the skull is cracked, but so far as we can ascertain the bone is neither misplaced nor splintered. Apart from the damage to his head, there was only one other mark on him, a bruise on the point of his right shoulder. I should say at a guess that he fell on to the stone border of the pool as he slipped off the bronze, and that would account for the bruise on the shoulder. Certainly there's nothing to indicate a fight or any sort of struggle. You weren't entirely satisfied with the accident explanation, I gather?"

"How long has that pool been there—stone border, water nymph, and all?"

"Ten years at least."

"And nobody has ever fallen backwards in it before?"

"Not to my knowledge—but you've got to make allowances for nerves being at a stretch."

"Quite. If Mr. Montague had fallen into the pool I shouldn't have been so pernickety over it. He's clumsy on his feet and never looks where he's going. Fellowes seemed a neat compact lad, not the sort to fall about in heaps."

"You've got your job cut out to get anywhere nearer the truth than the Coroner got."

Macdonald looked at Saunders's steady light-grey eyes and solid close-cropped head, and there was inquiry in his own gaze. "Yes. Any advice to offer?"

"None. I'm a general practitioner, not a psychologist or neurologist. I gather that your presence here indicates a dissatisfaction with the verdict of suicide. It seemed to me to meet the facts."

"The worst of the facts in this case—from Ruth Surray's good-night speech to her mother to Fellowes's broken crown—is that you can take them to indicate either of two meanings. However, lest I come to the conclusion that the Coroner got as near the truth as I'm capable of getting, I'll try not to set tongues wagging."

Dr. Saunders arranged some papers on his desk, and seemed to address the table rather than his visitor.

"I liked Ruth Surray. I like Naomi even better. Simpler, less precious, less sure of herself. It'd be a pity to drive her to the same extreme as the other one. I take it you wouldn't regard that as a successful conclusion to your case?" He raised his head and met Macdonald's eyes at the conclusion of his sentence, and the latter said:

"Won't you be more explicit?"

"Ruth's death came as a severe shock to all of them, particularly to Naomi. She was precious near to hysteria and on the way to nervous breakdown. They all suffer from over-intellectuality—that is to say their nerves suffer. If it gets about that suspicion rests on Naomi—and it's damned idiocy to imagine she's implicated—you may find your case multiplied. Don't go out of your way to look for a hidden meaning in what I say. There isn't one—only for God's sake be careful."

"I see your point well enough—but, as I just said, there are two ways of regarding every issue in this case. You say, 'One sister committed suicide; it won't improve matters if the second one does the same.' I add to that, 'One sister may have been murdered. If nothing is done, there is always the possibility that a second murder may be committed.'"

"I know it's not my business to ask questions," said Saunders, "but is there any real justification for the murder hypothesis?"

"When you warned me just now of your fears concerning Naomi Surray, I didn't ask you if you had any positive evidence to justify your apprehension. I take it you have a hunch, based perhaps on a collection of 'ifs.' So have I—but I'll bear your warning in mind."

Driving over to the Langs' house at Stow, Macdonald wondered what would be the best manner of framing his inquiries, and found it exceedingly difficult to decide. A flimsy pretext, which might break down under subsequent examination, would be more harmful than simple straightforwardness; but it took him some hard thinking before he decided on his best method of approach.

Arrived at Prior's Place, the Langs' house, Macdonald was told that Mrs. Lang would see him if he could wait for a few minutes, and he was shown into "the parlour," a pleasant white-walled room with a great ingle-nook fireplace. There was a fine collection of old brass and copper, and the gleaming surface of the metals reflected the colour of the butcher-blue curtains and cushions. On the walls hung old maps of the district, and while he waited Macdonald was able to enlarge his acquaintance with the topography of the district between Stow, Moreton-in-the-Marsh, and Upwood.

When Mrs. Lang appeared she turned out to be a sturdily-built, weather-beaten woman of about fifty. She had a finely-shaped head, her curly grey hair being shingled almost to a close crop, blue eyes, and a wide, humorous mouth. She wore an evening dress of black satin, so severely cut that it gave a tailored effect, and a monocle dangled on a long ribbon round her neck.

"Mr. Macdonald—about the Nursing Association Fête in our garden, I take it?"

Her voice and manner gave Macdonald the impression that the lady he had to deal with was both alert and business-like, and he decided immediately on his method of approach.

"No. Nothing to do with the Nursing Association," he replied, and produced his official card, adding, "I have been asked by Mr. Richard Surray to undertake further inquiries into the matter of his sister's death. This is, of course a confidential matter. He gave me your name on this account: his youngest sister, Naomi, is away in the Hebrides, and he is loath to bring her back without necessity. Possibly you would answer a few questions about her visit here on the Sunday evening—the 29th?"

Mrs. Lang raised her monocle and studied the card; she then dropped it and studied Macdonald.

"This is rather a strange request," she said. "We were greatly troubled by a plague of newspaper reporters last week; one of them went so far as to tell my servant that he was from Scotland Yard."

"If you'll give me the name of his paper I'll look into the matter," replied Macdonald. "This is my warrant as a Police Officer. If you wish for any further reassurance as to my identity, you could ring up the Surrays—or, better still, Dr. Saunders. I have just left him, and he knew that I was calling on you here; in fact, he advised me to do so."

"Good enough. I'll take you for granted," replied Mrs. Lang. "What do you want to know?"

"Was Miss Surray's visit to you on the Sunday evening previously arranged? Were you expecting her, or was her visit a surprise one?"

Mrs. Lang stared at him with raised brows.

"Would it not be simpler if you asked Miss Surray that question?"

"Much simpler," agreed Macdonald, "only she is away— rather far away, too. It's like this: Dr. Saunders is concerned about her health after the shock of her sister's death. If it can be avoided it would be better not to send for her, and better not to have her interrogated again by the police."

"Quite, there's something in that; but I can't say that I'm enthusiastic about answering questions when I can't see where they're leading. However, in answer to your first one, Miss Surray had not made any previous arrangement to drive over on the Sunday, but as she is constantly in and out of the house while she is staying at home, her visit was no sort of surprise. The reason she gave me for coming was that she wanted a little common-place fooling. The party at Upwood was rather intense."

Macdonald nodded. "Yes, I quite see that. Would you tell me the names of any other visitors who were here that evening?"

"I suppose that I had better answer your questions without trying to reason out their appositeness," said Mrs. Lang, "though the question of my guests does seem to me to be very remote from the matter of Ruth Surray's death. She never came to see us herself. However, young Holmerton was here, from Guiting, and the two Laidler girls, and John Kelton, who was staying the week-end. That made eight altogether, counting my own three young people and Naomi herself. They were dancing, and I remember that they made an even number."

She got up here and reached for a box of cigarettes.

"Won't you smoke—and I think you might have the grace to furnish me with some sort of explanation for these abrupt inquiries. It's not very satisfactory for me to have to answer questions in the dark, so to speak."

"Thanks," said Macdonald, accepting the cigarette she proffered. "It's all a bit difficult. I am groping in the dark, too." He went on to tell her about Ruth's letter to Richard and its belated arrival, and ended up by saying, "The only hope of arriving at any conclusion is to make a more exact and far-reaching inquiry than was previously done. Like doctors in a case of smallpox, we have not only to consider the isolated case, but all possible contacts as well."

Mrs. Lang smoked away, consuming her cigarette far more quickly than was usual. "Excellent generalisms, I've no doubt," she said, "but your analogy doesn't seem very helpful. I remember that Naomi did not see her sister when she got home."

"While she was here," persisted Macdonald, "did Miss Surray use the telephone, or did any call come through for her?"

Mrs. Lang stubbed out her cigarette and lighted another before she replied, giving herself plenty of time to think over her answer. "Yes. As a matter of fact, she did," she replied at last. "I don't know who the caller was, though."

"Perhaps Ruth Surray rang up her sister," began Macdonald, but Mrs. Lang cut in:

"Ruth? Rubbish! Naomi would certainly have said so. Besides, it was a man's voice."

"Ah—you answered the phone," he put in quickly. "Did you recognise the voice?" She did not reply, and Macdonald went on: "Would it be easier for you to answer the question put this way: Was it Keith Brandon's voice?"

"I require notice of that question," she replied. "I'm out of my depth here, and you're being much too clever for me. I might be able to answer questions a bit better if you in turn could be franker. What connection *can* there be between Naomi's visit here and Ruth's suicide?"

"In my turn, I don't know how far you are acquainted with all the complexities of Ruth's character," said Macdonald, "and it's no part of my job to break confidences more than I must. Put it this way: perhaps Naomi Surray came over here to receive a telephone message which she did not wish to have at Upwood. In that message there may have been something to pass on to Ruth."

"I can see what you are driving at now," said Mrs. Lang, "and I'm quite certain that you are wrong. Anyway, I'm sure that it would be much better for you to ask questions directly from the person involved, rather than indirectly, through me.

If, for reasons of your own, you think that Keith Brandon telephoned to Naomi here, why not ask him? He, I assume, has not also gone to the Outer Hebrides?"

"Not to my knowledge," replied Macdonald. "The next two questions you can answer without any heart-searchings. What time did Miss Surray reach here on Sunday evening, and what time did she leave?"

"She got here just after half-past eight, and she stayed until shortly before ten."

"Did she say to you that she expected a phone call?"

Mrs. Lang looked troubled. "This is all very unpleasant for me. I hate having to answer questions about Naomi. I think that perhaps I had better consult with my husband about it."

"That is for you to decide; but there is this point: these inquiries which I am making of you have got to be answered, but it is quite conceivable that they may have no real bearing on the main issue. In that case, it would be best if nobody knew that they had ever been made. What you have told me—or what you may tell me—will certainly go no further if it proves irrelevant to the case. For myself, I should be very glad to forget that the necessity for this part of the inquiry ever arose."

Mrs. Lang pondered, as though weighing up the implications of Macdonald's speech.

"Well, it's true that if questions are to be asked I'd much sooner that you came direct to me and asked them than went to the servants. Not that there's anything to make a mystery about; it's simply that answering questions about that child makes me feel mean and uncomfortable. When she came, she did say to me, 'If a phone call comes through for me, will you be kind and let me know? Some one' (Tony, I think she said) 'may ring up at home, and I told them I was coming over here.' Some one rang her up just after nine—a man, as I said, but I did not ask for his name, neither, of course, did I hear the conversation. That's the utmost I can do for you, Inspector."

"Thank you very much," replied Macdonald. "I am sure you will regard this conversation as confidential. I should be very sorry if it became general knowledge that my department was making inquiries in this direction."

"It will not become known through me," said Mrs. Lang firmly. "The Surrays have had enough to bear, poor souls, without adding to their troubles."

Leaving Prior's Place, Macdonald drove towards Moreton-in-the-Marsh, in order to learn the distances between the Langs' house, Keith Brandon's cottage, and Upwood itself. Driving carefully in the narrow roads, he pulled up sharply as a car poked its nose too suddenly out of the lane which led to Mr. Flemming's cottage. The driver saw the headlights on Macdonald's car (it was twilight, the awkward hour between lights), pulled up abruptly, and stalled his engine.

Macdonald sat where he was, safely concealed by his own headlights, and in their beam he saw Vernon Montague's unmistakable head, while the publisher pressed savagely on his self-starter and started the car again with a jerk which nearly landed it in the opposite ditch. Eventually he manoeuvred it into the main road and drove off with Macdonald behind him, the latter reflecting that if he himself were a "traffic cop," he would certainly have summonsed the man ahead for dangerous driving.

Montague and Brandon, what did that imply? Both men,

it seemed to Macdonald, had something to conceal, and the latter was inevitably suspicious of them separately; now that it appeared the two had been consulting together, he was more than ever suspicious, but found it difficult to formulate any theory which covered Montague and Brandon together. Fiddling with his pieces like a chess player, Macdonald evolved theories of the Sunday evening which had ended in Ruth Surray's death.

Brandon, forbidden by Naomi to communicate with her at Upwood House, had managed to telephone to her at the Langs' (this obviously involved Naomi's connivance), and he might have persuaded Naomi to come out to meet him some time after the Upwood household had gone to bed. Brandon could not have met her earlier in the evening; he had undoubtedly been in London (in the foyer of the Duchess of Kent's Theatre) at eight o'clock, and it would have taken him over two hours to drive to Upwood, even allowing for the fact that he was a good driver and had a fast car. Naomi's inquiry as to whether Ruth had gone to bed was made from apprehension lest Ruth should be out in the garden, or at the post, and might observe her (Naomi) if she went out again.

Leaving Brandon and Naomi on his mental chessboard, Macdonald returned to Montague and Ruth. When the latter came down to go to the post with Richard's letter, Montague might have accompanied her on her walk, and during that walk it was possible that the two couples had become aware of each other's presence—that is to say, that Montague knew that Brandon was in the neighbourhood, close at hand, and that Brandon knew that the publisher had been out with Ruth late that night.

How could that theory be made to square up with sub-sequent events?

Brandon's attempt to prove that he was not in the Upwood neighbourhood on the Sunday evening might be explained in various ways: If it were proved that he had met Naomi, he would certainly have Richard Surray's wrath to face. If it were suggested that he had met Ruth, public opinion might have held him responsible for her death. In any case he might have had to involve one of the sisters in his own admission.

But what could have induced Montague to tell lies about the events of the evening? If he knew that Brandon were in the neighbourhood, if he even knew that Ruth Surray had gone out of the house again after she had said good-night, the only explanation of his denials must be that he was involved in her death. If, on the other hand, he knew nothing more than his evidence admitted, why this visit to Brandon, and why the accident to Fellowes? An accident Macdonald was willing to concede, but there must have been some predisposing cause, some state of tension existing between the two men to make the thing explicable. Macdonald had an exasperated feeling that he would like to get hold of his various witnesses and shake them as a terrier shakes a rat, in the endeavour to get the truth out of them; they were all holding up something— Brandon, Montague, and Stanwood. Fellowes was laid out in such a manner that his evidence might not be available for weeks; Naomi Surray, in the far Hebrides, was hedged round by Dr. Saunders's warning: "It won't help your case if you drive her to do the same thing that her sister did." Probably Saunders knew more than he had admitted of the troubles which had beset both sisters, but it would take a very clear statement of a case on Macdonald's part to make the doctor break confidence with a girl who was his patient.

Following in the wake of Montague's spasmodic speeding, Macdonald took himself to task. Had he got enough solid evidence to justify him in regarding this case as a murder case? Would all his unearthing simply result in a re-statement of the Coroner's verdict, coupled to infinite distress for everybody who had been devoted to Ruth Surray? Should he (Macdonald) return to London and report that there was not enough evidence to justify a continuance of the case? Mrs. Surray's unhappy face came into his mind: "What good can you do? All these questions can't bring Ruth back."

But with the stubbornness which is the very essential of the Scot, Macdonald knew that he would go on delving, worrying, inquiring; there *was* a case, he was convinced—a case not of suicide, but of subtle, well-planned, neatly-executed murder. In Macdonald's mind was a belief that murderers always make some mistake, always overlook something, which can be found if the searcher is only patient enough. Direct questioning had failed. The evidence given at the inquest would simply be handed out to him again and again. "I heard nothing. I saw nothing."

Sympathy seemed to be nothing but a weakness in this case. Richard Surray, tired and nerve-racked, might be holding something back; Mrs. Surray herself, quiet of speech and wary of eye, might be saying to herself, "I shan't tell him that. It's nothing to do with him."

Conscious that his day's inquiry had landed him in a confusion that was more exasperating than the mere emptiness of the original facts, Macdonald determined to pursue the case until he reached a solution—or until it "broke him" by its sheer imperviousness.

He had, as tangible evidence, a coffee cup which no one could explain, a will on which the Roman numerals might have been altered, and a sheet of manuscript paper which might have been cut down. For intangible evidence he had the feeling that everybody was concealing something, that Fellowes's accident was not fully explained, and that Montague's visit to Brandon was somehow connected with the case.

CHAPTER X

WHEN MACDONALD DECIDED TO WALK FROM UPWOOD House to the post-box shortly after midnight, he was simply putting into practice a theory of his own to the effect that if you want to see what a person might observe during a midnight walk, it was better to cover the ground at the same time that they had done rather than to inspect it at noonday. It certainly seemed probable that Richard Surray was right in his conjecture that Ruth posted her letter to him some time after the household had gone to bed. Macdonald, unknown to the Surrays, was prowling round the garden soon after eleven. He watched the lights being extinguished and noticed that the servants, who occupied the top storey, had all put their lights out by the time he arrived. A light went on burning in the Professor's study until midnight, and there were still two lighted windows on the first floor when Macdonald made his silent way round the house, until he reached the small conservatory door. From here he struck across the garden and out into the paddock, whose lower gate gave on to the lane leading to the high road and to the village. Using his imagination, because he had no other guide, he thought that this lane would have been a likely enough spot for Naomi to meet Brandon (if any of his guesses had hit the mark). Out of earshot of the house, and remote from traffic at that hour, it would have served their purpose admirably. Hither then came Ruth, but to make sense of the rest of the story, Montague must have walked with her—or was he behind her? Arguing the matter out at every step, Macdonald reached the junction of lane and high road; there was a cottage here, and a watchdog barked and rattled his chain as the quiet footsteps passed; a good watchdog that. Had he barked on that Sunday night?

There was only one other house to be passed before the pillar-box was reached, and Macdonald arrived there almost simultaneously with another man. The Chief Inspector flashed a light on him at once and saw Dr. Saunders, with a Dalmatian puppy at his heels. In reply to the doctor's expostulation, Macdonald switched the beam off, after having first let it play on his own face.

"What the deuce are you up to at this hour?" demanded the doctor irately. (No man likes to be the target of an unexpected flash lamp.)

"What you might expect," replied Macdonald. "I'm really looking for some one who is in the habit of posting letters at midnight. Did you post any about this time on Sunday night the 29th?"

"I did, but I expect that I was earlier than this," replied Saunders. "I generally go to the post at eleven, and take this hound for a walk. What about it?"

"Did you meet anybody or anything while you were out that Sunday evening?"

"Good Lord, how on earth do you expect me to remember?"

"I wish you'd try," said Macdonald. "As you walk back, think out what letters you posted on that night, and see if you get any answering chain of thought."

"I get you—but one thing I can tell you immediately: I didn't meet any one from Upwood House."

"That doesn't matter," replied Macdonald; "but try to remember if you met any one at all. Folks are mostly early to bed in the village, I expect."

"They are. Yours is a darned funny job, Inspector. Chasing shadows, so to speak."

"A shadow indicates two things: the presence of a light and the presence of a body which intercepts that light," replied Macdonald. "In my present state of mind I should welcome anything as definite as a shadow to give me a lead. You'll try to jog your memory for me?"

"I will. Let's be a little more exact. You want information about anybody—no matter who—who went for a midnight stroll that Sunday night?"

"That's just what I do want."

"I'm as likely to find that out for you as anybody. I'll do my best. That young chap Fellowes is going on quite nicely. He won't give us the slip this time; but I'll tell you one probability to save you from disappointment: as likely as not he'll have forgotten everything immediately preceding that knock on the head. He's badly concussed, and concussion plays tricks with the memory."

Macdonald chuckled. "So I've heard. Do you remember

those tomfool guessing games schoolboys play; the joker finally explains, 'I only put that in to make it harder.' This case is like that; everything's put in to make it harder, and when you've stripped off the possibles there's nothing left where the kernel should be. Thanks for your offer of help about the Sunday evening. I shall be very glad if you get at anything for me."

"I'm by no means sure myself if it's a good deed to help the law in this instance," retorted Saunders. "The law's a hass—as has been previously observed."

"Maybe—but it's not so asinine as it would be if every man made his own laws," replied Macdonald.

"Good-night."

Walking back, he encountered nobody. The same watch-dog advertised his presence at the corner, but the lane was very dark and still. Pausing in his quiet walk, Macdonald reflected that voices would travel a long way in the stillness, and the beams of a car's side lamps or rear lights would seem startling in that close darkness. Because he had determined to complete the walk both ways, he went up through the gate in the paddock and woke old Charity, who whinnied softly in the gloom. Glancing up at the house, he saw a light somewhere on the ground floor—not the steady glow of an electric lamp, but a flicker, like a candle flame. He quickened his steps. Anything out of the ordinary might be important just now, and if somebody in the house were doing a little investigation by candlelight, they were certainly worthy of attention. The window was dark again now, but Macdonald had judged its position; it was the one beyond the kitchen quarters, either the servants' sitting-room or the workroom.

As he drew nearer to the house the light appeared again, more strongly this time, but there was a quality about it this time which made Macdonald forsake his cautious method of approach and break into a run, full tilt across the flower beds. It was no candle flame flickering in a draught which was causing a glow behind the windows of the workroom, it was a fire. Small flames spurted up and seemed to die away, others gained fresh strength and burned more brightly.

Macdonald had a hope when he reached the window that the fire might be of such small dimensions that he would be able to deal with it himself and then investigate its cause. His hand was in his pocket, withdrawing a knife to force the hasp of the window when he realised that this plan was unworkable. Suddenly, without warning, the flames leapt up inside, no longer in small flickering tongues, but in a sheet of light, rising almost from floor to ceiling. It was a horrible sight, that fierce burning fire, leaping for the beams overhead, and Macdonald knew how an old house could burn. In a second his police whistle was shrilling its note, its vibrance making his own ears ring. No time now for finesse, wake everybody up and get them out of the house. Fire! Fire!

A window opened overhead. Montague's voice shouted, "What the deuce… What is it? What's the matter?" The whistle had done its work and the household was awake.

"There's a fire on the ground floor. Get everybody downstairs," shouted Macdonald. "Are you there, Dr. Surray? Open the front door for me."

He raced round to the main entrance; there were fire extinguishers in the hall and passages, and it might be possible to get the blaze under if they wasted no time. As Richard opened the door Macdonald said:

"Fire extinguishers—it's in the workroom. We may be able to do it. The lights are working—that's one comfort."

As he pulled down one of the extinguishers Macdonald heard a calm voice saying:

"I'll ring up the Fire Brigade, but they're never any good. Not enough water. See that all the maids are down, Father."

It was a girl with dark hair who spoke—Judith, in green pyjamas, with her baby tucked under her arm.

Macdonald and Richard, each armed with an extinguisher, ran down the passage towards the kitchen quarters, Richard shouting:

"You there, Robert and Montague? Get the extinguishers from upstairs and bring them to the workroom."

They heard the crackle of the fire as they hurried towards it; the door of the workroom was closed and bolted, and when Macdonald got it open the heat seemed to spring out at them as out of an oven. Everything seemed to be burning at once, the carpenter's bench, the trestle tables, the piles of wood and frames and oddments, and burning with a vindictive fury which betokened only one thing to Macdonald. He heard a cool voice saying behind him, "Sand's what you want here. There are buckets outside. Hell! That's the main cable. Lights gone."

It was an hour before they got the fire under. It burnt obstinately, coming to life again after it had seemed deadened. Richard and Robert Surray, the Professor, Montague, and Macdonald worked away, shovelling sand and passing buckets of water when the extinguishers had been used up.

In the bedrooms above, the servants worked with Mrs. Surray and Judith to get all possible furniture moved out, and poured water over the ancient floors to make them less inflammable. Macdonald asked once about the fire brigade, and heard Robert beside him chuckling:

"They'll get here by the time we've finished, and go on rolling up all night. Fortunately there's no water main, or they'd souse the place."

By the time the brigade did arrive, at least it was possible for the original fire-fighters to have a breathing space. The workroom had been reduced to an evil-smelling oven, in which reeking heaps still smoked and hissed and smouldered; the smell of burning, and that foul, sour smell of acrid smoke permeated the house, but there seemed no risk of another outbreak.

"Sodom and Gomorrah! Lead me to a drink," spluttered Robert at last. "God knows what all the jolly stink is, but part of it appears to be the glue-pot and old rubber tyres. This has got the out-patients' department beaten to a frazzle."

Leaving the local "firemen" (amateurs to a man) to watch over the ashes, the others made their way back to the hall, lit now by oil lamps. They made a fantastic group, all blackened and tousled out of recognition, with sweat making runnels down their darkened faces. Richard, still clad in scorched dinner jacket and blackened shirt, Robert in striped pyjamas, once mauve and green, with the jacket now in tatters. Vernon Montague had a silk dressing-gown wrapped round him, the wet, dirty, draggled piece of finery consorting strangely with his powerful head and sombre eyes.

All of them were parched and exhausted, and waited until

they had swallowed their drinks before saying much. Then Robert, refilling his glass, turned to Macdonald, saying:

"I've no notion who you are, but you're a stout fellow. Here's how!"

Explanations followed, and then the inevitable chain of surmise about the origin of the fire.

"Must have been a short circuit; no one's been into the workroom for ages," argued Robert. "The servants don't go in there; it's just cleaned once in a way."

"I was in there myself about lunch time to-day," said Macdonald. "Everything was all serene then."

"How did you come to notice the fire?" inquired Richard, voicing at last the question which Macdonald had been expecting. He looked round at the strange little group.

"You all know who I am, and what I am here for. I was outside in the garden just after eleven and about the grounds until nearly midnight. There was no sign of a fire then. I walked to the post and back, coming and going through the paddock. I first saw a light on the ground floor when I was a couple of hundred yards away; it was a mere flicker and I took it for candlelight. Then, all in half a minute, or less—say fifteen seconds—the flicker burst out into a blaze which filled the whole room with flame." He turned and looked at the Professor. "Do you know anything about the contents of that room, sir? Was there any petrol or paraffin there, any drums of inflammable oil, or cinematograph film, or anything else that would flare up in the way I have described?"

The older man shook his head. "I can't believe that there was anything of the kind. We are quite cognisant of the danger of fire in old houses of this kind, and there is a strict rule that all paraffin, turpentine, petrol, and such like, is to be kept in the outhouses. I don't know who was working in the room last, but I don't believe that they would have left anything inflammable carelessly exposed."

"Wire fused," put in Montague. "Probably smouldered for hours and then burst into flame when everything got hot together. I've seen it happen before. Amazing the way a fire will get hold. Everything's dry with the hot weather. Like tinder. Ready to catch."

While Montague spoke, Robert Surray caught Macdonald's arm.

"I want to try to get the old boy back to bed. He's had a doing. Let's P.M. on our own accounts, but get him out of it first." Then, raising his voice, he said, "We can see about all that later. What about a spot of bed for those who feel like it?" He touched his father's arm. "It's safe enough now, and there'll be plenty of us watching. Can you persuade Mother to go and lie down again?"

The Professor got up with an unconscious, long-drawn sigh, like a man who has shouldered a burden too heavy for him, but he seemed glad of the opportunity of shelving any further discussion.

"Yes," he said. "You're right. No use getting more exhausted than need be." He turned to Macdonald. "We are grateful to you, Inspector. Had you not been there we should have had no roof to our heads, and possibly no need for a roof in future. Richard will see about anything we can do in the way of putting you up…"

His son took him by the arm and led him out into the hall, and Macdonald followed. Like the rest of them, he felt bemused and awkward; his eyes and lungs were still smarting from the smoke. He was battling between two impulses, the first an almost overpowering desire to go to sleep, the second a lively curiosity concerning the remains of the fittings in the burnt-out workroom. He heard Mrs. Surray's voice addressing him, almost apologetically:

"Is there anything I can do or get for you, Inspector? Are you hurt at all?" And he pulled himself together from the state of dizziness which was the result of heat and smoke and a long whisky and soda.

"No, not in the least, thank you," he replied. "I think you can rest assured that there is no further danger. We shall watch carefully, of course, and the local men will stand by. The smell is very horrible, but the house is safe enough now, I think."

"Oh, the house!" she said sadly. "I loved it so much. Now I'm beginning to hate it."

Judith's clear voice put in behind her mother, "I think the bathroom in the west wing's still functioning, Inspector. The others seem waterless. Mother, I've had some mattresses and a camp bed dragged out on to the lawn. I can't bear the smell of the house, and the infant can't, either. Wouldn't you rather come outside?"

Macdonald left them, thinking what a sensible, practical creature this married daughter seemed to be. On his way back to the workroom wing he turned into the kitchen and put his head under a tap which "still functioned," and felt better after he had washed off the grime and cooled down a bit. Then, hurrying along the passage, he found the super-intendent of the fire brigade, and once more impressed on him that nothing was to be moved among the charred débris of the workroom unless it was necessary owing to a renewed outbreak.

"I want to be able to find out what caused the fire, and the less things are stirred up the better," he said, and the superintendent (an astute old gamekeeper) nodded his head.

"Ay, I'll see to it as far as may be, sir, but you'll find it's them wirings, sure enough. Time and again it's happened in these old houses. The gentry, they puts in central heating and they puts in electric wires, and everything's lovely till something goes wrong with the works. It was the same at Stoke and the same at Abingdon and the same at Lord Plumstead's house in the Shires. Just asking for trouble."

Returning along the passage, Macdonald almost cannoned into Robert Surray, and the latter said:

"I've brought you another coat. Yours is only worth keeping as evidence for the insurance people. What about a stroll outside? We can keep an eye on the dust and ashes from the garden. Richard's staying in the bedroom just above, lest there's an outbreak there. You never can tell with these old houses."

Macdonald agreed and walked out into the garden, saying, "You're a physician, are you not? Do you think your brother is all right? He looked pretty poor when I saw him on Saturday, and this business hasn't been exactly helpful." He paused for a moment, and then added: "That room he's in now was Miss Surray's bedroom, the one in which she died?"

Robert waited before he answered, as though to gather all the meaning implicit in the words, and then said:

"Richard's all right; I don't think you need worry about him. He won't conjure up ghosts. It only occurred to me when you mentioned it that the room up above the holocaust was Ruth's—and the other one Naomi's."

He produced a cigarette-case and held it out to Macdonald, switching on his lighter to illuminate his action. (He had changed into flannel slacks and a shirt when he went upstairs.) "To put it in plain English, you think this evening's little to-do was arson and not accident? Deliberate fire-raising, in short?"

"I think it must have been," replied Macdonald. "I was in the workroom myself this morning. I examined the bench and fittings, and I know what was there. There was nothing to account for a fire of that intensity at that spot. There were sacks of sawdust and shavings, and a lot of the odd litter you get in a workshop, but none of it was piled under, or upon, the bench. It will be difficult to see how things were placed when it all cools down, but when I looked through the window I saw flames reaching right up the wall above the bench."

"Pretty grim," said Robert quickly. "It means that somebody in the house decided to burn us out—or at any rate burn Ruth's room out. You were in there this morning, though, weren't you? You'd have known if there was anything—to hide?"

Macdonald waited before he answered this time.

"I didn't find anything in there, neither did I expect to after this lapse of time. I could kick myself for a fool," he added, "not on this morning's account, but because I followed my instinct this evening. There was a fire, and the thing wanted putting out, so I rushed off with you to fire-fight. That's instinct, old as the hills—if there's a fire, go and put it out. If I'd stopped to think, I should have left the fire to you people and tried to find out if there was an intruder in the house. It did occur to me when the lights went out. You said, 'Main cable burnt through.' I thought,

'Main fuse tampered with.' It was too late to do anything else then but what we were doing."

Robert gave a long whistle, dolorous as a groan.

"This is all too damned beastly for words, whichever way you look at it. Has some one got such a down on us that they'd burn us all out—Judy and the kid, and Mother? If you hadn't spotted that burning fiery furnace we might all have been for it. Doesn't bear thinking of."

"Think of it another way," said Macdonald. "None of you in the house smelt any smoke or had the faintest suspicion that a fire had occurred until I gave you warning? Surely if it had been as Mr. Montague suggests, a slow charring of dry wood, some one would have noticed it? You weren't all early to bed to-night. There were lights burning until after midnight. Isn't the only possible explanation that there was no previous charring, no smoke? It all happened at once, and when it did start burning it flared like hell."

"If you're right, somebody must be raving mad," said Robert. "No one in their senses could plan out a piece of devilment like that."

"Every man who commits a murder is mad to some extent," said Macdonald. "That's why we dare not let them escape if there's any possibility of catching them."

"Then you believe that Ruth was—murdered?"

"With every hour that passes I'm more disposed to believe it. After the Coroner's verdict the murderer would have felt perfectly safe. Everything had gone according to plan; but as soon as the inquiry was reopened, danger threatened. This fire was the result—or one of the results."

"It's damned hard to keep one's head and not to rage

furiously, like the heathen," replied Robert. "I was talking the whole thing over with Judith—Mrs. Beech, you know. She's got the clearest head of the lot of us and manages to keep calm while she looks at things. If your idea of murder is right, the murderer must have been staying in the house that Sunday night, and must have been in the house to-night."

"The first point isn't established," replied Macdonald. "If Miss Surray went out to the post she may have met somebody; she may even have brought them back to the house with her, but certainly the murderer must have been in the house some time during the night, in order to place those papers by her bedside, unless that was the work of an accomplice."

Robert swore beneath his breath—a sound that was half groan, half violence. "It's all unspeakably hellish," he replied. "Do you wonder that Richard looks like a death's head? If this case were presented to him as a clinical problem, he'd hand you out the probable answer, complete with motive, accomplices, and opportunity. He can see it with the most damnable clearness, and the best answer to hope for is Broadmoor—for one of us."

"It's not come to that yet," replied Macdonald quietly. He knew that Robert was thinking of Naomi and Keith Brandon. "There may be quite different aspects to consider. Psychologists have a tendency to overstress the sex motive, because they find it the driving power behind such a lot of queer manifestations."

"That chap Brandon—do you know anything about him, where he is now, or what he's up to?"

"Yes. He's under observation, as the doctors say." Macdonald drew a deep breath of the cool night air, adding,

"I don't know about you, but I feel less woolly in the head and more steady about the knees now. I'd like to go in and inspect the electrical doings to see if I can find any signs of interference. All the smoke and heat and fumes resulted in making me feel temporarily tight."

"I know," replied Robert. "I could have fallen asleep standing up, and my eyes wouldn't see straight. I hope to God you find something to prove your theory of an interloper. Otherwise you're bound to conclude that some one in the house did the fire-raising. Incidentally, I managed to ask the servants if any of them had been in the workroom to-day. They said they hadn't, but Gladys, the housemaid, said the door was ajar when she was locking up this evening. She shut the door and bolted it. It was fastened when you got there, wasn't it?"

"Yes. Bolted. Have you any theories on deferred fire-raising?"

Robert whistled. "A slow match—time-fuse—something like that?"

"Something less obvious than that. If the door was left open it would have had to have been something that wouldn't be noticed if anybody had gone into the room. A time-fuse gives off fumes as it burns."

"Good Lord! I've remembered a trick I played at school once—in the lab. I got a bit of potassium, and arranged a tilted beaker under a dripping tap. When the beaker overflowed a dribble of water ran down to the potassium. It flares when water touches it—you remember? I'd put some cotton waste above the potassium and the fire started just in the middle of a dull chemistry lesson, as per arrangement. It was a great do."

"That's a good example of a method no one could spot until the fire actually began," said Macdonald. "A dripping tap—nothing to suggest fire. Another method by which water could be utilised would be to disturb the rubber insulating of an electric flex and leave it to get wet gradually until the wires fused and got hot. They would ignite something like a rag soaked in petrol very easily, and the subsequent bonfire could have been organised in advance. Wood shavings all handy, sawdust soaked in paraffin, and so forth. When we got in there the glue pot had discharged itself over every-thing, and there was some rubber burning, too. In fact, the general stink made it impossible to recognise paraffin fumes, or petrol either, or any of the other jolly messes which might have been used."

"Electricity has many points in its favour," murmured Robert fatuously. He was so much relieved by Macdonald's theory over "deferred fire-raising" that his spirits had gone up with a bound. "Every ass in existence knows something about short circuits and whatnots. I once worked out a glorious 'defective' about a chap who listened to the wireless in his bath."

"What is a defective?" demanded Macdonald, who knew quite well in reality.

"Family description of detective—on paper," replied Robert. "A lamp is indicated here, and the main fuse and other doings are in the first cellar under the pantry."

"I know they are, and I know the main fuse is blown," replied Macdonald. "The point is, if my short circuit theory is any good, the main fuse should have blown earlier in pro-ceedings. I want to trace the entry of the cable and find out what happened when the lights went, and why it happened."

Macdonald and Robert Surray between them had a good working knowledge of electrical installations, but they found nothing in their researches at Upwood House which was in any way suggestive or helpful. They traced the cable through the cellars and noticed where it ran up through the workroom floor, where the wires branched out to the various rooms above and around, but since the wooden cases were burnt away from the wiring in the burnt-out room, it was obvious that the insulation would also have been destroyed.

Macdonald studied the remains of the workroom wiring as best he could by the light of his torch. The room was still very hot, and the smoke made his eyes stream and his head dizzy. He turned to Robert Surray, saying:

"I've got an idea which is trying to come to the surface, but I've also got such a thick head that I can't think clearly. The best thing we can do is to lie down and go to sleep for a couple of hours. It'll be full daylight then, and our wits will be in better working order."

"Also the ex-furnace will have cooled down a bit and we can sift the ashes," replied Robert, "or don't you sift ashes in reality?"

"I'd sift with the best if I had any hope of finding anything," replied Macdonald. "What would you look for—a detonator?"

Before he went to lie down for his short night's sleep, Macdonald looked in to Ruth Surray's bedroom, where Richard still sat on the window seat.

"I think everything is safe enough now, Dr. Surray," said Macdonald. "There's no real need for you to sit up any longer."

"And there's no real object in my going to bed," replied

Richard. "Sleep won't come my way to-night. Was this fire part and parcel of our other troubles? Perhaps it would have been better if I hadn't shown you that letter after all."

"You're in no state to discuss it now," replied Macdonald, "and neither am I. I'm stupid with sheer tiredness. It's not my province to give you advice, but surely it would be better to lie down and rest, even if you can't sleep—and in any room but this one."

"Rooms mean nothing to me—in that sense. I've never been conscious of the supernatural. I'm just trying to puzzle things out in my own way. Thanks for all you've done—and are doing. Can I get you anything?"

"Nothing, thanks. I'm going to lie down in the next room for a couple of hours."

Macdonald felt more sorry for Richard than for any of the others at that moment, but he left him without saying anything else. Indeed it was difficult to know what to say.

CHAPTER XI

MACDONALD, SEARCHING AMONG THE MALODOROUS débris of the workroom in the early hours of Tuesday morning, hardly dared to hope for any clear indication of how the fire had started. Remembering the flickering flames he had seen when he first came within sight of the window, he wondered whether he ought to accept the obvious conclusion that some one had gone into the room shortly after midnight, arranged a bonfire with some petrol to expedite matters, lighted a small heap of shavings, and had then beaten a hasty departure. It was not necessary to assume that the fire-raiser had slept in the house. Upwood House, with its many windows and doors, would not have been a difficult house to enter, and during the confusion of the fire, when the lights were out and the doors open, it would have been easy enough for the intruder to make good his escape. That the fire had been deliberately engineered Macdonald was certain, for, in spite of ashes and charred rubbish, there was evidence that the contents of the room had been moved since he examined it that morning.

One thing he found which made him ponder for a long time. The fire had at one place burnt away the wooden wainscot, and an electric switch which had been affixed to the wainscot had fallen away; it was a solid brass fixture, whose metal, though blackened, had not been otherwise affected by the fire, and the button of the switch was still pressed down. Holding it in his hand, Macdonald looked round for a stove, or any other fixture which could have been connected with it. Eventually Robert Surray came to his assistance.

The switch was a power-switch, with a two-way plug, and various gadgets had been connected with it—an electric lathe, a fretwork saw, an electric fire, an electric kettle, and a small cylindrical heater used for melting glue, or boiling up paste, or other decoctions.

The lathe and the fretwork saw were ruled out as possible agents on account of the noise they made while working. The electric fire was not found in the room at all, and Mrs. Surray said that it had been moved into another room the previous spring and had not been returned to the workroom. The electric kettle testified to its own innocence because it stood on a shelf at the end of the room farthest from the fire and still contained some water in it.

There remained the little round heater. This was eventually found deep buried in the piles of charred wood and ashes which had once been the carpenter's bench. It was capable of adjustment to three degrees of heat—low, medium, and high, and its indicator still pointed faithfully to "high."

"Well, there you have it," said Robert. "It's a much simpler method of 'deferred fire-raising,' as you call it, than anything you and I suggested. All you've got to do is to put a few shavings or a bit of newspaper over your heater, put down the switch and walk away. In about a couple of hours the metal plate will be hot enough to ignite anything, and there you are, with a lovely alibi. In two hours' time you can get quite a long way from the scene of action."

"Two hours," said Macdonald thoughtfully. "That's approximate, I take it? If we get another of these stoves from the makers we could time it exactly. I saw the fire beginning at half-past twelve. If this was the method used, the current must have been turned on between ten and eleven."

"Not later than half-past ten," said Robert. "I'm certain it would take a good two hours for the plate to get hot enough to ignite anything. Possibly longer. When you were in here yesterday morning did you notice whereabouts the heater was standing?"

"No, I didn't see it anywhere, but I didn't search the room in any sense. I only looked around," replied Macdonald.

"Mine's not to reason why," replied Robert, who would have dearly loved to know why the contents of the workroom should have interested the Chief Inspector yesterday. "Would it be a good idea if you were to find out what everybody in the house was doing between ten and eleven last night? If that heater caused the fire, it must have been switched on by eleven o'clock. It takes a long time to warm up."

"Go ahead," replied Macdonald. "I expect you have been doing a certain amount of reconstruction."

"So far as ourselves are concerned, yes," replied Robert. "After dinner Montague borrowed the car and went to Oxford. He came in about ten. Richard, Father, and I were in the study together from dinner time until Montague came in. He joined us in the study and stayed there talking to Father, while Richard and I went into the drawing-room where Mother and Judith were sitting. We were in there until half-past ten, when we went into the dining-room and made tea—rather as people used to do during the air raids, to show how jolly and normal they felt. Judith and Mother went upstairs just before eleven, after we'd been out on the terrace. By the way, there's a point here which might interest you. We went out on to the terrace because Judith noticed a couple of rabbits giving an entertainment on the lawn. Any reaction?" He paused here and looked quizzically at Macdonald, who replied:

"I noticed that the garden is wired all round against rabbits and that you have notices at every entrance that the gates are to be kept shut. You mean that the rabbits indicated that a gate had been left open?"

"Yes. It's a bit thin as an argument, but when you know the way gardeners wage war against rabbits, the reaction to seeing a couple of bunnies on the lawn is that some damn fool's left a gate open. I know Montague shut the drive gate, because I asked him. However, that brings us to eleven o'clock. Mother and Judith went up to bed, and Richard and I went into the drawing-room and talked for another twenty minutes. Then he went up, saying he'd got a report which had to be written out. That'd made it nearly eleven-thirty. I went to say good-night to Father. He and Montague were still in the study. They didn't go up till nearly twelve." Robert broke off here; he had managed to keep his voice to a normal tone of narration, as though he were discussing something of merely abstract interest, but his face and voice changed as he added: "I don't want to stress the obvious, but it may have occurred to you that one of us is a criminal lunatic. *Qui s'excuse s'accuse*, and all that. At least it's a crumb of comfort to know that everybody's doings can be accounted for until nearly midnight."

"Thanks," replied Macdonald. "Questions have to be asked, and it saves a lot of wear and tear if people take your method and recognise the necessity."

"Meanwhile, shall I go and forage for breakfast? The servants have come down, and you might like to talk to them straight away."

From the servants Macdonald gathered that none of them was in the habit of going into the workroom. It was a rule of the household that nothing in the room was to be moved and no cleaning was to be done without specific orders to that effect. He next inquired when last the room was known to have been used, and was told that Miss Naomi had been in there doing some bookbinding in the week before Miss Ruth died. The parlourmaid remembered that she (Naomi) had been in the workroom some time after tea on the Saturday before the tragedy, and that "one of the gentlemen" had been talking in there with her. Who this had been Macdonald could not ascertain. So far as he could gather, no one else had been observed in there since.

With regard to the previous evening, all the servants had been in their bedrooms by half-past ten. This was easy to ascertain, because each of them shared rooms with another one. The cook and the "sewing maid" (who was also Mrs. Surray's personal maid) were sisters and shared one room. The parlourmaid and the head housemaid shared another, and the kitchenmaid and the under housemaid shared a third.

It was Gladys who had done the locking up on the ground

floor the previous evening, and she told Macdonald that she had seen the door of the workroom was ajar when she was going her rounds. She had not gone inside the room, only shut the door and bolted it.

"How did you know there wasn't anybody in there?" he inquired. "You might have locked somebody in."

"There wasn't a light in there," she answered, "and the bulb in the passage had gone—fused or something. It's always dark there in that passage even when the sun's shining outside." She gave a little shiver and added: "I've been that nervous since last week. I know it's silly, but I can't help it. I generally get Mabel to go round with me in the evenings, but she was feeling poorly yesterday. I didn't think anything about that door being open," she protested. "I knew you and Mrs. Surray had been round in the morning, and I thought you might have left the door open."

Macdonald knew that he had closed the door after he had been in the room at mid-day, but he could get no information about whether it had been seen standing open since. As Gladys said, it wasn't wide open—only just ajar—and no one used the passage leading to it unless they were going into the room.

After he had finished talking to the servants Macdonald went back to the workroom, examining the bulb in the passage on his way. Taking it down and examining it he found that it was burnt out, the glass was blackened and the filaments within broken and rattling faintly as he shook it. Examining it out of habit he noticed that the voltage mark on the bulb was 225, and that the make was an Osram.

Shortly after seven o'clock two men from the local police

force came to assist in the search among the ashes. It was not for any tiny object that Macdonald was looking, and he was pretty certain already that he would not find it. When he had first come into the workroom with Mrs. Surray, he had at once noticed the "sewing frame" used by bookbinders, and it was on this account that he had returned to the room to look for something else. The Surrays took their hobbies seriously and had supplied themselves with all the equipment necessary to do the work properly. Examining the end of the heavy bench Macdonald had found the long blade of a paper-cutting "plough" fixed into its socket. He had seen one of these instruments in use and knew that all serious bookbinders had a plough in order to cut their sheets and boards accurately. There had immediately come into his mind the realisation that here was a means whereby the sheet of manuscript paper on which Ruth Surray had written her farewell message could have been cut down to the dimensions of the smaller block, and cut so accurately as to defy inspection. It was only necessary to place one of the smaller sheets over the larger one and to fit it to the metal straight-edge of the plough and lower the knife; by that means alone could the cutting be done in such a way as to defy discovery.

When he had first found the plough, Macdonald had thought he might be farther than ever from any conclusive proof of his theory. If the sheet of paper which he was sending up for microscopic examination had been cut in this manner by a skilled hand, the microscope would reveal nothing for the simple reason that the cut sheet would be identical with the others of the smaller block. All he would have would be a possibility; the means could be proved to exist, but not the employment of the means. Now, however, he believed that his case was made clear. The bench had been burnt, and burnt so thoroughly that it had fallen to pieces and its fittings scattered among the ashes, but the knife of the plough was not among the other fragments; whoever had lighted the fire had first unscrewed the long knife and removed it. That, to Macdonald's mind, constituted the first proof in his line of reasoning.

Leaving the search to his two helpers, Macdonald found Robert Surray again and asked him what was the present voltage of the electric supply and if it had been recently altered. Robert replied that the voltage was now 240, but that until a year ago it had been 225. In the previous summer the Wessex Electricity Company had brought their cable through Upwood, and the electric plant which had previously supplied the house was now disused; the voltage of this plant had been 225. In reply to further questions he said that it was more than probable that old bulbs had been left about in the workroom cupboards or on the shelves. To Macdonald's mind it seemed clear enough that the old bulb had been fitted to the fixture in the passage to ensure darkness for the person who went into the workroom to remove the plough and switch on the current.

Macdonald's next activity was to telephone to the inn to find out if any message awaited him from Reeves. The Chief Inspector thought it probable that Reeves would have rung him up last night to report on Montague's visit to Brandon. It came almost as a shock to Macdonald to realise that it was only last night that he had driven so peacefully to Stow; the events of the night seemed to have spread themselves over an interminable length of time. There was no message at all from Reeves, and Macdonald felt faintly perturbed. He wanted to know what Brandon was doing, and more especially what he had been doing during the midnight hours.

As he left the telephone Richard Surray appeared at the door of the room and said, "Can you spare five minutes? I hoped to have seen you last night, before all this added confusion. Can you tell me if you have come to any conclusions at all?"

"I have drawn certain conclusions in my own mind, but I can't confide them to anybody because they are merely hypothetical," replied Macdonald. "The only way to carry on is by close examination and comparison of statements and evidence. One essential thing is concerned with your younger sister. I shall either have to go north to see her, or she must return home. The latter course would be better; I want to reassemble the party who stayed here over the week-end."

"Then if that is the case, it would be better for one of us to go up north and bring her back," replied Richard.

"Why not telephone to her, or send a wire? You can understand that the less discussion of the evidence, the better. If one of your family travels south with her, you will inevitably discuss the case; you wouldn't be able to help it. The more discussion there is, the more probability that the original evidence becomes confused with the addition of afterthoughts."

Richard shrugged his shoulders—a despairing sort of gesture. "What you really mean is this. You have satisfied yourself that Ruth's death was due to foul play and every one of us is suspect to you. You are really warning me that this inquiry—which I asked for—is now out of my hands. Any activities on my part will be unwelcome to you."

"I think it is a very difficult position for all of you," replied Macdonald. "That is an understatement, I know. You are faced with the possibility that much painful matter may have to be attested in public. You can't help wishing to avoid it. I am still in a state of complete ignorance as to the author of these crimes, but I can at least say this. If the upshot proves that Miss Naomi Surray had no connection with the case, I will do my best to assure that she shall not be involved in the final statement—if such ever materialises. But there must be no more 'reticences.' I've got to get at the root of things myself."

"I will get my mother to send her a wire," replied Richard. "I have been trying to face the whole thing more reasonably, and though…" He broke off. "It's no use talking," he added wretchedly. "You don't want opinions. You want facts."

That was a statement in which Macdonald heartily agreed, and his next inquiries were short and to the point. He asked Professor and Mrs. Surray if any members of the week-end party had shown any interest in Naomi's bookbinding activities and if any of them had been in the workroom with her. Mrs. Surray shook her head in the manner Macdonald had got to know. It seemed to him that the action implied an obstinate refusal to consider the point at issue; the Professor, however, was more forthcoming and said that Naomi had been talking about her hobby at tea-time on Saturday and that Mrs. Trant had been discussing designs with her and urging her on to a more modern style, as opposed to the traditional manner of decoration she employed. "Ask Montague. He was talking about it, too. He's quite good at the job himself, I believe. We were laughing at him over the idea of a publisher binding books in his spare time."

Macdonald was surprised. It had not occurred to him to connect Montague with any handicraft; the man's big clumsy hands seemed but little adapted to the nice use of tools. Montague, when he entered the study, seemed more than ever ill at ease. He listened to Macdonald's polite questions with a puzzled air, his big ears twitching a little.

"Yes. I remember they were talking about bookbinding," he admitted. "I'm interested in the subject myself. Once tried to do a bit, but I was the world's fool at it. Never could get any common sense into my hands. I didn't actually go along to the workroom, though I believe Mrs. Trant did. You're not going to suggest that they did any damage to the wiring, or anything like that, are you? Why, it's more than a week ago." Montague got up and started prowling round the room in his restless, ungainly way. "Can't believe any one would be such a devil as to fire a house and risk burning people to death. Horrible idea. Must have been an accident. Must have."

"I don't think it was anything of the kind, Mr. Montague."

"Damned nasty lookout for me, then," mumbled the other. "Look here, Chief Inspector, do you believe that I'm the man you're after or not? If so, say so."

"I've no more reason for believing you are a criminal than I have for believing that any of the other seven people in the house that night were criminals," responded Macdonald, but the publisher went on:

"Yes, you have. I was here last night, too, and you believe that fire was arson. I knocked Fellowes into the pool, or you believe I did, and stopped you asking him questions. Now, you're trying to prove that I've had a chance of monkeying in the workroom."

"Yesterday I asked you if you knew Keith Brandon, and you said that you only knew him slightly; have you anything to add to that?"

Montague's look of perplexity was almost comic. "No. Why should I have?"

"Because you went to see him last night."

Montague ceased his prowling and looked down at Macdonald, who was seated at the table.

"Yes. I heard he'd got Flemming's cottage. Nothing to do with you, though."

"You know that Brandon was on intimate terms with Miss Surray. If you believe or know that he met her on the night of her death, the sooner you say so, the better. I can't imagine that you have any motive for protecting him beyond that of saving yourself from suspicion."

Montague sat down and mopped his forehead. "You're wrong there," he said earnestly. "I'm not any more anxious to be accused of murder than any other man, but it wasn't my own skin I was saving. The real crux of the matter is that I didn't want to see all the gutter press putting Ruth's death down to a broken heart, because that animal had let her down. I'd hang to prevent his name being coupled with her. Can't you understand that?"

"I think that you're all so obsessed with keeping her memory sacrosanct that a small point like discovering who murdered her seems immaterial to you," retorted Macdonald. "Did Fellowes know that Brandon had been here late that Sunday night?"

"No. He believed that I was downstairs talking to Ruth," said Montague, and his unexpected admission nearly took Macdonald's breath away. "You see it was a bit awkward for me," went on the other, in that maddeningly vague way he had. "Fellowes and I were talking and he got excited; so did I for that matter, and he tripped up and fell backwards. I had nothing to do with that—never touched him until I dragged him out of the pond. I was a bit knocked endwise. Didn't want you to think I'd knocked him over the head because he'd got a bee in his bonnet. Now I suppose I've made things worse. No proof of any of this. No reason why you should believe it. You're the sort of chap who wants hard facts; you've not enough imagination to see that there's something in a man's make-up that doesn't care a damn for facts."

"It doesn't take a great deal of imagination for me to see that some people don't care a damn for a solemn oath," replied Macdonald. "You say that Fellowes heard—or thought he heard—Miss Surray talking to you, after everybody had gone to bed. Yet he swore at the inquest that he had heard nothing—just as you swore it, and Stanwood."

Montague's jaw dropped. "Good Lord!" he groaned. "I've let Fellowes in for it. I didn't think of that. Look here, you'll have to wait until he's capable of speaking for himself. One thing I'm certain of, whatever he said, it was from decent motives. He wasn't going to make the public a present of sensational disclosures, any more than I was."

"Don't you think it's time you told the truth about what *did* happen on that Sunday night?" asked Macdonald. "In due time every one of you will be cross-examined again in the witness-box, and the counsel for the prosecution won't consider your susceptibilities or any one else's when he examines you. Your hush hush policy won't even have success to recommend it; if you'd all told the truth in the first place you would have saved a deal of subsequent trouble."

Montague's face was puckered into a heavy frown.

"It's always a mistake to get talking," he said at last. "Fact is, I've got to the state when I don't know what I'm talking about. If you've anything against me, arrest me, and get it over. I've nothing more to say. Just been blethering. Sorry, but there it is."

"If you won't be more explicit, I shan't have any option but to detain you," retorted Macdonald.

Montague made a further effort to extricate himself from the impasse he had unthinkingly created.

"I've given you a wrong impression about Fellowes. The fact is I didn't take in what he was trying to tell me. I'm not going to make trouble for a man who's got himself laid out and can't speak for himself. It doesn't make any difference anyway. You'll have plenty of time to ask him what he *did* say. Neither of us is likely to do a bolt."

"If you conceal evidence in a murder case you thereby make yourself accessory after the fact," replied Macdonald, and Montague retorted:

"Tell me something I don't know. I'm convinced that Ruth Surray took her own life. I've got the Coroner's verdict to bear me out."

"The Coroner was naturally unable to get at the truth of the matter if the witnesses gave perjured evidence. There are two questions you've got to answer, Mr. Montague. The first is, what statement did Mr. Fellowes make to you immediately prior to his accident? The second is, have you any reason for believing that Mr. Brandon was in this house on the Sunday night when Miss Surray's death occurred?"

"In answer to the first, wait until Fellowes is able to speak for himself. In answer to the second, I've every reason to believe that Brandon was not in this house on the Sunday night, and I'll add this: You say you're working on a murder case; if you suspect me of murder it's your business to warn me before questioning me."

"I don't seriously suspect you of murder," replied Macdonald. "It seems to me that you're not sufficiently capable of carrying out a logical sequence of planning. I may be wrong in that. As for warning, here is a plain one. I do not intend to lose sight of you; you will have to expect police supervision from now onwards. It will be better for you to return to London and to stay in your own home. If you are unwilling to do that I shall obtain a warrant for your arrest on the charge of obstructing the police by keeping back information relevant to the inquiry."

A twinkle appeared for a second in Montague's eyes, the first sign of mirth which Macdonald had observed in his heavy countenance.

"I was born a mug, Chief Inspector. I'm like the chap in Browning who chanted 'No end to all I can not do.' I've only one saving grace. Give me a manuscript and I'll tell if it's worth publishing, either because it's so good that it'll do me credit as a publisher, or so bad that it'll be a best-seller. That's my job, and I claim that I've made good my boast. Your job is spotting criminals. If you've spotted me as one, then I have the consolation of knowing there's one bigger fool than myself in the world, and that's you. At least I'm reliable at the only thing I say I can do. You, apparently, are not."

"It's the old conundrum again, Mr. Montague. Is it better to look a bigger fool than you are, or to be a bigger fool than you look? There's one particular type of foolishness which I cannot afford to indulge in, and that is the luxury of accepting my fellow men at their face value."

When Macdonald left Upwood House, one of the county detectives was detailed to keep Montague under supervision, while others were still busily engaged in examining the débris of the workroom. Macdonald had worked out an idea of his own about the fire-raising question. At first he had been puzzled that no smoke had been observed in the house from the slowly heating pile of débris above the electric plate, until he remembered a case of arson where impregnated charcoal had been used. If this material had been put on the hot plate it would eventually have glowed and become red-hot but there would have been no smoke until the whole carefully prepared bonfire burst into flame.

While he drove towards Moreton-in-the-Marsh, Macdonald's mind was busy with the problem, trying ideas and then discarding them. The motive of his present journey was to get into touch with Reeves and learn what he could of the Montague-Brandon meeting of the evening before. It was unlike Reeves not to have reported progress in some way, and the Chief Inspector was anxious to get in touch with him.

Approaching the lane which led to Brandon's cottage, Macdonald sounded a special horn which was fitted to his car, the note whereof was known to all members of the C.I.D. He pulled up for a while and then drove on slowly, sounding the horn at intervals. There being no answer of any kind from Reeves, Macdonald drove his car down the lane, past the cottage (it was called "Faraway") and noticed that its front door was shut and the windows also. Leaving the car a little way past the house, he got out and went back to prospect, but could see no sign of life. It appeared that Brandon had departed, Reeves presumably following him.

Macdonald turned away, but some disquietude in his mind made him change his mind, and he walked up the garden path and knocked at the front door. If Brandon were in, he would have a few more words with him. If Brandon were not in, he would have a look at the cottage. The sound of his knocking died away, and he stood listening. There was certainly some noise going on in the cottage; some one was hammering—a heavy, muffled sound came through the solid old door, and then, in addition, a sound which Macdonald recognised at once, that of a police whistle. The latter came from inside the cottage and instead of blowing his own whistle in reply, Macdonald gave a rapid series of "long and short" on the knocker, which implied "Help coming." Then, without further finesse, he sprang to one of the side windows, smashed it without ceremony, undid the latch and swung his long legs over the ledge as soon as he had raised the sash. A tattoo from the passageway guided him to a door beneath the stairs; it was a very solid, ancient door and the big key was still in the lock. Turning it, Macdonald got the door open and Detective Reeves emerged, looking rather green in the face and owlish about the eyes. He blinked in the clear daylight and said:

"I made a proper mucker of it that time. Been in that ruddy hole all night."

"A spot of breakfast seems indicated then," replied Macdonald. "Come along into the kitchen. I expect there's something in the food line if we look for it."

He put his hand under the other man's arm, for Reeves seemed a bit shaky on his legs and led him to the kitchen and pushed him into a chair. Drawing a flask from his pocket, Macdonald drew some water from the pump at the sink and handed over a pick-me-up, and then filled the kettle and put it on the primus stove. Reeves looked distinctly the better for his drink, saying:

"There wasn't room to lie down in there, nor even to squat properly. What you'd call a poor night. I tried to be too clever for once. About nine o'clock last night a man drove up here in a car. It was Mr. Montague, who was at Upwood. I knew the front door here was open and I thought I might get a chance to hear what he'd come to say. I got in the house all right and I'd have sworn no one saw me from inside, and when I was in the passage I heard Brandon say, 'I'd better shut that door. Don't want any one mooching round in here.' I was just by that door under the stairs and it was open. I slipped in to get out of the way and the next thing I knew was that the door was slammed on me and locked from the outside. I was pretty sick, but I didn't believe Brandon had spotted me; I didn't see how he could have, so I just stayed doggo. I thought I knew enough about locks to be able to get out of a cupboard when I wanted to, but I couldn't move that damned contraption. Came out of the original ark, I reckon, with rust of ages to help. I'd landed myself, sir. You said, 'Don't let him spot you.' I thought I'd managed that part of it and I wasn't going to kick up a racket and give the whole show away."

"Bad luck," said Macdonald, busy pumping the primus. "As a matter of fact, I expect Brandon *did* spot you. He's got a sort of extra sense and can smell when he's in danger, that's why he's such a fine explorer. Did you hear anything at all of the evening's doings?"

"I heard Montague going. They swore at one another and shouted a good deal, but I couldn't make out a word of it, except just before he went I heard Brandon shout at him, 'Tell that to your friend, the hangman.' Then the door slammed. About half an hour later I heard the engine of the Humber start; the car was in the stable, up against the wall of the house and she backfired as he got her out. Then I reckoned the coast was clear and I tried to manage the lock. I'd got a small pair of pliers and an electric torch, but the key was too large and the pliers too small. I couldn't get a grip. As for kicking the door down, I nearly bust myself, but it wouldn't budge."

"When they built this cottage they used the right sort of stuff," replied Macdonald, as he made the tea. (He found tea and sugar on the chimney piece and bread in the pantry.) "That door's been there for three hundred years, or I'm a Chinaman. As for the lock, it would resist a battering-ram. Get outside some of this" (indicating the tea and the loaf), "and I'll have a look round to see if there's anything worth seeing. What time was it Brandon went off—about ten?"

"Ten-fifteen, sir. I'm sorry I made a hash of it. Let you down all right this time."

"Oh, bunkum. Any one might have been had that way. I'm glad it was you and not me. There's been some more dirty work at Upwood. Arson this time."

"The bastards!" said Reeves indignantly, and Macdonald left him swallowing a scalding saucerful of tea.

"Nothing doing," said Macdonald a few minutes later. He had looked round the cottage, but found no signs of Brandon's occupation. "My car's outside. We shall have to get on to the fellow's tail and see what he's up to. You can have the pleasure of tailing him again when we pick him up. If he's gone in his car he'll be easy enough to find."

"By gum, I owe him one," said Reeves wrathfully. It would be a long time before he forgot the ignominy and discomfort of twelve hours spent in the cramped quarters of Flemming's wine cellar.

CHAPTER XII

THE KEYS OF RUTH SURRAY'S FLAT HAD BEEN HANDED over to Macdonald by Richard, who had said that none of her papers had been removed, since Montague, as literary executor, preferred to examine them in Ruth's study rather than to remove them to his own office. Macdonald regarded that statement with an open mind; it might be true, but since Montague had had plenty of time to destroy anything which he wished to destroy, the statement carried no weight.

The flat was at the top of a lofty block in Portland Place; it was situated at a street corner and consequently had windows on two sides, the north and the east. Ruth's study faced north, and the windows beyond her writing desk opened on to an immense panorama of unexpected beauty. In the foreground, beyond the leaded roofs of Nash's Crescent, spread the level green of Regent's Park with the waters of the lake shining white around the little islands; the Mappin Terraces at the Zoological Gardens showed their absurd crags above the trees, and far away to the north the ridges of Hampstead and

Highgate stretched across the immense skyline. Spires shone white in the sun; trees in surprising numbers still embowered the houses which were set on the far-off hillside, and in the clear summer air the northern heights of London had so fair an aspect that Macdonald stood by the window, forgetful for a moment of everything but delight in that surprising vista. Raised high above the traffic and the din of busy streets, the window offered an outlook of peaceful serenity, but after a moment or two Macdonald's eyes no longer registered what they saw. Intent on his case, as a hound on a fugitive scent, he was summing up his data before he set to work on searching the drawers and cabinets of the peaceful room.

Having driven up to town with Reeves, the Chief Inspector had gone first to call on Mrs. Trant, the only member of the week-end party at Upwood House whom he had not yet seen. A practical, sensible, well-balanced woman he had found her, but she could tell him little that was of any direct assistance. The chief points which had emerged from the conversation had been summarised by Macdonald thus: (1) Mrs. Trant had been in the workroom with Naomi on the Saturday evening before Ruth's death, but she did not know if any of the men in the party had been in there; (2) Naomi had been binding a copy of *Last Leaves*—the book on which Ruth Surray had written a criticism dealing with posthumous publications; (3) Mrs. Trant was obviously familiar with bookbinding tools, but as she had been in London on the previous night she could have had no hand in the matter of the fire. Apart from these points she told Macdonald a good deal about her fellow guests at Upwood House. Fellowes she classified as a healthy, normal, successful young man, somewhat obsessed by a hopeless passion for Ruth Surray. Of Montague she spoke with warm affection and admiration, deploring the fact that his devotion to Ruth had prevented him marrying some "commonplace woman who would look after him and send his clothes to be pressed when they needed it, tell him to go to the barber's, and see that he kept his appointments." Of Stanwood, also, she spoke with liking and respect, telling Macdonald of his early struggles, when, as the son of a poor provincial printer, he had toiled at the hackwork of journalism, and of his efforts to earn money to keep a tuberculous wife. The latter had died before Stanwood attained success, and Mrs. Trant spoke warmly of his devotion to her in those years of poverty. "I never sat at Ruth Surray's feet and adored her, as most people did," said Mrs. Trant. "I knew she was really a self-centred woman, but I do think that the way she backed Stanwood was one of the most admirable things she ever did. He spoke of her as though she were an angel—small wonder."

Turning at last from the window, Macdonald began his task of searching the drawers of the writing desk. Admittedly he did not expect to find much to guide him, but even the absence of certain things could be useful in assisting to formulate a theory. First he wanted to find Ruth Surray's engagement book. He knew that she had kept one, and believed that he might learn quite a lot from it. Next, he wanted to examine for himself the essay entitled "Man's Right to Die," which had been found by the police when they searched the flat before the inquest.

Macdonald's early suspicions about the nature of Ruth Surray's "farewell message" were steadily crystallising into logical form. He believed that the will had been obtained by suggesting to Ruth the possibilities demonstrated in the publication of *Last Leaves*—the book which she had so strongly deplored. The "farewell message" was a sheet of manuscript cut down to serve its purpose. Possibly the essay entitled "Man's Right to Die" had been "planted," in order that its bitterness and disillusionment might add to the weight of evidence which pointed to suicide as the explanation of Ruth Surray's death. The essay had been found, Macdonald learnt, in the middle drawer of the writing table. It was in typescript, but certain alterations had been pencilled between the lines in Ruth's neat writing, and her signature was written (also in pencil) at the end. Macdonald, all his scepticism aroused, formed a cautious judgment about that essay. It might have been written by the murderer, and handed to Ruth Surray for criticism and comment; this explanation might account for Ruth's signature and pencil notes.

On searching the flat for a typewriter, the only one Macdonald found was a full-sized Remington in the secretary's office. The essay he had been considering was obviously not typed on this machine but on a smaller model—probably a portable. There were, however, several examples of the smaller typescript among the papers in the filing cabinet, and Macdonald guessed that Ruth herself had occasionally used the smaller machine for her own private purposes. He put together various sheets for the experts to examine, but drew a blank so far as the machine itself was concerned.

Macdonald next turned his attention to the engagement book. This was no small pocket-book affair, but a solidly bound volume giving a page to every day, and he knew at once that it was a private book, kept for Ruth's personal use, because some of the entries were in her own system of shorthand.

Macdonald sat and wrestled with the complexities of this volume for over an hour; by that time he had learnt quite a lot about Ruth Surray's activities prior to her death. He had previous knowledge of certain exact dates—on the first Tuesday in July Ruth Surray had dined with Keith Brandon, and Macdonald was thus able to recognise the symbol she had used for further entries of his name. Brandon had said that he had only met Ruth twice, but Macdonald found entries showing that the pair had met nearly a dozen times during the early part of July. Ruth had evidently not trusted her own memory very far, because she wrote down details of times and places and distances. She and Brandon had spent evenings together on the river, it seemed, meeting at Sonning and Bourne End. Hampton Court was once mentioned and the Silent Pool near Clandon. Macdonald was far from being an unimaginative man, and remembering what Richard Surray had told him and what he himself had surmised, of Brandon's transference of his devotion from one sister to the other, Macdonald felt an ever-increasing disgust. He tried, in this as in all cases, to keep his personal likes and dislikes from influencing his judgment. There were, he realised fully enough, at least three possible explanations of Ruth Surray's death which did not involve Keith Brandon at all, but the big man seemed to spread his shadow over the case at every turn.

Having finished his examination of the engagement book, and having looked through the tidy drawers which spoke so eloquently of Ruth Surray's businesslike habits,

Macdonald tried to sketch to himself the attributes of the murderer against whom he was pitting his wits. The scheme had been, in the first place, the work of a subtle and calculating intelligence. There was a diabolical cleverness in the way the evidence had been obtained and planted, but later developments showed different qualities. It was as though the murderer had been cool enough before the act, and cool enough when the Coroner's verdict had crowned his—or her—scheme with success, but there was clumsiness, as well as brutal disregard of human suffering, in that matter of the fire. Macdonald pulled himself up here. The clumsiness had become apparent because the fire had been discovered; if he had not happened to be in the garden, and the house with its inmates had been destroyed, there might have been a very different problem to face. Could any sane man have planned that callous attempt to destroy a whole family by fire? Was it not the act of a madman whose actions were unpredictable? Throughout the case was the curious combination of extreme cunning—both the original murder and the fire showed evidence of cunning scheming combined with reckless stupidity or carelessness. With a sense of exasperation Macdonald wondered if there would ever be any definite proof by which he could convict the criminal.

He was almost glad when the ringing of the front door bell interrupted his thoughts and he went to the door to find Robert Surray standing outside with an attaché case in his hand.

"Richard told me that you might be coming in here to-day, so I thought I might find you," said Robert. "May I come in?"

Macdonald drew back from the door. "Yes. Do. You might

be able to help me. I've been up against a few fair-sized problems in my time, but I've never felt in a more glorious muddle." He closed the door and the two walked down the passage towards the study. "I went to see Mrs. Trant," went on Macdonald. "She told me that my case resembled an impression by Picasso, half interior and half exterior. For a woman who boasts that she has no brains I thought the remark a shrewd one."

"She's as shrewd a body as ever I met, and a good judge of character, too," replied Robert. "To hear her and Ruth arguing was really amusing—two quite incompatible methods and points of view, the instinctive and reasonable. May I dump this case somewhere? I'd got some of Ruth's books which I'd borrowed and they're on my conscience. Her library is to be valued, and I thought I'd better put these back. One or two may be valuable."

"You've got a sensitive conscience," observed Macdonald. "There's hardly a man in the world who's honest when it comes to books."

"As a family we're averse from pinching from libraries," replied Robert. "We've suffered too much that way ourselves." He opened the case and drew out a pile of books and Macdonald picked them up one by one.

There was an early edition of Bacon's *Advancement of Learning*, a copy of *The Way of all Flesh* by Samuel Butler, one of *Bitter Herbs* by Geoffrey Stanwood and one of *Last Leaves*, the posthumous book of which Ruth Surray had left a review among the papers which Montague had collected in her bedroom at Upwood.

Robert pointed to Stanwood's book. "That may be valuable

if the chap keeps up his form," he observed. "He's only just got into the limelight, and people are rushing round asking for copies of his earlier ones. My bookseller tells me that *Bitter Herbs* is unobtainable now. It'll be reprinted, of course, but the first edition only sold two hundred copies and the rest were pulped. That's one of the original ones—I've been meaning to return it for months—Ruth didn't even know I'd got it."

Macdonald picked up *Last Leaves*.

"Do you know anything about this? Was it a review copy? Did you know that Miss Surray wrote a notice of it, protesting against the indiscriminate publishing of a man's slighter works after his death?"

"Good Lord!" Robert's face showed the astonishment he felt. "I'd no idea. What was Ruth's notice published in?"

"It wasn't published. It was in manuscript, among the papers in her room at Upwood."

"Are we all going morbid and following our own imaginations? When you think it out, doesn't that indicate her line of reasoning in altering that will?"

"Yes. I think it may. When did you borrow that book from your sister?"

"At Upwood, when we were all there on my mother's birthday. She shoved it into my hands just as I was going and said, 'Write and tell me what you think of this.' I didn't think much of it, so I didn't write. Oh Lord! I wish I could make out what you're really driving at."

"So do I," replied Macdonald. "However, let's leave that. Can you tell me if Miss Surray had a portable typewriter with her at Upwood?"

"I don't know. I expect so. She generally had one among

her traps, although she didn't use it a great deal. If she had one there, it would be in her room."

"There wasn't one in her room, or I should have seen it. I've been looking for it here and I can't find it."

"You can telephone to Upwood and ask my mother. She would know. Look here, I've been thinking things over and I want to know your opinion on this point. I'm not happy about the family being at Upwood. If last night's little effort was intentional and not accidental, I think they'd better clear out of the house for awhile, until you've got things sorted out. If there's a criminal lunatic about, anything may happen."

"I had thought a bit about that problem myself," replied Macdonald. "It's a point of view which has to be faced, but I think they're quite as safe there now as anywhere else. The house is under close supervision and they are, if anything, safer in their own surroundings than in a strange house, or in an hotel."

He broke off as a telephone bell shrilled somewhere in the distance. Robert gave a jump at the unexpected sound and said, "The phone's in the typist's room, along the passage. Are you going to bother about it?"

Macdonald went and answered it. In a few minutes he returned to the study and said:

"More trouble, I'm afraid. No, not another tragedy—not quite. Stanwood has been picked up in the street, semi-poisoned with some opiate drug, and your brother has had a dose, too. I think they have both been treated in time."

Robert groaned aloud. "My God, what next? How did it happen?"

Macdonald was looking round the room, packing up the things he wanted to take with him.

"I must go along and find out. Apparently Stanwood and Montague met at your brother's rooms after lunch for a conference with him. Stanwood was taken ill in the street shortly after he left, and your brother was found by his servant. There's no news of Montague being affected."

"This is simply too bloody awful," groaned Robert, as one bereft of appropriate words—and Macdonald did not contradict him.

CHAPTER XIII

WHILE MACDONALD WAS BUSY AT RUTH SURRAY'S FLAT, two taximen were standing by their cabs at a rank near the junction of New Cavendish Street and Portland Place. The older of the two, a weather-beaten Cockney named Herbert Harris, was examining a couple of half-crowns he had taken from his pocket.

"'Ate 'alf-crowns. 'Ate 'em, I do. Been 'ad three times by the ruddy things. Every fare I've 'ad to-day seems ter me to've paid me in one er these same bitchy bits. I'll swear this one's a dud. Take me oath on it. 'Ad that one from an old gel I dropped in 'Arley Street. 'Alf dead she looked, too."

"Tell you what, Herb," replied the other driver—a young man with a smart new Austin cab, "I'll make you a sporting offer. I'll buy your rotten half-crowns at two bob apiece. You cuts your losses and I takes the risk, see? That's fair, ain't it?"

Harris laughed, the wheezy laugh of a bronchitisy man, and spat on the coins before he put them back in his pocket.

"Nothing doing, Jock. 'Eard of Aberdeen before, I 'ave. Lummy, cocky! look at that bloke crossin' the road. 'E's a deader... no, 'e's not. Wouldn't I like to've 'eard what that lorryman said? Drunk, 'e is. Not 'alf. Drunk as a lord!"

The pedestrian who had attracted Harris's attention had been coming from the direction of Upper Marylebone Street (the continuation of New Cavendish Street to the east, across Portland Place). He had hesitated for some time before he crossed the wide roadway of Portland Place, and then, instead of crossing straight over, he had swerved across the tarmac in the characteristic roll of a drunken man who is unable to control his direction. As he staggered, a lorry driver approaching from the north only managed to avoid the pedestrian by swinging abruptly on to the right-hand side of the road and taking the refuge on the wrong side. Fortunately Portland Place was wide, and at that time fairly empty, or such a manoeuvre would not have been possible, and the lorryman's mate leant out and poured forth a stream of objurgation as the lorry swung back on to its own side, leaving the pedestrian unscathed, still making his erratic way across the road.

"There's a fare for you, Herb," chuckled the younger man. "Take the poor boob home and help him up to bed. He'll be run in, or run down, or run over, sure as eggs is eggs."

"Don't want no drunks in my keb," retorted Harris. "'Ad some of that before, I 'ave, and don't want no more. There's a cop on point duty at the 'Arley Street corner. That's a job for 'im, that one is."

Meantime, the staggering pedestrian had reached the western side of Portland Place in safety and was standing by the railings at the street corner, holding on to them with one hand, while with the other he was making passes across his eyes, with queer clumsy gestures.

The younger taximan stared.

"He's not drunk, Herb. Never seen a drunk like that. Look at 'is dial. Ill, that's what '*e* is!"

Hastening up to the man by the railings, Jock Somers put a hand under the man's arm.

"Feelin' queer, sir? Better get home, y'know. Taxi?"

"Can't see you. Can't see anything. Blind." The man spoke in a queer, thickened voice, his lips seemingly stiff and unmanageable. He made an effort to go on speaking. "I've been poisoned. D'you hear? Poisoned. Must be. Get to hospital. Doctor. Quickly. Doctor." He made a step away from the railings but would have fallen if Somers, with the help of Harris, had not caught him. "Doctor," he repeated thickly.

"Well, there's plenty o' them about in this neighbourhood," said Harris. "That's a doctor's, ain't it, Jock?"

He pointed to a brass plate in a nearby house, but Somers shook his head.

"That one's an oculist. Better get him to 'ospital. Gawd! He'll be a goner in a minute."

The unfortunate man was sagging down between them, and at that moment the door of the oculist's house opened and two men appeared, one elderly and bareheaded, the other just setting his hat on his head as he held out his hand and said, "Well, good-bye and many thanks."

Somers, still clutching the arm of the now half-unconscious man, let out a yell.

"Hi, doctor! Accident! Chap says he's poisoned."

Dr. Fratton, the grey-haired oculist, gave a start, as a man well might, seeing a casualty almost on his doorstep.

"Good Lord! What's all this about?" He hastened towards the three men, saying, "Let him down on the pavement—gently, now. No use holding him up like that."

The sick man made another effort to speak. "Name's Stanwood. Must've been poisoned. Gone blind. Ask Surray." He swallowed convulsively and licked his lips. "Richard Surray," he gasped out. "Been to see him. Poisoned."

His head fell back and Dr. Fratton leant over him as they lowered him on to the pavement. He lifted one of the eyelids and saw the dilated pupil, and noted the dry tongue moving feverishly over the parched lips. Then he straightened himself quickly and said, "He's been poisoned all right. Granelly, the toxicologist, lives a few doors along. This is his pigeon. Lift him inside my door—I'll go and see if I can rout Granelly out. If too much time's wasted there won't be any case to treat."

He spoke to the younger man, who had been taking his leave when the taxi-driver hailed them. This was Basil Lathom, a barrister, and he stood looking down at Stanwood for a second or two with eyes that were bright with interest. Lathom had caught the two names— Stanwood and Richard Surray—and his interest was well aroused. Like most other intelligent people he had read the evidence given at the Coroner's inquest on Ruth Surray's death with much interest.

"We'd better get him inside Dr. Fratton's house," said Lathom. "We shall have a crowd in a brace of shakes and then a bobby, and by the time the bobby's taken all our names and addresses, this chap will have passed out."

They lifted the now unconscious Stanwood between

them and carried him into Dr. Fratton's consulting room. By the time they had laid him down, the oculist came running back with another man—this being the famous toxicologist, Granelly, who had come post-haste to assist at this unexpected consultation.

By this time the expected police constable had turned up, attracted from his beat further down the street by the report of "corpse at the next corner" yelled cheerfully by another taximan *en passant*. When the constable arrived, the "corpse" had been carried indoors, but the small crowd attracted by Stanwood's collapse still clustered about. "Tell 'em to move along," urged Herbert Harris, "they don't know a thing abaht it, not one of 'em. Just starin'. Indecent, I call it."

Basil Lathom took matters in hand. "Come inside, constable, and bring the two taximen. They're quite right. They were the only ones on the scene when the chap collapsed."

As was only to be expected, the constable took a lively interest in "the chap" and looked with some suspicion on the ministrations of the toxicologist and his assistant. To the constable's mind it would have been more "in order" to get the casualty to a hospital as promptly as possible, or into the hands of a police surgeon.

Dr. Fratton was short and to the point in dealing with the constable and his note-book.

"Get your police surgeon, or whoever else you fancy. Tell him the man's been poisoned with atropine, and if we'd waited for the official red-tape our services would only have been required at the inquest. The man's name is Stanwood—here's his card. He's a member of the Novelists' Club. Provided you don't interfere, he's not going to die. You'll be able to ask him all the appropriate questions later."

With the assistance of the taximen, Constable Stone got down his "times and particulars," and then turned to Lathom, who was at last able to get in the piece of evidence which seemed important to him.

"This man, Stanwood, said, just before he became unconscious, 'must have been poisoned. Ask Surray. Richard Surray. Been to see him.' Do the names Surray and Stanwood convey anything to you?"

The man scratched his head with a pencil and merely looked blank. Lathom went on, "There was an inquest a week or so ago on a Miss Ruth Surray, who died from an overdose of thalmaine. Stanwood, the man who has just been poisoned, was staying in the house when Miss Surray died. The mid-day editions have a report of a fire at Upwood—the Surrays' house—last night, and also suggest that the police are thinking of reopening the case. Don't you think you'd better report immediately to Scotland Yard, and suggest that somebody goes to see Richard Surray?"

Constable Stone was slow, but not altogether foolish. It took a little while for Lathom's suggestion to sink in, but then he acted promptly, and Macdonald's department lost no time in getting into contact with the Chief Inspector and with Richard Surray himself.

The latter was at his Bloomsbury flat, but when the C.I.D. inquiry came through, Richard was in no state to answer it himself, being indeed, reduced to the same condition as Stanwood.

The psychologist had come up to town from Upwood that

morning, and had asked Montague and Stanwood to come to see him after lunch, with the intention of discussing the problem of Fellowes. Richard had believed that Montague and Stanwood could throw more light on the problem if they were tackled together in the right way. This much he had confided to Robert.

When the latter, with Macdonald, arrived at the Berry Street flat, Richard was in the hands of a doctor who had been summoned from University Hospital nearby, and such evidence as was obtainable came from Harrow, Richard's servant, who with his wife ran the flat and acted as valet and occasional chauffeur. Harrow said that the two gentlemen (Stanwood and Montague) had come within a few minutes of one another, about a quarter past two, and that coffee and liqueurs had been served on their arrival. They left about half-past three, and it was a few minutes later when Harrow had gone into the study to fetch the cups and tidy the room. He had observed then that his master looked ill, and had expressed concern at his appearance. Surray had admitted that he felt "rotten," but said that he had had a sleepless night and consequently a vile headache, adding that he was a fool to have drunk black coffee when he was off colour—it always affected his liver. Harrow had left him sitting in an arm-chair. Some minutes later, just before four o'clock, the bell had rung from the study and Harrow had gone up to find Richard in a state of collapse; the latter had barely been able to speak, but had managed to tell his servant to ring up a Dr. Wilmot and to ask him to come quickly. "Tell him it's poison, probably atropine. I'm half blind," had been his last words, save for an interjection of "Montague" a minute later.

"Have you washed up the coffee cups?" demanded Macdonald and the man nodded.

"Yes, sir. I'm sorry, but how was I to know? The missus washed them up as soon as I took them downstairs."

"Have there been any other visitors to-day?"

"A Mr. Brandon, first thing this morning, sir. No one else to-day barring the two gentlemen I told you of after lunch."

"Mr. Surray was away when Mr. Brandon called this morning, I take it? Did he—Brandon—come in to the flat or just go straight away when he heard that Dr. Surray was out?"

"He came in to write a note, sir, when I told him that Dr. Surray expected to be back during the morning."

"Where did he write his letter? In the study?"

"No, sir. In the dining-room. I was doing the study with the Hoover. I'd seen Mr. Brandon before and knew he was a friend of the doctor's."

"Dr. Surray had the note?"

"Yes, sir. As soon as he came in."

Macdonald went in to see Dr. Wilmot; Surray was in a state which looked like complete collapse and all that Macdonald asked for was his coat and waistcoat, in order to be able to go through the pockets and note-case, in order to find Brandon's note if it was still in existence. He found it eventually—or rather the fragments of it—torn into tiny pieces and thrown into the waste-paper basket. It took him a long time to piece together the tiny scraps, but at length he got them into order sufficiently to read them.

"Dear Surray.—I'm sorry to have missed you. If we could have had a talk we might have cleared up some

of this ghastly misunderstanding. I know you've set the C.I.D. on my heels, and you're absolutely at sea if you think I'm at the bottom of all this tragedy. Next time we meet I hope to be able to clear away the misunderstanding, but do, for God's sake, try to keep Naomi's name out of it. She knows no more about it than I do. In haste. K.B."

Having read this and cursed himself for wasting time on something which threw no light on his immediate problem, Macdonald only waited to discover one thing. This was the fact that the sugar served with the coffee was kept in the cupboard of the sideboard in the dining-room. The bowl which held it was now almost empty, but Harrow told him that it had been nearly full when he put it on the coffee tray; but Richard Surray always took a great deal of sugar in his coffee, especially when he drank it black, in fact he liked it like syrup. Asked whether all three coffee cups had been used, Harrow replied, "No, only two, but three liqueur glasses had been used."

Robert stopped Macdonald in the hall, just as he was leaving. "I wouldn't have believed it possible, but there doesn't seem to be any way out of it. Montague must be at the bottom of all this. The man must be raving mad—first Ruth, then Fellowes, then the fire to burn the lot of us, and finally this. Do, for God's sake, get him quickly, before he does any more damage. I've rung them up at home. They're all right now, but you can't tell what devilment a madman's planned. Atropine, too. The very poison he'd be likely to know all about."

"Why?" asked Macdonald.

"He's as short-sighted as a bat, always having trouble with his eyes, and he's one of the people who react to atropine—a trace of it poisons him. He'd made a study of the drug as a sort of academic exercise. He got on to the subject with me one day and asked me every damned thing that was known about it. I told him, too. It's the very thing he would have chosen. Bunged it in the coffee and went off chuckling. The man must be raving mad. I shan't have a moment's peace until I know that you've got him locked up."

"It might have saved a lot of complications if I'd taken the bull by the horns and locked him up before this happened," said Macdonald, "but you've got to have something more than suspicion to go on before you charge a man like Montague with murder and arson." He looked at Robert Surray's agitated face, and added, "I don't know if you'll take my advice, but the best thing you can do is to go home and stay there—not to Upwood, but to your own rooms. Your brother will be moved into hospital and kept there until he has recovered. He'll be safer there than here. When you get back, you'd better make certain that there haven't been any visitors admitted who could have been preparing surprises of this kind for you. I must hurry off now. There's the deuce of a lot to be done."

Leaving Robert looking as though his one desire was to commit a murder himself, Macdonald hastened off to Montague's office in Holiman Street. Since the publisher was under police supervision, with a C.I.D. man at his heels, it had been easy for Macdonald to ascertain his movements. When the message came to Ruth Surray's flat that Surray and Stanwood were both laid low, Macdonald had given an order that Montague's "shadow" was to be found and a report on the publisher's movements supplied. Since Montague had gone direct to his office when he returned to town and his only activity since had been the short journey to Richard's flat in Berry Street, there had been no difficulty in obtaining a prompt report of his movements.

When Macdonald was shown into Montague's office, the publisher looked up at him with the nervous twist of his features that was so characteristic.

"What the devil do you want now?" he asked. "So far as I'm concerned I might as well offer to come and sit in a police cell. Might save you a few journeys, and give me a little peace and quietness."

"I'm disposed to agree with you, for more reasons than one," replied Macdonald. "You went to see Dr. Surray after lunch to-day. I should like an account of that interview, please."

"Then ask Surray for it," retorted Montague. "You suspect me of murder and arson. Childish to ask me any more questions when you don't believe a word I tell you. Ask Surray. You don't suspect him of murder, I take it—nor of burning his own people's home."

"I can't ask Dr. Surray questions because he is at present in no state to answer them," replied Macdonald. "Both he and Mr. Stanwood were poisoned some time this afternoon. You are the only person who remains to answer questions about your joint interview."

"Poisoned! Good God Almighty!" Montague's startled face was almost ludicrous in his expression of horror. "Poisoned! D'you mean dead?" He shouted the question at Macdonald, pushing back his chair with a violence which overturned the small table beside him, scattering papers and boxes in its fall.

"No. Not dead." Macdonald waited for his words to sink in. "By good fortune they both obtained treatment in the nick of time, but understand this. The three of you met for a consultation, and you are the only one to escape harm. It's no time for equivocation now, Mr. Montague. At that interview coffee was served. Did you drink any of it?"

"No. Never drink it," groaned Montague. "You mean I poisoned them?"

"I can't afford to disregard an obvious suggestion just because it *is* obvious," replied Macdonald. "You were at Upwood on the night of Miss Surray's death. You were there last night when the house was set on fire. You were with Mr. Fellowes when his accident occurred. I have no proof that you were responsible for any of those happenings. I have no proof that you attempted to kill Dr. Surray and Mr. Stanwood, but it's quite plain that you had the opportunity, since you were on the spot on each occasion."

"The whole thing sounds like raving lunacy," said Montague. "This afternoon Surray asked Stanwood and me to come along and talk. Talk! I'm sick of it!" he groaned. "Richard's in the state when he suspects everybody, myself included, and now you come to me and suggest that I poisoned him and Stanwood... I didn't do it, God knows—but who did?"

He stared at Macdonald with a heavily frowning face, his restless fingers twisting a piece of paper into knots round and round, until it split under the strain and he flung the pieces away.

"Are you telling me the truth?" he demanded. "They're alive, both of them? They're not going to die?"

"They are both alive, and I don't think that either of them will be much the worse in twenty-four hours' time," replied Macdonald.

"Then you can wait and ask *them* questions!" retorted Montague. "So far as I'm concerned, you can arrest me. I may be a fool, but I'm not such a damned fool that I can't see you've got a case against me." He broke out laughing, not mirthfully, but with a sort of bitter fury. "It's damned funny!" he shouted. "Damned funny! Fellowes goes and splits his head open and you ask me, 'What did he say?' and I tell you to wait until he can answer that question himself. Then Surray and Stanwood get laid out, and you ask me what *they* said, and I say again, 'Wait until they can answer that question themselves.' If you think I'm a murderer you must think I'm a damned incompetent one. Three tries, and not a score to my credit. Don't you ever laugh, you owl-faced policeman?"

Montague's hands were shaking, and Macdonald realised that the man was in such a state of nervous tension that he hardly realised what he was saying, when he would be capable of breaking out into the wildest assertions, or even admissions, to which no weight could be adjudged.

"Try to get a hold on yourself, Mr. Montague. Hysteria won't help anybody," he said quietly. "On the face of it, I've a good enough case to justify me in arresting you, but I'm going to do this instead. I'll see you back to your own rooms and leave you there, provided you'll undertake not to go out and not to communicate with anybody unknown to me. There are two ways of looking at this business; the obvious one, which demonstrates that you have had the opportunity for each of these crimes, and the unobvious one, which shows you as some one else's scapegoat, or as in a position of sheer bad luck. I'm not going to waste time asking you questions which you're in no state to answer. I'll give you twenty-four hours to think things over, and then you can answer my questions or face the consequences."

Montague sat with his head in his hands, a rigor shaking his big frame occasionally.

"The whole thing's like the devil incarnate," he said. "That fire!—I've a horror of fire. Gave me the blue devils. Didn't know what to think. Now this business. There's no way of proving anything. In twenty-four hours' time it'll be just the same—unless some one else is killed before then."

"Well, you're all as safe as I can make you," said Macdonald with a flash of grim humour. "Fellowes, Stanwood, and Dr. Surray are all in the keeping of one doctor or another. The people at Upwood House are under police supervision and so will you be. I ought to be able to get a few hours' peace and quietness to sort things out after this."

Montague was recovering from the spasm of nerves which had shaken him, and he asked an abrupt question without looking at Macdonald.

"Naomi Surray—has she come back home yet, or is she on her way home?"

"Neither," replied Macdonald. "Naomi Surray went out with the fishing fleet a few hours before her mother's wire arrived. That means a few days' delay before she can possibly get back—but she ought to be safe enough, anyhow," he added, as an afterthought.

"And Brandon?"

"Is roaming the world on his own account. If that were not so, things might be even more trying for you than they are at present," retorted Macdonald. "I asked you once why you went to see him and you refused to answer. I shan't ask you again until I have his version to check yours."

"He's quite as capable of holding his tongue as I am," flared Montague, and Macdonald replied:

"In certain respects you resemble one another. You're experts on your own jobs, and singularly lacking wits in other directions. Further than that I won't go. You've got twenty-four hours, Mr. Montague. You'd better go home and think things over."

"Things can't be much bloodier than they are now," replied the publisher gloomily. "The Surrays used to be reckoned the world's luckiest family by every one who knew them. The devil must have laughed to himself one day—reversed the deal and left them to stew…"

Macdonald saw Montague back to his own quarters and left a C.I.D. man installed there. It was an unusual proceeding, but it had certain advantages from the Chief Inspector's point of view, and Montague raised no protest. He had relaxed into a state of dumb apathy, as though the weariness and the nerve strain of the preceding twenty-four hours had exhausted his energies. When Macdonald left him, he sat down in an arm-chair with his head slumped forward on his chest, a very picture of dejection and weariness.

CHAPTER XIV

DETECTIVE REEVES, DETAILED FOR THE JOB OF TRACING Keith Brandon, had for his starting point the garage in Twist Street where the Humber had been left in the small hours of the morning. Reeves was a man of great common sense; apart from the quickness of perception and neatness of action which made him one of the Yard's most efficient shadowers, he had enough imagination to think himself into another man's place.

Although he had believed that he had shadowed Brandon to "Faraway" in such a manner as to have made it impossible for the explorer to have been aware of his follower, Reeves was willing to accept Macdonald's estimate—that Brandon was one of those men who have an additional sense, similar to that sensitiveness which makes some people aware of the presence of an unseen cat; a sensitiveness which in his case was coupled to the scout's ability to read a trail, added, perhaps, to the guilty man's expectation of apprehension.

Reeves believed that he had approached the cottage so

circumspectly that Brandon could not have seen or heard him, but when he slipped inside the wine cupboard he had drawn the door a little closer than it had previously been set. Thinking things over, he came to the conclusion that Brandon had left that door ajar on purpose. The explorer had thought it possible that Macdonald would be on his heels, and the cupboard was a very good booby trap. Brandon might easily have made some mark on the floor to denote the angle of the open door; on going into the hall after Montague had arrived, the alteration in the angle would have been enough to tell him that the bird was limed, and the quick shutting and bolting of the heavy door must have caused him a grin of complacency.

Leaving the garage after a quick inspection of the car, Reeves went into a neighbouring tea-shop to think out his plan of campaign. He began by putting himself in Brandon's place—a man in London in the early hours of the morning, not wishing to go to his own rooms, which might be watched, and unable to go to a hotel whence he might be all too easily traced. There seemed to be two probabilities to Reeves; Brandon might have walked until such time as trains and buses were running, or he might have gone to a railway waiting-room—those at the main line termini being open all night.

Knowing Brandon's record and physique, Reeves inclined to the idea that the man would rather have walked than merely waited. He might have set out along the Dover Road, if he intended to make a bolt for the Continent, and walked for several hours southwards, until such time as it was convenient to take a train from some station on his route to the coast, or until the bus services could take him unnoticed on his way. Reeves made a neat list of all the possibilities which occurred to him along this line of thought, and then returned to Scotland Yard to set in motion the machinery for following up his ideas. He was a very thorough and pertinacious worker, and knew that time can most often be saved in detective work by going about a job in methodical fashion.

This done, he followed up his other idea—that of the station waiting-rooms. He began at Victoria and worked his way round slowly, finding out who was responsible for occasional inspection of these melancholy apartments where travellers are often forced to spend miserable hours of the night, waiting until the railway authorities who landed them at such deplorable hours were ready to take them on their way again. It was slow work, for Reeves had first to find out who had had the opportunity of observing the waiting-rooms, and then to seek out that individual at his home, since those on night duty took their rest in the daytime. The detective was patient to an astonishing degree; he knew that he would get information if Brandon had been noticed leaving the country by either airports or seaports, but until then his only means of following him was by this slow method of inquiry, working on doggedly from one disappointment to the next. Victoria, Waterloo, Charing Cross, and London Bridge were ticked off his list, and he next set to work on the northern group—St. Pancras, King's Cross, and Euston. It was at the last of these that he got news of Brandon, and unexpectedly explicit news. A porter who had been on duty when an excursion train from the north had arrived at four o'clock in the morning had both seen and recognised the explorer. The porter (Simpson by name) had had Brandon pointed out to him as a notability when the former had returned from a journey to Edinburgh in the summer, and Simpson was quite certain that the big fair man he had seen, hunched up in uneasy slumber in the waiting-room at Euston, was Brandon and none other. It was not until later that Reeves learnt of Brandon's visit to Richard Surray's flat. At the time the detective struck the trail of his quarry at Euston, Reeves simply concentrated on the probabilities evoked by the possible journeys from the terminus of the London, Midland, and Scottish line. Reeves knew the outline of Macdonald's case, for the Chief Inspector believed in sharing the available facts with the subordinate who was working with him, and Reeves had proved his own trustworthiness by several years of work in his department. He was not one of those who have no control over their tongues, and he was trusted by his superiors as a safe man in a difficult case. Therefore he knew quite well that Naomi Surray was up north in the Island of Uist, and when he heard of Brandon's presence at Euston, Reeves made two guesses at the man's probable objective—one was Liverpool, whence Brandon could take ship for almost any part of the world, the other was Scotland, whence he could reach the Hebrides.

Armed with the photographs which Macdonald had given him, Reeves tackled the booking offices. Once again he needed all the patience which he possessed, but he eventually got his facts. Brandon was a noticeable person, his height and good looks made him easy to remember, and the clerk who had booked his ticket remembered both his face and his impatient, overbearing manner. The explorer had taken a ticket to Glasgow, about a quarter to ten that morning. Once more Reeves set out in search of porters, ticket inspectors, and barrier men, and spent a hectic time interrogating them. If Brandon had decided to travel north on the spur of the moment, so to speak, he could not have reserved a seat, and the trains at this season of the year were so crowded that a traveller arriving at the last moment without a reservation might well have had some difficulty in obtaining a seat. This reasoning bore fruit. A porter who had settled "a party" in reserved seats remembered having to re-stack the hand luggage in a first-class compartment in order to accommodate a tall, impatient gentleman who was quite unable to find another seat to his liking. This porter, having examined Brandon's photograph with maddening deliberation, at length decided "that was 'im. Remember 'is long ears. Funny ears, 'e 'ad. Dressed in a grey flannel suit, with a raincoat over 'is arm and a yellow 'ide suit-case. Just the one I remembers. Thought 'e was the Prince o' Wales and Mussolini, too, that one."

At this news Reeves's spirits went up with a bound. It was now nearly four o'clock in the afternoon, but since Brandon had not left London until the ten o'clock train, it was still possible to warn the authorities at Glasgow to look out for him when that train arrived there, and to see what was his next move. If he tried to leave by sea, it was possible to have enough difficulties put in his way to detain him until Reeves could reach Glasgow. Macdonald was willing to take the risk of detaining Brandon for an inquiry into his movements at the time of the fire. Reeves himself could give evidence that the car had been taken out of the garage at Faraway soon after ten in the evening, and that it had not returned there during the night.

It was at this stage in his report that Reeves returned to

Scotland Yard to report. Brandon's train would reach Glasgow at 5.55 p.m.—if Reeves followed him by train, the detective could not get there before six o'clock the following morning, there being no trains to Glasgow from London between the early afternoon and the evening. And the detective knew that if a man like Brandon once got away into the happy hunting ground of the Western Highlands, he could lead the authorities a merry chase with all the odds in his favour. It was essential for Reeves to obtain fresh instructions and clear authority for his next step.

Reaching Scotland Yard again by five o'clock, Reeves heard of the added complications to the case. Macdonald was busy at that time with his inquiry at Richard Surray's rooms, and by the time Reeves got through on the telephone, the Chief Inspector had left in pursuit of Montague. Reeves scratched his head. He wanted the Chief Inspector's authority behind him to get Brandon held up at Glasgow, and it was beginning to look a close thing. It might take too long to get in touch with Macdonald, so Reeves put his case to the authorities at the Yard. While he was thus employed Macdonald rang through, and at his instructions the Glasgow police and the authorities at the Central Station were communicated with. Brandon was to be detained "pending inquiries." No arrest was to be made if he showed himself willing to stay quietly in Glasgow until the Yard emissary arrived, but he was not to be lost sight of.

This matter having been arranged, Reeves treated himself to a large tea. He was very tired, but there was a sense of satisfaction dawning in his mind which did something to mitigate the disgust and exasperation which had been brewing in his mind ever since the door of the cupboard had closed on him the previous night. Drinking his strong tea, he sat and waited until Glasgow should report. The rest of the case sank into insignificance; Brandon *was* the case to Reeves, and the sturdy little detective felt that life would be very sweet when he faced the big fair man and requested him to return to London for an inquiry into his recent doings.

It was not much after half-past six that the Glasgow authorities rang through to say that they had carried out instructions. The "wanted" man had been spotted at the barrier and challenged by the Inspector detailed for the job—and had promptly endeavoured to make a bolt through the crowd. The resulting scene had occasioned considerable excitement and disorder in the crowded booking hall, but the result had been satisfactory from the police point of view. They had their man and they were able to detain him at police headquarters under the temporary charge of "obstruction." The Yard would find him safely housed when their representative arrived to make an interrogation. Brandon had not denied his identity. On hearing that Scotland Yard wished to question him he simply turned obstinately silent and refused to utter another word.

Reeves, to his great joy, was offered the job of going north to fetch his man back. He fairly chuckled to himself now, as he began to piece together the evidence against Brandon. The chap might be a superb mountaineer and a famous explorer of unmapped territory, but when it came to matching his wits against the police he was no expert. His original alibi for the Sunday night of Ruth Surray's death was a clumsy, incomplete affair which would convince no one. As for his alibi at the time of the fire, Reeves chuckled more. That night on his own in the cramped misery of the wine cupboard had not been wasted. He could swear to the fact that the Humber had been taken out of the garage; there was no second car housed there, for Montague had left his in the road. Brandon had left Faraway at half-past ten and he had not returned there. Finally there was Brandon's visit to Richard Surray's this morning. No wonder the chap decided to bolt, thought Reeves to himself.

Unable to get a sleeper on the night train, the detective curled himself up in a corner and went to sleep. He could have slept on a stone pavement if necessary, so weary was he after his unhappy night and his day of patient inquiry, and the rhythmic throb of the train seemed as comforting as a lullaby.

It was barely eight o'clock when Reeves, after a good breakfast and a shave and brush-up, arrived at Police Headquarters in Glasgow to interview the detained man. The interview was perhaps the briefest of the kind ever held. The big fair man who was sitting consuming the breakfast sent in for him raised a jaunty eyebrow as the C.I.D. man was shown in. Reeves's face spoke volumes.

"Who in hell is that?" he demanded, his previous satisfaction vanishing like smoke in the wind. "That's not Brandon."

"Who in hell said it was?" demanded the detained man affably. "You cops want a lesson. Fancy yourselves no end. You've made a bloomer this time. You've got nothing on me."

Reeves withdrew into the passage and the door was closed on the large blond gentleman who was consuming his breakfast.

"You've got some blasted card-sharper or confidence man who kicked up a shemozzle to let his mates get through without being noticed," said Reeves, when he had swallowed down a few lurid words to relieve his feelings. "Hell! Can't I see it! There was a gang of shysters on the train, and this one was sent ahead to make a diversion and let the others slip through under cover of the mess-up. My man must have walked past while you were busy seeing to this one. You've collected a crook all right—only too pleased to be charged under a name that wasn't his own. I've met that game before. Neat and not noticeable, as the devil said."

Once again Reeves sat down to think. His luck was out, dead out, but he was not going back to London to admit defeat without further effort. Brandon had travelled on the ten o'clock train from Euston, and his trail had to be picked up somehow. Reeves once again cudgelled his brains for a sequence of possibilities. There were the steamship companies to be notified again, the Glasgow hotels, garages, bus depots—endless work, but the local men would put that through. Last, and most important of all, was the possibility that Brandon had gone on to the Hebrides, and it was this idea which Reeves determined to examine himself. He had spent more than one holiday on his motor-bike, exploring the west coast of Scotland—from Glasgow up through Crianlarich and the Pass of Glencoe to Fort William, and on through Glenfinnan to the coast, Arisaig and Mallaig and the Kyle of Lochalsh.

Sitting chewing his pencil, he worried away at Brandon's probable movements after he left Glasgow if the Hebrides had been his objective. There was Oban, with its frequent steamer services to Skye and the other islands to the north-west. Oban was the most obvious route (inquiries should be put on foot at once); but Oban at this time of year was crowded, and full of the very people who might be Brandon's friends. It seemed to Reeves that his man might well avoid Oban lest he fell in with the acquaintances he would wish to avoid. Might he not prefer to try his luck at one of those remote spots like Mallaig, the little fishing village at the very back of beyond, divided from the busy crowds by the hazardous road through Glenfinnan—a road of moor and forest and tors, swinging its narrow course round hairpin bends, clinging to the steep fell sides with a precipice below and a wall of rock above?

Thinking of that well-remembered road, Reeves lifted his head and felt hope coming into his heart. Outside a howling west wind was blowing through the busy streets—it had been blowing all night, tearing in from the stormy Atlantic. If the wind held, no vessel could put out that day from the smaller ports like Mallaig; the crashing seas were too perilous for anything but a heavily-engined vessel to make headway against them.

The London detective made a good impression on the Scots police. Cockney he might be, a southerner bred on foreign ground, speaking with a clipped speech which seemed devoid of R's and A's, but he knew the north-west coast. He had climbed the Ben and scrambled in the Coolins, and knew the rocky coast between Arisaig and the Kyle of Lochalsh, and when he said that he was going a-hunting to Mallaig, the shrewd Scots police saw his point at once.

"Anyway," said Reeves, "I know the blighter by sight. Even if he's wearing a black beard and sun glasses he won't come it over me. I'd know his shoulders among a thousand, be damned to him!"

It was true, as the Glasgow men pointed out, that if Brandon reached Uist it would be easy enough to take him there, but Reeves still hoped that he might stop the big man before he left the mainland. The detective did not confide his ideas to the shrewd members of the Glasgow force, but he had very real apprehensions on the subject of Brandon's intentions. The death of Ruth Surray and the attempted destruction of Upwood House and its inhabitants argued the mentality of a devil or a madman. Reeves had not forgotten that he himself had been locked up into a hole from which he could not have escaped by his own efforts. If Macdonald had not come to seek him, but had assumed that he was following on the trail of his suspect, Reeves might have died miserably beneath the stone stairs of Faraway. Added to these devilments came the poisoning of Richard Surray and of Stanwood. If Brandon were intent on killing the whole family of the Surrays, he might well make Naomi his next point of attack. She was safe enough for the moment, away with the fishing fleet (Reeves suffered a qualm when he thought of the howling gale—had they run for shelter, or were they "riding it out" on that tempestuous sea?), but if she returned and Brandon found her, it seemed to Reeves that another murder might crown the first.

Leaving the Glasgow men to pursue their inquiries, Reeves set out for Fort William. By the time he reached there the police might have got on Brandon's trail and be able to indicate his further movements. He would have had to get a car or a motor-cycle to negotiate the road through Glenfinnan, and it would have been hard to do so without leaving a trail which the police could pick up.

As the train took him northwards, Reeves worried over his problem. He could have done nothing more by staying in Glasgow, and at least it was a consolation to be moving and exploring one possibility. If Brandon had chosen the Fort William route on his journey north-west Reeves was bound to hear of him—at the worst it would be one possibility examined.

It was not until late in the evening that Reeves arrived at Mallaig. Hope was in his heart again, for the police reports at Fort William told of a motorist answering to Brandon's description "who had been held up for repairs to his car" at a local garage early that morning, and Reeves reasoned it out that Brandon, having observed the "shemozzle" during the arrest at the Glasgow station, had argued that the railway was no place for him. He could have hired a car and driven up through Glencoe, and if the man seen in Fort William in the early hours was really Brandon, it seemed almost certain that Mallaig would be his objective—and the wind was still blowing with gale force.

The long northern evening was dimming to a grey twilight when Reeves called on the constable in the little port and told his business. If Brandon had been at the place during the day, he had been careful not to advertise his whereabouts, but Reeves had the consolation of learning that no boats had put out from Mallaig that day. The wind was falling now, and the "morn's morn" would see the normal service working again. It would hardly have been necessary for any man with Brandon's experience of the sea to inquire if there were any sailings on a day like this— the churning waters, coupled to the gale whose force had almost prevented a man from standing erect on the quayside, answered the question before it was asked. But the wind was abating now, and Reeves had a feeling that Brandon—if he was in the neighbourhood—would be tempted to the quayside to watch events. Sailors reckon by tides, not by landsmen's hours, and at the turn of the tide some stout-hearted seamen might venture out again.

After an enormous meal, which included good Scots pies and scones of an excellence seldom met with over the border, Reeves went out into the gusty evening and prowled about by the quayside, listening occasionally to the fishermen's talk, most of it incomprehensible to a Londoner's ears, and then he heard the chug-chug of an approaching motor-bike. His cap pulled down, his collar turned up to his ears, he slouched along the quayside, watching, as a cat prowls around a room where a mouse has passed. He saw the cycle pull up and the cyclist alight and prop up his machine, and he knew that his journey had not been fruitless. Only one man in the world had quite those broad shoulders, sloping down from the long neck, with the head held at that arrogant angle.

Following Brandon up the quayside in the grey twilight, out of earshot of the group of men below, Reeves drew closer to his man. While the detective was still some paces behind him, Brandon turned round, with the swift movement of a startled man, and faced his follower.

Reeves drew closer. "Mr. Keith Brandon? You're wanted."

It was already half dark, but Reeves could see the exasperation on the fair, mobile face as the English voice uttered its unwelcome message:

"And who the deuce may you be?"

"Detective Reeves, Criminal Investigation Department. You are wanted to give evidence about your movements during the last two days. I have authority to detain you if necessary. You will have to return to London for interrogation."

Brandon drew a cigarette-case from his pocket.

"Have you a warrant for my arrest—and, if so, on what charge?"

"I have no warrant for your arrest. That will be issued if the authorities are not satisfied with your account of yourself. The police, as you know, have the right to detain a man for interrogation. If you refuse to comply with their request you can be arrested for obstructing the police in the execution of their duties."

"Oh, parrot talk!" The other laughed almost good-humouredly. "You can hold up a tramp or a communist agitator, but when it comes to a man like myself, you've got to give a few reasons to back up your request. What's the song about?"

Reeves was certain by now that Brandon knew him—certain, too, that the big man had locked him in the cupboard and was laughing to himself. Reeves was not going to mention that cupboard; he had had no warrant to enter Faraway, and the incident would never be mentioned—officially—by himself. He replied in the same stolid official manner he had used throughout:

"You are wanted to give evidence concerning an attempt to burn Upwood House, and also concerning an attempt on the life of Mr. Richard Surray."

"Good God!" There was consternation in his voice, and

astonishment as well. "There must be a madman about! I don't know anything about either of the crimes you mention. This is ludicrous. Do you seriously mean that you expect *me* to come back to London to answer for crimes I've never even heard of?"

"Those are my instructions," replied Reeves. "I should not have been sent north to find you without good reason on the part of Scotland Yard."

The two men stood only a few paces apart in the fading light. Behind them the group of fishermen had moved farther away, and Reeves suddenly realised that the other man was playing for time. Looking small and stolid and clumsy by comparison with his companion's height and grace, Reeves was chuckling inside. Brandon was going to go for him, waiting his chance until they were alone, unseen and unheard. Reeves, the best exponent of jiu-jitsu in Scotland Yard, was not afraid of his large opponent. Let the chap try it and he'd have the surprise of a lifetime. To attack a policeman in the execution of his duty was crime enough to put a man in the wrong without further evidence against him. If Brandon tried that, he would know what handcuffs meant for the first time in his life, if not for the last.

"Come on!" said something inside Reeves's mind. "Come on! You try it!"

"There's the constabulary close at hand, sir," he said politely. "If you want further evidence of any authority, you can get it there. The police up here have instructions to detain you."

Brandon swore. His temper—never his strong point in

dealing with his fellow men—was going. Was he to be brow-beaten by this small fellow mouthing out his official jargon with a cockney accent?

"You'd best come quietly, sir," said Reeves, and laid his hand on Brandon's arm. The policeman's speech and gesture were too much for Brandon's temper. He flung the arm off with violence.

"Keep your filthy paws to yourself!" he flared.

Reeves resumed his grip. "None of that," he said sharply—and then things began to happen.

Brandon, for the first time in his life gripped by the hand of a policeman, saw red. He lunged out, and Reeves's grip did not relax. Using Brandon's own weight and impetus scientif-ically, the small one had the big one at his mercy. Conscious of a sickening pain in his arm, caused entirely by his own struggles, Brandon swung round violently, tripped up over Reeves's foot and crashed down on to the pebbles with the small man still gripping his opponent's arm.

"Police, there, police," yelled Reeves, and to his struggling captive he said cheerfully:

"You've only got yourself to thank for it. You'll be hurting yourself if you don't keep quiet."

The large Scots constable came hastening up from the farther end of the quay, where he had been patrolling, ready to assist the Yard man in case of need. If Brandon could have got his arm free from the grip of the jiu-jitsu expert he might have succeeded in throwing two policemen simultaneously over the jetty, but he was beaten by the application of a science worked out by ingenious small men to protect themselves from the onslaught of more powerful ones.

He fought to get free, being as reasonable by this time as an angry bull, but his efforts availed him nothing. Every sailorman on the quayside was ready to assist the arm of the law. Brandon had committed an offence in the presence of witnesses—he had attacked a policeman; in the eyes of the massive Scots constable the big fair man was "nought but a fulish body."

CHAPTER XV

IT WAS ON THE MONDAY NIGHT THAT THE FIRE HAD broken out at Upwood, and on Tuesday that Reeves set out in pursuit of Brandon. On the Tuesday evening, after Stanwood and Richard Surray had been declared out of danger, and Montague had been left under supervision in his own flat, Macdonald proceeded with the investigations which had been interrupted by the news of the poison mystery.

The thought of the fire was uppermost in the Chief Inspector's mind. He was satisfied that the theory of accident—urged by Montague—was untenable, and that it had been caused deliberately by some one who had pressed down the electric switch and left the heater to do its work until it ignited the inflammable material placed above it. How he was ever to prove who was responsible for that devilish intention, Macdonald did not know, but at least he could eliminate those who could not have been at Upwood at the time of the fire.

With this intention in his mind, Macdonald went to

Denham Court, where Stanwood lived. This was a huge pile of flats overlooking the Marylebone Road, and Macdonald introduced himself to the porter on duty at the door giving on to that section of the block where Stanwood's flat was situated. The porter, by name William Sharp, looked at the C.I.D. man with much interest and led him into his cubbyhole by the entrance, where Macdonald proceeded to explain the purpose of his inquiries by a complicated theory of "impersonation." Some person was alleged, said the Chief Inspector, to have impersonated Stanwood during a raid on a club in North Kensington—not a very important matter, but one which it was desirable should be cleared up by "independent evidence." Sharp, a large and good-looking member of the Corps of Commissionaires, at a first glance belied his name. He did not look "sharp"—all beef and no brains might have been the first verdict of any one regarding his massive person and good-humoured countenance, but Macdonald saw the intelligence which underlay the man's ponderous movements and slow speech. Sharp nodded his large head slowly over Macdonald's story, and accepted it with a polite "Yes, sir, I see the idea." But he saw a little further, too, Macdonald guessed. "You're from the Yard, sir. That's good enough for me," he added.

"I want you to tell me what you can about Mr. Stanwood's movements yesterday—Monday. Did you see him go out or come in—if so, at what times?"

Sharp sat and pondered; he was not the type of witness who believed in answering hurriedly, and his answer when it came was deliberate, but very clear:

"Mr. Stanwood went out yesterday morning between ten

and eleven. He told me on his way out that he was expecting a packing case of books—he's only had his flat for a fortnight, and his things are still being moved in. He asked me to see that the case was taken up to his flat. I didn't see him again until he came in about quarter to seven in the evening. He asked me if the case had come, and I told him yes. Then he asked me if I'd got any time that was my own, so to speak, if I could come up and give him a hand with moving some heavy stuff. As it happened, I was due for a couple of hours' free time, eight till ten, and I said I'd go up at nine."

"And you went up as arranged?" prompted Macdonald.

"Yes, sir. I went up just after nine, unpacked the crate and moved a bookcase for him. He'd got a visitor—a Mr. Franks from number twenty-one—and we got the job done between us. A big heavy bookcase it was—one o' them mahogany things with cupboards down below. When I left, after clearing up the packing from the case, it'd've been half-past nine."

"And Mr. Franks was still there?"

"Yes, sir. They was playing chess when I came down—great chess player, Mr. Franks. Looked like a long sitting."

"Thanks very much. That's very satisfactory from my point of view," said Macdonald. "It's important for us to get the evidence really clear, and your statement is just what was wanted. Is Mr. Franks in now, do you know? A word from him would complete that side of my case."

"I think you'll find him at home, sir. I saw him go up in the lift about an hour ago. Funny thing you should be asking me about Mr. Stanwood. There's a lady up in his flat now—his sister-in-law, she said she was—and she's in a proper stew about him. He said he'd be in by teatime, and he's not turned up. The lady's been down twice to ask me if there weren't no message about him."

"Is the lady staying with Mr. Stanwood?"

"That I couldn't say, sir. She came this morning and brought a small bag with her, so maybe she is. Perhaps you'd look in and see her, sir. If so be as Mr. Stanwood's met with an accident, you could advise her how to act about making inquiries—begging your pardon for the liberty, but I'm sorry for her, and that's a fact."

"I certainly will," replied Macdonald; "and bear this in mind: there's no need to tell anybody about these inquiries I've been making. If Mr. Stanwood was at home all yesterday evening, he doesn't touch my case. It always annoys people to learn that inquiries have been made about them, even though it's necessary from our point of view."

"That's all right, sir," replied Sharp. "I've been on this job long enough to know when to keep a still tongue in my head. There's more harm done by talking than there is by keeping quiet, I reckon."

Macdonald went upstairs in the lift, thinking how circumstances alter cases. The "speech is silver and silence is gold" adage did not always apply in police work. If everybody, including Richard Surray, had told everything that they knew before the Coroner's inquest it might have been better for all of them.

Mr. Franks turned out to be a tall, thin, elderly man, pleasant of voice and reserved of manner. Macdonald found out later that he was a poet, well known among scholars for some of his classical translations. To him Macdonald told a story which was nearer the facts of the case than the subterfuge (calculated for Stanwood's benefit) that had passed muster with the porter.

"I must ask you to regard this visit as confidential," began the Chief Inspector, after introducing himself. "Mr. Geoffrey Stanwood has met with a curious and disturbing accident, and I am in charge of the inquiry concerning it."

"I am very sorry to hear that. What's happened to him?" returned the other.

"He has been poisoned. Since you are a friend of his, it is probable that he will tell you the circumstances later. My point in visiting you is this: I want to know whether a certain individual could have called on Mr. Stanwood yesterday evening. I have already made inquiries of the porter, and he told me that you were in Mr. Stanwood's flat yesterday evening."

"I was, but not for the purpose of poisoning him," replied the other dryly. "I went in to play chess with him—he is a very fine player. Our game did not begin until rather late, as he had taken into his head to move some of his furniture about. However, we got settled down about half-past nine and played until after midnight. During that time he certainly had no visitor of any kind. His flat is a very quiet one, and we should undoubtedly have heard if anybody had called, as we had the door of the room open in order to get as much fresh air as possible."

"Thank you very much. That was the point I wished to get clear—that no visitor called on Mr. Stanwood between those hours."

"You can take it as certain that they did not. And now, Chief Inspector, since I have answered your questions, I take

it that you can answer one of mine. Is Stanwood in a dangerous state?"

"Oh, no. I might have reassured you on that point earlier.
He collapsed in the street, but fortunately help was forthcoming in time, and he is now in no danger—but neither is
he in a state to be questioned. In a day or two he should be
quite normal again, but we can't afford to wait a day or two
before setting inquiries on foot."

"Obviously. Do you connect this dastardly outrage with
the Surray case?"

Macdonald had been about to take his leave, but the last
question brought him to a halt.

"Why do you ask that?" he inquired.

Franks gave a slight shrug of his shoulders.

"I was interested in the matter of Ruth Surray's tragic
death—as all writers were interested. Stanwood talked about
it a little last night. He felt her death very keenly, as he well
might. I understood from him that further inquiries were
being made, and he confided to me, in absolute confidence, a
curious theory he had formed. Since you say that his recovery
is certain, I do not feel justified in breaking that confidence.
You will be able to question him on the point yourself."

"I think that you had better reconsider that decision, Mr.
Franks," replied Macdonald. "It is only by chance that Mr.
Stanwood obtained expert help in time to save his life. If you
have any evidence to offer which may assist us in the search for
his would-be murderer you are bound by the law to state it."

"I have no evidence, Chief Inspector, merely supposition,
and that of a sort which would not be admitted to any court
of law. Stanwood and I were discussing the psychological

matter of the case, and his supposition involved the presumption of insanity in one of those witnesses in the case you are investigating."

"And who did he consider was the insane person?"

"There I find myself in a quandary. I have already told you that I should not consider myself justified in breaking his confidence. I might ask you a further question. Who was the visitor whom you suspected of calling on Stanwood last night?"

Macdonald's wits were working hard. He did not wish to waste time arguing with another of these "conscientious objectors" who seemed so prevalent in this case, and his hypothetical visitor had been suggested only as a means to an end; the non-existent visitor theme was developing unexpectedly.

"Obviously I wished to find out if any person connected with the case had visited Mr. Stanwood," he said, "but it is hardly expedient for me to mention names. Suspicion is bound to be wide in a case of this nature, where we have very few facts at our disposal. As you have been discussing the case with Mr. Stanwood you would know the names of those persons who have been interrogated. Since Mr. Stanwood met certain of these only yesterday, he would hardly expect a visit from them in the evening."

Macdonald was talking to gain time while he thought. Was it possible that Stanwood's theory fitted in with an idea which he had been exploring himself? He risked the allusion to watch his companion's reaction.

"I should not have been surprised if Dr. Richard Surray, for instance, had called on Mr. Stanwood. I may tell you in confidence, however, that Dr. Surray has fallen a victim to the same form of attack as Mr. Stanwood himself."

"Good heavens!" The other man's surprise was obvious, but after a moment he added, "Dr. Surray is also recovering, I take it?"

"Yes. He is still ill, but no longer in danger."

"Ah!" said Franks thoughtfully, and studied Macdonald's uncommunicative face. "I think we understand one another, Chief Inspector, without further elaboration."

"I hope that you understand this, too," said Macdonald, "that to give voice to suspicions to the police is one thing, but to express them to anybody else is quite another."

Franks smiled. "You can hardly accuse me of lack of circumspection. I have belied my name even to you—but I am interested in seeing the workings of the expert mind."

Macdonald laughed. "I can only advise you not to jump to conclusions. Good-evening, Mr. Franks—and I am giving you sound advice when I warn you to forget this visit of mine completely—or at least not to mention it to anybody. It is easier to be drawn into an admission than it is to check the results of it."

Leaving the grey-headed man smiling to himself, Macdonald went up in the lift again to Stanwood's flat and rang the bell. The door was opened to him by a tall dark young woman with a white face and anxious eyes. "What is it?" she asked quickly.

"I have come about Mr. Stanwood, who has been taken ill in the street," began the Chief Inspector, and she cried out:

"Tell me, he's not dead?"

"No, neither is he in any danger," replied Macdonald. "I am

an inspector from Scotland Yard. May I come in a moment?" He held out a card, which she took and glanced at quickly, and then stood away from the door.

"Yes. Do come in. I have been so worried, not knowing what had happened to him." She led the way across the small entrance hall into a sitting-room, where books stood in piles about the floor and on tables and chairs, as though they were in process of arrangement. "My name is Elsa Wentworth, and I am Mr. Stanwood's sister-in-law," she said as though to explain her presence in the flat. "Whatever has happened to him?"

"He was taken ill in the street about four o'clock this afternoon," said Macdonald. "I am afraid that he was poisoned—deliberately; but there is no need for you to be anxious over his health now. The doctors are quite satisfied about him. He is now in a nursing home in Beaumont Street. I am sorry that no message was sent to relieve your anxiety. Mr. Stanwood was too ill to think coherently, and he was understood to say that he lived alone and that no message was necessary. The effects of the poison probably clouded his mind."

"How did it happen?" she demanded, her long fingers twisting themselves together in agitation.

"We can't be quite certain, Miss Wentworth. He went to see Dr. Surray, and both of them were taken ill in the same way about half an hour after they parted."

"I must go and see him," she said. "There may be things he will want. You can tell me where he is?"

"He is at 190 Beaumont Street. I don't know whether you will be allowed to see him to-night—"

"Oh, but I must go; of course they'll let me see him, even

though he may not talk. You can't imagine how I have been worrying about him. He said he would be in by four o'clock; we were arranging these books and he was going to see me to my train at seven o'clock. I knew something had happened."

Her words came in a rush, almost incoherently. She was a striking-looking creature, with a thin nervous face, in shape a beautiful oval, clean-cut features, very dark eyes and a magnificent dark head. Her throat was very slender and her black hair was twisted into a great knob low down on the base of the white neck. A woman who lived on her nerves, with no great reserves of physical strength, Macdonald guessed.

"If it will relieve your anxiety just to see him and to talk to the matron at the nursing home, by all means go," he said kindly enough, and she snatched up a hat that was lying on top of some books.

"Of course. Poor Geoffrey! He's always been so kind; he was an angel to my sister. I don't know what I should have done… I can't bear to think about it… 190 Beaumont Street, you said? That's just across by High Street, isn't it? I can't rest until I've seen him."

"I could come with you—or if you'd rather, I will ring up the matron and tell her that you are coming—"

"Yes, please do, ring up, I mean," she said in her breathless way. "Don't bother to come with me. I can't bear to talk, somehow. I'm sorry, but I've been feeling so awful. If I can only see him and *know* he's safe I shall be all right again. Will you ring up now—they'll be expecting me when I get there?"

"Don't get run over crossing the road," adjured Macdonald as he stretched out his hand for the telephone which stood on a side table. "That wouldn't help Mr. Stanwood at all. You'd better have a taxi."

"Oh, no! It won't take me a minute; I shall run. Please don't think I'm as mad as I seem. I'm quite sensible, really, only I was so dreadfully worried."

She was out of the room in a trice, her hat pulled on anyhow over the noble dark head which seemed such a contrast to her agitated speech and fluttering hands.

Macdonald, putting his call through to the nursing home, said to himself, "Sensible? She's as much sense as the Mad Hatter. Leaving me in charge of Stanwood's flat without a thought of further possibilities. If any one had wanted to plant evidence here with that poor thing in possession, they'd have done it as easily as the chicken crossed the road."

He got through to the matron of the home, warning her to expect an agitated visitor. "Don't let her talk to him," he added; "she's nearly beside herself with nerves."

"You leave that to me," replied the matron. "Number Eighteen's picking up nicely, though. His pulse is still incredible, and he can't see much, but he's fairly clear in his head."

"Pack Miss Wentworth back here as soon as you can," replied Macdonald. "She's left me here as a sort of act of faith. Some minds can't cope with more than one idea at a time."

As he hung up the receiver and looked round the untidy room Macdonald realised that he had performed an "act of faith" himself. If Miss Wentworth had been anxious to escape from further contact with Scotland Yard her behaviour could be construed as that of a guilty party—in which case she would not now be running down Marylebone Road towards Beaumont Street—but Macdonald did occasionally let his instinct guide him. He had felt instinctively that the dark-eyed young woman was possessed by one idea only—anxiety about the fate of Geoffrey Stanwood. Macdonald went as far as to say to himself, "Well, perhaps I was the mutt that time—but since I am here I might as well look around."

The latter process was easy. Stanwood appeared to have been rearranging not only his books, but his papers and belongings in general. Nothing was locked. His desk, with its closed flap and many drawers, was open to inspection, and bundles of letters and papers lay around, as though their owner had been interrupted in a determined attempt to get his possessions into order. The typewriter—a full-sized Remington—stood uncovered, with sheets lying beside it indicating that a catalogue of books was being undertaken. Macdonald gathered from the state of the room that its owner was one of those untidy people who make occasional feverish attacks on the accumulation of years, and who generally end by ramming everything back into the handiest receptacle in sheer despair at achieving order out of chaos.

The waste-paper basket was jammed with a multitude of papers, and among these Macdonald fished out some torn sheets covered with Stanwood's sprawling writing. He had evidently been attempting drafts of a letter, and had torn the sheets in half and flung them into the basket without destroying them further. "Dear Jack," began one attempt. "I can't rest for worrying myself over this ghastly tragedy. I'm hag-ridden by suspicions, but I haven't anything tangible to go upon. I believe you're in S.'s set. Can you find out—" Here it broke off, and another began: "Dear Jack—Thanks for your letter. The whole thing is ghastly beyond words. Nerves play the devil with all of us, and mine are no exception. Were you in London on the evening of Sunday, the 29th? I know it's safe enough to ask you questions. You're not likely to think I'm demented. For my own peace of mind I want to find out what S. was doing on that Sunday night. Can you get any information...?"

Pocketing the tell-tale fragments, Macdonald walked quickly round the rest of the flat. It was compact enough—small lounge hall, sitting-room, bedroom, bathroom, and kitchenette. The bedroom also was stacked with books and a pile lay on the bedside table—travel books, Macdonald noted. Burton's *Pilgrimage to Mecca*, and Doughty's *Arabia Deserta*.

There was also a box of "Medinal" Tablets, which bore mute witness to the fact that Stanwood's nerves had begun to keep him awake at night. After a moment's thought Macdonald removed them. If Stanwood were feeling depressed and melancholy after his dose of atropine—as well he might—it would be better for him not to find any drugs at hand when he returned home.

A few moments later there was a ring at the front door bell, and Macdonald went to open it, and found Miss Wentworth standing on the threshold.

"I forgot that I hadn't a latchkey," she explained in her quick, agitated way. "It's kind of you to have waited. I suppose the porter would have let me in, but it's so difficult explaining things. I saw Mr. Stanwood, just for a minute. They only let me just have a look at him. Oh, dear! I can't make it all out. It's so dreadful and mysterious. However did this dreadful thing happen? If you know, won't you tell me?"

Macdonald closed the door behind her and drew her into the hall as though she were a child.

"I don't know, so I can't tell you, Miss Wentworth. The whole thing is a complete mystery at present." She looked so unhappy and bewildered as she stood there that Macdonald was constrained to ask, out of common humanity, "And you? Will you be staying here, or are you going home? Now that you have seen Mr. Stanwood, why not go back to your own people? It's very comfortless for you here by yourself."

"Oh, that doesn't matter. I shall manage somehow," she said vaguely. "Geoffrey—Mr. Stanwood—was going to let me have his flat while he was away. I live in lodgings in Birmingham, but I was coming up here next week. I think I'd better stay here and try to get the place tidy. He's such a dreadful muddler, and I'm not much better. Thank you very much for thinking about me," she added, with her quaintly childish air, which consorted so oddly with the dignity of her dark head.

Macdonald was sorry for her; she seemed so helpless and agitated. He expressed sympathy with her over her worries and left her standing with her hat in her hand looking round the little entrance hall as though she wondered if the ceiling would fall on her. He was glad that he had taken away the "Medinal" Tablets. Miss Wentworth looked just the type of being "to take several of the silly things" in the determination to get a night's sleep somehow.

On his way out Macdonald asked the porter to go up and inquire if Miss Wentworth needed anything. He felt certain that the thought of a meal would never occur to her unless some one suggested it. Stanwood evidently had his meals sent up, or else went out for them; there was no food in the flat, Macdonald had observed. The thought of Elsa Wentworth's white face had been in his mind when he glanced into the empty cupboards of the kitchenette. There had not even been a milk bottle, and she seemed to have made her tea from some queer beverage made from the contents of a tin labelled "Health Coffee," which claimed to have the flavour and aroma of coffee without its dyspeptic effects. Apparently she had not even found a biscuit to sustain her, and Macdonald urged Sharp to order a tray from the kitchen and to see that she had all she needed.

"Very good, sir. I'll tell the manageress. I thought the poor thing looked all flamboozled," said the porter sympathetically. "Sorry to hear Mr. Stanwood's had an accident," he added.

"He's in a nursing home in Beaumont Street. The matron was on the phone just now," replied Macdonald. "I expect he'll be back to-morrow or the next day."

Leaving Denham Court, the Chief Inspector walked across to Beaumont Street and interviewed the matron. "If it's possible for Mr. Stanwood to talk, I think I'd better see him," he said. "I'll be guided by you, of course, but it's very important that we should get a statement as early as possible."

"Well, I don't suppose it'll hurt him if you're careful not to excite him," she replied. "I'd rather have kept him quiet, of course. His pulse rate is still ludicrous, and he's pretty exhausted. He's had a doing, with the actual poison and the drastic treatment to get rid of it."

"Yes. I realise all that, but when a man's been poisoned the sooner he makes a statement, the sooner we can get things straightened out," said Macdonald. "Is he quite clear in his mind now?"

"Not quite—I went up just now. I think he's still a bit muddle-headed and excitable, so don't put too much reliance on what he says. Now I'll give you five minutes, and when I tell you to go you can do as you're told without arguing," said the matron, with a touch of waggishness often displayed by those who have dealings with the sick and helpless.

Stanwood, clad in a pair of borrowed pyjamas, looked a very sick man as he lay back on the pillows. There was a touch of hectic colour on his cheek-bones, but the face seemed to have fallen away, leaving the nose and temple bones jutting out sharply from the hollowed cheeks and cavernous eye-hollows. He looked much more ill than Macdonald had expected to find him, judging from the reassuring reports he had received. The matron went up to him and said in her voice of professional cheerfulness, "There's a visitor for you, Mr. Stanwood. Do you feel up to talking a little?"

Stanwood opened his eyes; the pupils were still dilated to pools of blackness and his voice was husky and indistinct.

"Tell 'em to go to hell. I feel bloody," he groaned thickly.

"I'm sorry to bother you, Mr. Stanwood," said Macdonald. "I want to find out how this happened."

"Who are you? Curse it, I can't see a thing," replied Stanwood, passing a limp hand across his eyes.

"Inspector Macdonald. Can you remember anything about your visit to Dr. Surray's?"

"Ask him. He knows," replied Stanwood. "At least he ought to know. Made a muck of it and didn't finish the job. Coffee…foul stuff. Montague wouldn't drink it. He knew better. Talking about Fellowes…but Montague did that, he knows, too. Oh, hell! Never mind what I'm saying; brain's gone. Elsa's waiting for me somewhere. I meant to ask. She'll get lost; always gets lost in London. Go and find Elsa, there's a good chap."

The incoherent voice died away, and the matron bent down and laid her fingers on Stanwood's pulse, then she frowned at Macdonald. The latter said:

"Miss Wentworth is at your flat, Mr. Stanwood. She knows all about your accident, and she is quite safe."

"Might have got her, too. Meant to do those books. Look here, I've left all those books." He jerked himself up on his elbow. "Awful mess; I must go and see about it. Elsa can't…"

The matron and the nurse at the other side of the bed made Stanwood lie down again, and Macdonald went out quietly in response to a gesture from the former.

"If a man's mind goes, it's like that…mad, and everything gets in a mess…" Stanwood's husky voice was trailing on as Macdonald went into the corridor with the matron behind him.

"I'd better get doctor to have a look at him again. He's worse than he was an hour ago," she said. "He was a bit delirious at first—I believe atropine causes delirium, but it's a most unusual poison."

"He is certainly in no state to be questioned now," said Macdonald. "Can you send another nurse up and let me see the one on duty, if I wait?"

The nurse in Stanwood's room was not a member of the Beaumont Street staff; she was an infirmary sister on duty for the C.I.D., and it was her business to take note of anything that her patient said. When she came down to see Macdonald in the matron's sitting-room she said, "There is nothing to report. At first he wasn't comprehensible at all, because the poison had affected his throat. Then he talked about some one called Marion, and said that she was dead. Then he babbled on about mountains and climbing. Nothing coherent. No mention at all of what happened to-day. I imagine Marion was his wife, or his sister. He was quite quiet and seemed to be going on satisfactorily until you spoke to him. That excited him and caused his pulse to quicken again."

"Do you know anything about the usual after-effects of atropine poisoning?"

"Nothing but what the text-books say. It's a most unusual drug for a poisoner to get hold of, and I have never heard of a case before. He must have swallowed a very big dose of it to be reduced to that state. Delirium would be expected after a large dose, I believe. However, he had been quite quiet for an hour before you came in; he was only light-headed for a short time, but his mind was clouded as though he found it difficult to get words in their proper order. Here are my notes. I'll let you know at once if he says anything relevant."

"He looks pretty bad to me," said Macdonald.

"You'd look pretty bad if you'd been through what he had," she replied, "but he's getting on all right. He'll be quite rational in the morning, so doctor says."

As Macdonald went out he allowed himself to yawn—a very large yawn. He had had two hours' rest on the previous night, and, like Reeves, he felt that a little sleep was indicated.

"They're all doing nicely this end," he thought to himself; "and Brandon can come back and complete the party. It might have been worse."

Richard Surray meanwhile, his brain clouded by the potent drug he had swallowed, kept on repeating "It's atropine... I can't see. Tell them it's atropine..."

CHAPTER XVI

MACDONALD WAS HAVING HIS BREAKFAST ON WEDNESDAY morning when he heard two pieces of news over the telephone which caused his long thin face to look a little more saturnine than usual. One was from Glasgow, to the effect that the man detained by the police was not Keith Brandon, and the other concerned Richard Surray, whose state of health was far from satisfactory to the doctor who had charge of him. "You won't be able to ask him any questions to-day, Chief Inspector," said the doctor's voice. "If he's not kept quiet it'll be touch and go with him. He's been overworking for months, and the shock of his sister's death hit him when he was in no sort of state to stand anything of the kind. On the top of that you have the strain occasioned by the new inquiry you've set on foot, and this last business has about put the lid on it."

"Nervous breakdown, in short?" inquired Macdonald.

"Nervous and physical, too. He's in the state when he'll develop pneumonia at any moment—shock and poison acting on a system already undermined. I've seen it happen before, just when you think a man's out of the wood. You can have another opinion if you like, but you won't get any change out of it."

"Your opinion's good enough. If I can't see him, I can't," replied Macdonald. "Good-bye."

From the nursing home in Beaumont Street came more hopeful tidings. Stanwood was better after his night's rest and would be able to see the Chief Inspector and answer his questions.

Nine o'clock found Macdonald at Richard Surray's rooms. Here he found Robert Surray, whose frowning face expressed a question; he followed Macdonald into his brother's study, and the Chief Inspector answered the unspoken question immediately.

"I have made no arrest. Until we get more definite evidence, we cannot charge anybody. The point is, how could either of the suspects get hold of a drug like atropine? It's a most unusual poison."

"It would be infernally difficult," said Robert. "I've been making inquiries about it. The ordinary chemist doesn't stock the actual alkaloid, or if he did, he wouldn't sell it. He'd only sell it in solution or as tablets for making ophthalmic drops. Hospitals would have it—but the most likely way of obtaining it would be through a firm of manufacturing chemists—and then you'd have to steal it. That's not so impossible as it sounds, if you know any one who's an analyst at a pharmaceutical lab. Get yourself asked to tea in the lab. and lift the poison that comes handiest. Atropine in crystals is quite clear and colourless—it could be put into the coffee quite openly as sugar if the poisoner were neat in his actions."

"That's a point that's being gone into—who could have got possession of the stuff," said Macdonald. "Meantime, since your brother is ill, I should like to look through the papers in his desk."

"I can't quite see the point," said Robert. "You're hardly likely to find anything bearing on this problem. Poisoners don't write warnings of their intentions."

Macdonald studied the troubled face, and realised that Robert, too, was showing the signs of nervous tension. His ability to think clearly had markedly diminished and he went on irritably:

"I don't like the idea of you—or anybody else—going through my brother's papers while he's ill. There may be a lot of confidential stuff there which no one should see but himself. It's a difficult point. If he had had anything relevant to this inquiry, he would have shown it to you."

"What I really want are some specimens of typescript," said Macdonald unexpectedly. "I found some typed notes at Miss Surray's flat which may have concerned your brother. I can't ask him about them, but I can see if the typing was done on his machine."

Robert stared. "You haven't got a bee in your bonnet by any chance? I'm damned if I can see what you're getting at."

"I'm simply trying to collect data. I can't tell you my reasons for doing so—take it that it's routine work. Do I understand that you have any objection?"

Robert stood and looked out of the window with his shoulders hunched up; when he turned round again his face was white, but he answered quietly, "None whatever. If you take anything away, however, I should like to know what it is. Richard's typewriter is in his secretary's room in Harley Street, if that's what you want."

Macdonald's eyes had been studying the room as he stood by the fireplace, and he replied, "Isn't that a portable typewriter under the desk there? I might take a specimen from that to start with. I didn't think of it when I was here yesterday."

Robert Surray went and lifted the case containing the light Corona on to the table.

"This is—was—Ruth's," he said. "Oh, for God's sake, say what you're getting at!" he burst out. "This talking in riddles is enough to drive a man demented."

"The only thing that I can say at this juncture is that every scrap of evidence has to be examined without prejudice," replied Macdonald. "You have nearly all the evidence at your disposal and you have had the same opportunities as myself to examine it. I cannot, in common justice to everybody, neglect to examine any point which may be relevant, out of consideration for your own feelings or for those of your brother."

"Evidence," cried Robert. "I've been thinking over it until I'm sick at heart, and I realise well enough the manner in which it can be twisted, one way or another..." He broke off abruptly. "I'm sorry. I've been behaving like a fool. One can start dispassionately enough, but a succession of events like those we have suffered is enough to get under any one's skin. I'll leave you to it. Here are Richard's keys."

"I think I may not have to trouble about the desk. It was the typewriter I was thinking about," rejoined Macdonald. "If you'll give me some paper I can take a specimen myself. There are a few questions I must ask—but if you would rather not answer them..."

Robert Surray had got control of himself again now. "Carry on," he said quietly. "If I know the answers I'll tell you them. If I don't, you can ask elsewhere."

"Do you know if Miss Ruth Surray was in the habit of taking her typewriter with her when she went away? For instance, did she take it to Upwood House with her?"

"If she was going to be away for a goodish time she would probably have taken it," replied Robert, "but there would have been no point in her taking it to Upwood. There's a machine there if she wanted one. As for the rest of your question—I think you mentioned it before—since no one at Upwood saw her typewriter there, neither our own people nor the maids, I think one can assume that she didn't take it with her."

"Then it remained at her own flat," replied Macdonald. "Presumably your brother brought it here. You did not hear him mention it?"

Robert looked at the neat little machine for a moment or two before he answered:

"In reply to your question, no. I did not hear him mention it, neither can I imagine that he would have taken that thing from Ruth's flat and brought it here. He never uses a type-writer himself if he can help it—loathes the things."

Macdonald slipped a sheet of paper into the machine, but before he used it, he inquired, "Why are you so certain that this typewriter is your sister's? Has it any identifying mark?"

"Yes. The scraping on the case in front. I did that damage myself, some time in the spring—kicked the whole thing over when it was standing on the floor, just as it is now. It ought to have the remains of an orange label underneath it somewhere."

Robert stood and watched while Macdonald typed out his specimen and then said, "Is there anything else I can tell you?" and Macdonald replied:

"Not just now, thanks. Can I see Harrow?"

"I'll send him in. I shall be staying here, by the way, until Richard's out of the wood. I don't want to alarm my mother by sending for her; she's had quite enough trouble for the time being."

A few minutes later Harrow entered. Macdonald placed the Corona on the floor under the desk, and he asked the man if he could say how long it had been there. Harrow looked puzzled.

"I don't remember seeing it before, sir, but I can't be certain. Dr. Surray often put cases under his desk just there, but I don't remember seeing that one before. It wasn't there yesterday, that I do know—not yesterday morning when I did the room."

"Did either of the gentlemen who came yesterday carry a case when they arrived?"

This the man was unable to say; Macdonald, watching him, realised the type of witness he was—cautious and conscientious, but neither very observant nor a good visualiser. Two gentlemen had come by appointment to see his master; he had admitted them without giving much thought to them.

"Mr. Stanwood came first," he said, "at 2.15 to the tick that was. I showed him into the study. Dr. Surray was in his bedroom, and I told him Mr. Stanwood had come. Mr. Montague came in five minutes later—I'd seen him before. I think he was carrying something—an attaché case maybe, but honestly I can't say for certain, sir, and that's a fact."

"And you did not take the coffee tray in until both visitors had arrived?"

"That's right, sir. The tray was in the pantry, and I took it in when Dr. Surray rang."

Taking the portable machine with him, Macdonald went on to Beaumont Street to see Stanwood. The latter was now sitting up in bed, looking drawn and haggard, with his eyes still black and strange with their immense pupils, but it was obvious at once that he had recovered to a degree that was remarkable, considering his state of collapse the previous evening.

"I'm glad you're better, Mr. Stanwood," said Macdonald, and the other man replied:

"I seem to have been through a dreary sort of hell since yesterday; however, I suppose I'm lucky to be alive at all. You came to see me last night, didn't you? I remember trying to talk, only the words wouldn't come straight."

"I want you to tell me about your interview with Dr. Surray, and to know, of course, if you can throw any light on the poisoning episode."

"Well, the latter's obvious enough, isn't it? It must have been the coffee. Was Montague done in?"

"No. He was immune."

"Exactly. He didn't drink any of the blasted stuff—and I'll swear to this, he never touched the tray at all. Never went near it. What about Surray?"

"He was poisoned as you were, and he's still laid out with like results."

"Poor devil!" said Stanwood. "Not that I'm feeling charitable, but it's a grim business."

"It is. What was the nature of your conversation during your meeting?"

"I'll do my best to tell you, though honestly I only remember things through a sort of haze. Surray began by saying that he was convinced somebody was concealing something. He admitted that he himself, having accepted his sister's death as suicide, had endeavoured to get through the inquest without having too much probing done. Now he intended to follow a different course. He asked both of us—Montague and myself—if there was nothing we could add to what we had said."

"And the answer was?"

"I had nothing to add. I told Surray—as I told you—that I had thought that his sister was unhappy and perturbed in mind when I went to see her that Tuesday, but of the actual night of her death I could say nothing. I had no evidence at all. Montague then put his word in. He said that Fellowes, just before his accident, had accused him, Montague, of being downstairs talking to Ruth Surray after every one else had gone to bed that Sunday night. Montague denied this, of course. He said that he had not left his room. He'll have told you this himself, though."

"Yes. More or less—but I want to hear your version."

"Montague then admitted that though he had heard nothing consciously, he believed that some one was awake and moving about in the house. He said that at night, when everything else in the house is quiet, it is possible for the subconscious mind to be alert. He talked a lot of stuff along these lines, and though it's not evidence, I'm inclined to believe what he says. Possibly he did hear a sound without registering it—the sound of Fellowes shutting his door."

"Did you hear that?"

"No—but Fellowes had told me of his belief that Montague was talking to Ruth that night. I don't believe it was Montague at all."

"You think Fellowes was either mistaken or lying?"

"God knows. I keep on going over the evidence and asking myself the same questions, as you must have done. Who knew that Ruth Surray took sleeping draughts? Who knew the contents of her earlier will? Last night, when Upwood House nearly went up in smoke, who was on the spot to start the fire?"

"In reply to all those questions, several people," answered Macdonald.

"Then take this last effort which laid me out. How was Surray found when he was taken ill?"

"He rang for his servant and told him to send for a doctor. Actually he—Surray—was able to name the drug responsible for his condition. He said, 'I've been poisoned, probably with atropine,'—but any medical man would recognise the effect of that particular drug. Its action on the eyes is unique."

"Yes; any doctor would know it, though it's not a poison which is familiar to many laymen, and it's not an easy drug for a layman to get hold of, I imagine, not in lethal quantities, that is. Then a doctor would know that atropine poisoning, if taken in time, can be counteracted by a well-known antidote. If it's not taken in time, you just pass out, painlessly, like Ruth Surray."

He paused and studied Macdonald with his haggard eyes. "Does it strike you as odd that Surray and I should have been the victims and Montague immune? There was a mistake somewhere."

"Whose mistake?" asked Macdonald.

"Haven't you really decided that in your own mind already? Isn't it reasonable to suppose that the dose I got was meant for Montague?"

"But you said that Montague did not take coffee, so the poison could not have been intended for him."

"I know he didn't take it, but I know that the cup of coffee I drank was poured out for Montague. He let Surray pour it out in that absent-minded way of his and then said he wouldn't have it. I refused the coffee straight off—I very seldom drink it—but before I left, I took up the cup of coffee which had stood untouched on the tray. Surray said, 'Don't drink that. It's cold. I'll pour you out another cup,' but I drank it *because* it was cold—I was thirsty and I took up the damned cup, thinking, 'Well, I'll risk it for once. I've got a head that's fairly splitting'—but that cup hadn't been intended for me."

"And you think that it was intended for Montague?"

"Obviously. I can't see any point in taking all that trouble on my account. Surray asked us both to come to his rooms because he wanted to find out if either of us could produce anything new in the way of evidence. I had nothing to tell him, but Montague produced this story about Fellowes hearing some one downstairs talking to Ruth Surray that night. Montague was guarded enough in what he said, but I got the impression that his generalities about the subconscious covered an idea which he was guarding for purposes of his own."

"I thought something of the same kind myself," said Macdonald. "Montague has been concealing something—either evidence or an idea which is based on evidence, but whether for his own interest or that of somebody else, I haven't decided."

"If one could only look at all this in the same spirit of detachment that one looks at a chess problem it would be a fascinating topic," said Stanwood, his voice telling how very far he felt from any spirit of detachment himself. "You have the Surrays, a family whose intellectual attainments are famous, whose whole tendency is to control the emotions and treat the study of them as an academic exercise. You have Montague, a creature of intense feeling and natural simplicity hidden beneath a clumsy manner and the same veneer of philosophy. Montague adored Ruth—you'd only got to see them together to recognise it—but he was devoted to Surray also. Now he's in a cleft stick; he's fumbling after the truth and afraid to admit it even to himself."

"That's only one reading of the problem," replied Macdonald. "You are arguing along the lines that Richard Surray is demented, and you fit your arguments to agree with the theory. To my mind, an even stronger case could be argued against Montague himself—and there is another factor which you haven't had the opportunity of studying."

"The unknown quantity which all the Surrays were intent on concealing? You couldn't have been in that house, as I was, without realising that everybody was guarding something. The two sisters—Naomi and Judith, Mrs. Surray, and the clear-headed Robert, they were all alike in that. I was an outsider—but I felt that carefulness."

"And ascribed it to the fact that the whole family shared your own suspicions and dreaded to express them?"

"No. Not quite that. There was a secret somewhere, a secret connected with Ruth."

"That being so it seems to me a more logical line of thought to disinter the secret than to build up a theory with mania as its starting point."

"And trace the whole thing to the fact that Ruth had a lover who tired of her?"

"Had she? What do you know about that?"

"Nothing—but since Ruth Surray had all the success that the world could offer along most lines, there remained only one way in which life could have let her down. She *was* depressed—that's why I originally accepted the theory of suicide."

"But you don't do so any longer?"

"No. There's madness afoot. The fire, and then this poisoning effort. You've got to find some one who could have been responsible for both."

"Yes—and some one who could have induced Ruth Surray to rewrite her will and to leave that farewell message. No theory is any good which disregards those points."

"And who could have induced her to write them? Obviously one versed in the practice of hypnotic control. That's the only possible explanation. It may sound crazy, but when every other theory fails you have got to fall back on the only possible explanation."

At this moment the nurse knocked at the door and came in, saying, "I'm sorry, but orders are orders. Time is up and the patient must rest."

It was true that Stanwood looked exhausted, and Macdonald got up at once, saying:

"I won't bother you any longer just now, Mr. Stanwood. Miss Wentworth will be glad to know that you are better. She is camping out at your flat, by the way."

Stanwood looked up in surprise. "Miss Wentworth? Good heavens! I thought she had gone back yesterday. My brain seems to have got addled."

"She came to see you last night, only you were too ill to know her."

"Good Lord! One's brain plays tricks. I thought she… Never mind."

He leant back with his eyes closed and Macdonald obeyed the nurse's imperative nod and went out. It was curious, he thought to himself, that Stanwood had mentioned that idea of hypnotism; Richard Surray had spoken of it, only to scout it as impossible. "Hypnotic control," he had said, "can only be assumed with the co-operation of the individual to be hypnotised. The popular fallacy about hypnotic powers is an old wives' tale"—something to that effect.

Macdonald was not the type of "practical common-sense investigator" who dismissed a theory because it was, at a first glance, fantastic. In the course of his career he had met too many strange happenings to say "that is fantastic, therefore I won't consider it." That Surray's dictum about the limitations of the hypnotist was true, Macdonald did not doubt, but there still remained the possibility that Ruth had consulted her brother, and had agreed to a suggestion that her sleeplessness should be treated by hypnotic suggestion. Such a course had been proved beneficial by certain psychiatrists, especially in those cases of obstinate insomnia which occasionally follow a severe operation or other shock to the system, and the degree of control and suggestion varied enormously according to the patient's degree of co-operation and concentration. Macdonald felt that he was examining the idea only with a view to dismissing it, but there was at the back of his mind a recollection of the impression Richard Surray had made on him on the night of the fire. Surray, sitting hunched up in his chair in Ruth's room, had seemed strange and abnormal; his nerves had been strung up to a pitch which had made Macdonald fear for his reason.

It was with a sense of relief that Macdonald reached Scotland Yard and turned to the study of those practical matters which come under the heading of "routine." It was a comfort to be in contact with the realities of tangible things after all his groping among confusing theories of a deranged mind.

CHAPTER XVII

IT WAS ON WEDNESDAY NIGHT THAT REEVES ESCORTED Keith Brandon southwards, and on Thursday morning that the latter was brought into Macdonald's office to be questioned again as to his own possible share in the Surray case.

After his abortive struggle with Reeves, Brandon had wasted no more energy in either physical resistance or verbal argument. His first furious rage dissipated, a measure of common sense seemed to have returned to him. He realised that he had played into the hands of the C.I.D. man by striking him, and that no amount of argument could help the man who had been rash enough to lose his temper and hit a policeman. "All right, muttonhead. I'll come quietly. One Chief Inspector's going to lose his rank over this and that I promise you," was the purport of his further remarks.

Yet when Macdonald had stated his case, Brandon sat and looked out of the window with less confidence in his bearing, and for the first time a troubled look began to appear in his eyes.

Macdonald went through his facts succinctly; first the suspicions aroused by the belated arrival of Ruth Surray's letter to her brother and the probability that she had gone out on the Sunday evening to post it. Next the probability that the "farewell" message had been adapted to play its part; the fact of the fire at Upwood House and the poisoning of Richard Surray and Stanwood were then mentioned, and Macdonald went on:

"You told me that you had spent Sunday night, the 29th, in London. You were, however, seen in the Upwood district on that night. After I saw you at The King's Arms on Monday last you went on to Mr. Flemming's cottage, Faraway, where Mr. Montague visited you in the evening. You left the cottage shortly after ten o'clock and your doings between that time and three o'clock in the morning are unknown to us. It was between those hours that the fire occurred at Upwood House. After spending some hours in the waiting-room at Euston, you went to call on Dr. Surray, who was away. You were admitted by his servant and left to write a letter in the dining-room, thus having the opportunity to poison the bowl of sugar which was afterwards used to sweeten his coffee."

Macdonald paused here and then continued:

"In spite of the fact that many of your actions seem calculated to arouse suspicion, you may yet ask what grounds have we for connecting you with Miss Ruth Surray's death? The answer is that you were on intimate terms with her, and met her very frequently during last month. Her own diary testifies to that fact, although you yourself have denied it. It can be reasonably assumed that you grew weary of that intimacy and transferred your attentions to her younger sister."

The level voice was interrupted by a violent oath from Brandon; he had been listening quietly enough up till now, but rage got the better of him at Macdonald's last phrase. He swallowed down his furious words, however, and bade Macdonald go on. The latter continued:

"One of the problems in this very difficult case has been to assess the probabilities of Naomi Surray's part in it."

"She had no part in it," said Brandon.

"That remains to be seen. On the Sunday evening—the 29th—you telephoned to her at Mrs. Lang's house at Stow. Later you met her near Upwood House—at the same time that Ruth Surray went out to the post."

"Since Naomi has told you that, there's no object in my concealing it any longer," said Brandon, and the flush had died away from his face. It was white now. "*She* did not see Ruth," he added slowly. "I saw her—but without her knowing it."

Macdonald, even in the heat of a difficult case, was a fair-minded man; he would bluff in order to gain his point, but he would not ascribe to Naomi Surray a part she had not played.

"No. She did not tell me that you two had met on that night," he replied. "I guessed it. It was pretty obvious after I had learned about the telephone call at Mrs. Lang's and knew that Naomi Surray was in a state akin to nervous collapse the following morning."

"May you be everlastingly damned!" said Brandon fiercely, and Macdonald went on.

"Seeing that the facts can be interpreted in a very ugly way, not only for yourself but for Naomi Surray also, don't you think that you would be well advised to change your mind and tell the truth—assuming that you are innocent of the crimes for which it appears you had both opportunity and motive?"

"Why don't you charge me with them?" demanded Brandon, his eyes ablaze again.

"I'm quite willing to explain my own unwillingness to do so," replied Macdonald. "It's because a logical case can be made out against you, with Naomi Surray as your accomplice; such a logical case that even though you were both found innocent by a jury there would still be a large proportion of people who would believe you guilty. It's no part of our job in this place to seize on a probable person and pin the guilt on to him in order to give the impression of smartness on the part of the police. It is much easier to charge a man on probabilities than it is for him to prove—in the eyes of the whole world—that he is innocent of that charge."

Brandon's face looked both wary and puzzled, and he replied, "So you are going to trap me into admissions to reinforce your case in the eyes of the jury. I haven't much patience with the psychological rubbish which Richard Surray expounds, but I know one thing which sheds a light on your lofty motives. You disliked me at sight, as I did you, and you've been cooking a case to meet your own humours."

"That line of argument won't get us any further, but since you've stated it, I'll give you the only answer I can, Mr. Brandon. It's mainly because I dislike you that I want the balance to swing evenly. Perhaps that's beyond your comprehension, but you aren't too dense to see that there is a case against you, and through you, against Naomi Surray. At present there's no charge formulated against either of you." Exasperation broke the level quietness of Macdonald's voice.

"Can't you see that if you're both innocent, the only way of proving it is to tell the whole truth? You're a very clumsy liar. Why give me the chance of telling you so? I'm ready to listen to you with an open mind, not for your sake, or even wholly for my own peace of mind, but because the Surrays have had enough to put up with. Do you want to see that girl beside you in the dock?"

Brandon's face twitched. "God knows I don't. I'd rather hang for a thing I didn't do."

"If you hang, you will involve her in something which will break her as surely as if you'd accused her in your own words," said Macdonald. "You say that you've no hand in it, and that Naomi Surray has had no hand in it. It is because I hoped that she had no contact with the case that I did not send a man north to bring her back, as you were brought back. If you can clear up this misunderstanding, as you called it in your letter to Dr. Surray, you'll do more than save your own skin."

There was a silence between the two men for a few seconds; they sat facing one another, Keith Brandon's angry blue eyes, bloodshot and fierce, meeting the steady gaze of Macdonald's stone-grey ones. At last the latter said:

"What about it? You've been responsible for a good deal of trouble—and you're likely to be responsible for more, if you can't see sense."

Pushing the papers together on his desk, Macdonald reached out his hand towards the bell-push beside him and then Brandon said:

"All right. It's a bloody mess either way—I can see that. I'll tell you what happened, but I did not kill Ruth, and neither did Naomi."

Macdonald was conscious of swallowing a sigh of relief. This interview was anything but orthodox, but if it enabled him to get at the truth he felt that his conduct would be justified. He sat back and listened.

"If I'm going to tell you anything at all, I'd better start at the beginning and go through with it," said Brandon. "Whether I shall make things better or worse I don't know, but if you charge me now, knowing enough to make things look their blackest, it'll mean hell for Naomi.

"I first met Ruth Surray at the American Authors' dinner at Grosvenor House. I fell for her—and she for me, since you want the naked facts. I'm not justifying myself over any part of the story, but there was this about it. Ruth was a beautiful woman and she had a reputation for being too lofty for any man's aspirations. Some fellow once said to me, 'Ruth Surray writes about human passions as a physician writes about mortal disease—a state he has observed but not experienced. She is as immune from emotion as a toothless man from toothache.' When I found that her immunity was not so complete as her reputation suggested, I pursued her. She..."

He hesitated here and Macdonald put in, "She was in love with you. I'll accept that as data."

"It's no use putting it as simply as that," said Brandon. "She was too complex for any simple statement to describe her. If she had been in love with me—as I understand the word, I should have been her lover, but I wasn't. That's the point. She wasn't a normal woman in love; she wanted to talk about passion, to dream about it, but never to be logical over it." He shrugged his shoulders. "Either you can understand the exasperation aroused by a situation like that or you can't. From being mad for her—just at first—I became mad with her. I cut away and then she pursued. Illogical again. She wouldn't go through with it, but she couldn't leave it alone. I told her, at last, that I was through, and there was no object in our meeting at all. Then I met Naomi." Again he paused, his hot blue eyes staring out of the window. "I can best explain it like this: Naomi was the first woman I ever wanted to marry—make love, pursue, all the rest of it, dozens of times before, but not marry. There's a lot of difference." Once again he met Macdonald's steady eyes. "I'm giving you stronger reasons every minute for believing that I killed Ruth. I didn't. I've this much in common with the moralists—I couldn't marry a woman if I'd murdered her sister to get her."

"No," said Macdonald. "In spite of the fact that I disliked you because we're innately different, I'm willing to believe that; but it's a subjective point. You'd better get on to the main facts which I'm investigating."

"A few days after I'd met Naomi, Richard Surray called on me and warned me off. I didn't argue. I knew he could do me harm if he set about it, and I wasn't giving him the chance. He and I see life from different angles, like the Roundheads and the Royalists. I meant to marry Naomi first and argue with her brother afterwards; but Naomi began to avoid me. I couldn't get at her, and she wouldn't write. I couldn't go to Upwood House and risk meeting Ruth again. Then at last Naomi wrote and told me to telephone to her at the Langs' house on Sunday evening. I took the chance and left London in time to get best part of the way to Stow before I rang her up. Then I persuaded her to meet me in the lane leading to Upwood about midnight. I think we were both a bit crazy by that time. If I was in love with her, she also was in love with me."

Macdonald sat quite still, his face expressionless. Whatever was his own opinion of the man before him, he did not show it, and Brandon blundered on with his statement:

"I drove like hell that night. I can't think why I didn't crash a dozen times. I got to Upwood by half-past eleven and left my car in a coppice just off the main road. I walked up the lane and through the paddock, because I knew Naomi would come that way. When I got into the lower garden I heard somebody moving, and just before I spoke I saw a light. It wasn't Naomi; it was a man. He was turning away from me and I only saw his figure for a second as he lighted a cigarette. It was a dark night and he was standing under the beech trees. I knew that I hadn't made a sound as I came up and he didn't know that I was there, only a dozen yards away. I didn't know who the fellow was, but the last thing I wanted was to butt into any of the party at the house, so I just stood and waited. After a minute or so I heard footsteps coming from the house and then Ruth's voice spoke: 'Who's that? Who is it?' The fellow with the cigarette answered, 'It's only me. Sorry if I startled you.' And she said, 'You! How funny. I thought it was some one else—a ghost, perhaps.' He laughed and said, 'Do ghosts walk—in your garden? Surely not. If you're going for a stroll, may I come with you? I wanted to talk to you about my trilogy idea.'" Brandon broke off for a minute. "I think those were their exact words. After that I don't remember so well, but the gist of it was this: Ruth said, 'Yes, I'm anxious to hear about it; but time seems to have gone so quickly. Don't come with me now.

I like a stroll by myself; I'm like a cat of nights. Anyway, a walk helps me to sleep. If you're still about when I come back—I shan't be long—we might talk for a bit.' And he said, 'I shall be about all right. I can't sleep in the country; it's too quiet.' She laughed at that and said, 'By the way, you'll be interested to know I've rewritten my will. I can die in peace whenever I like now.'"

Macdonald broke in: "And, knowing all that, you could still keep quiet and say nothing…"

Brandon interrupted in his turn; "There was Naomi."

"No time for post-mortems now," said Macdonald, swallowing down his disgust with the other. "Do you know who the man was who talked to Ruth Surray that night?"

"No. I've no idea. I didn't see his face. But I should know his voice again."

"Go on," said Macdonald. "What happened then?"

"He answered—after her saying she could die in peace, 'Well, I've seen to it that I shan't be exploited posthumously. I'll stroll around for a bit and hope to see you later—if you're sure you don't mind losing your sleep.' Something to that effect. She answered, 'There are times when I can't sleep. To-night's one of them, somehow. I'll come into the study when I get back.' She walked down towards the paddock, and he went up towards the house, and I waited where I was. It was just midnight when Naomi came; she'd got a torch with her, and when she lighted it under the trees I saw her. I made her come right across the garden to the little coppice on the west side lest Ruth should find us." Still Macdonald was silent, and Brandon went on: "I tried to make her—Naomi—come away with me, then and there." Macdonald interrupted:

"It was as well for both of you that she didn't agree to that. How long did you stay there with her?"

"Until nearly two o'clock."

Macdonald made an abrupt movement of exasperation.

"How, in God's name, do you expect any jury to believe this? If you'd told the whole story as soon as you heard of Ruth Surray's death you might have been believed. Now you've left it too late. If you swear to the voice of the man who met her in the garden, it's only your word against his."

"If I had gone to the police and told them that I was at Upwood that night it would have meant involving Naomi," said Brandon stubbornly; "moreover, her own people believed that Ruth had committed suicide. The last thing they wanted was a public inquiry into her relations with me. When I heard the news of her death I phoned to Upwood to try to speak to Naomi. Richard Surray spoke to me; he spoke in German lest he was overheard by the exchange, and he said, 'Haven't you done harm enough? For God's sake keep out of it and hold your tongue.' I knew what he meant."

"I know what he meant, too," said Macdonald; and there was something in his voice which made Brandon move restively, a scorn and disgust which had the quality of a lash, and then Macdonald went on in his official voice, "There are other points on which you can explain your own version. What were you doing in the Upwood district last Monday?"

"I drove down there to find out where Naomi was. You set your man on my heels and I didn't want him following me round. I stayed in the cottage, and then Montague came. He—like you—believed that I had been at Upwood to see Ruth on the Sunday night, and that she had killed herself in consequence. I told him that I had met Naomi, and that if he chose to tell you so he would do more harm than good. He believed—as I did—that Ruth killed herself."

"The motives of everybody involved in this case would take an alienist to unravel," said Macdonald. "The next point is: What were you doing between ten o'clock and three the next morning?"

"After I locked your man in the cupboard?" said Brandon coolly. "Nothing like telling you the whole story. You'd set him on my heels when I least wanted him. He had no warrant to enter the house, and he asked for what he got. I learnt from Montague that Naomi was up north at the Hebrides, and my first idea was to drive straight up there. I set out northwards, and the more I thought about things by that time the less I liked them. I made up my mind to go back to town to see Richard Surray. If I had found him that morning I should have told him the whole story as I have told it to you, and he could have chosen his own course. It's all very well for you to sit there looking like a censorious elder," he burst out, "I may have behaved like a lunatic, but, by God! I felt one by that time. I could see a noose for Naomi as well as for myself— all because Ruth Surray took it on herself to teach me the meaning of spiritual values—"

"If there are any reasons to be adduced, you can spend the rest of your life arguing them out," interrupted Macdonald. "The thing I want to know is an obvious fact—your route from Faraway when you left it just after ten o'clock on Monday night?"

"I drove up to Rugby and got there at midnight," replied Brandon. "I had to get more petrol and the brake wanted adjusting. I shoved the car into a garage in Wood Street, and by the time they'd finished tinkering with it I'd changed my mind and decided to drive back to town. I didn't go to my own rooms, because I didn't want to find you on the doorstep."

Once again Macdonald ignored the "because." It was obvious enough that Brandon's crazy-seeming behaviour could be put down to the fact that he had been in a frenzy of nerves and apprehension, not only for himself, but for Naomi. The one important fact which had emerged was his statement that he had been in Rugby at midnight on the night of the fire. Writing a brief note, Macdonald rang through to the office to have that point investigated. Then he sat back and thought, racking his brains for the possibility of further enlightenment, without leading his witness. The greater part of Brandon's story about the events in the garden at Upwood that Sunday evening might be mere fabrication, a clumsy story invented by a guilty man to lead suspicion elsewhere; what Macdonald wanted was some detail, no matter how trivial, to link up his own theory of possibilities. To prove that Brandon was lying was difficult enough; to prove that he was speaking the truth might be more difficult still. One sentence alone, of all that Brandon had said, led the Chief Inspector to believe that his own early suspicions were right, that the theory he had formulated was the truth. But how could he get Brandon to substantiate it?

At length he said, "Think back to that moment in the garden at Upwood when you saw that man lighting a cigarette. Did he strike a match?"

"No. He used a lighter—it was only a tiny flame."

"Did he stand with his back quite towards you?"

"No, not quite. He was turned half away. I didn't see his face because his head was bent, but I saw his hands cupped round the flame to keep it from the breeze." Brandon was frowning intently, as though he were trying to visualise the scene again, with the dark figure and the tiny flicker of light shining through the curved fingers, and then he went on:

"I saw his hands in the light. He was standing with his left shoulder towards me, and he wore a gold ring on the third finger of his left hand—a wedding ring. I remember seeing it glitter in the light. Is that any good to you?"

"It may be some good to you," replied Macdonald. "That recollection and one short phrase which you repeated may save you from the dock, because I don't believe you invented either item."

"Which phrase?"

"'I can't sleep in the country. It's too quiet.' That woke an answering chord in my mind. You're not out of the wood yet, Mr. Brandon, but you can help yourself a step further on the way. You will have to stay here for the time being, and I want you to do this: At a given time, when you are instructed, I want you to talk over the telephone to some one. I shall not tell you his name and he will not know yours. When you hear his voice you are to say, 'I can't sleep in the country. It's too quiet. I've seen to it that I shan't be exploited posthumously.' If he asks you what you mean, you are to say, 'I was in the garden that night, too. I heard your voice.'"

"And if the voice that answers isn't the voice I heard?"

"I think it will be. There is only one voice it could be if you have spoken the truth."

Brandon frowned. "It's a rotten thing to trap a poor devil—"

Macdonald fairly blazed at him, "It's not a rotten thing to poison a woman in her sleep, to fire a house at night, and to poison another man to complete the job? You have your own ideas of rottenness and I have mine. The less you use the word the better for you. Will you do what I ask or will you not?"

Brandon shrugged his shoulders in acquiescence. "You've got me in a cleft stick. I don't like your ways—"

"And I don't like yours," retorted Macdonald. "I've given you an extra fair deal, because I think you deserve a rope; but as the law in this country goes it seems you haven't earned it. There are some people I haven't any use for. You're in one category and murderers are in another. The world would be a more wholesome place without either of you."

And Brandon, sitting with his shoulders hunched up and his flushed face back-tilted, made no answer.

CHAPTER XVIII

"THE TROUBLE IN THIS CASE IS THAT THERE IS NO DIRECT way of getting at the facts. The evidence is mainly circumstantial—arguing from probabilities, and trying to guess at the truth in a maze of lies and half-truths. It is a horrible case in many ways, and the most damnable point in it is the fact that the murderer was willing to burn a whole household of people to save his own skin, or exact his own vengeance. That was a crime for which hanging is too kind a punishment."

Macdonald spoke as he felt, his voice incisive with condemnation, and Stanwood, who sat facing the Chief Inspector in the sitting-room of the flat at Denham Court, went on folding a piece of paper into tinier and tinier folds.

"Then you are no nearer the truth than you were before?"

"Much nearer to it," replied Macdonald, "yet still groping. The same facts can point at different individuals, but one narrows the issue at last, until motive is joined to opportunity by the length of a piece of string—which was burnt in the fire at Upwood House."

Stanwood looked up, and his questioning eyes met Macdonald's just as the telephone bell rang.

"Will you answer it—or shall I?"

Macdonald replied, "It's not my call. Answer it yourself."

Stanwood lifted the receiver, called, "Hallo," and listened. Macdonald saw him start, saw his face go rigid, and a pallor as of death creep over the lean cheeks. When he tried to answer, Stanwood's voice seemed to stick in his throat.

"I don't know what you're talking about," he said, and clapped down the receiver as Macdonald's voice said:

"You do know, and now I know that you know."

Stanwood, still standing by the shelf where the telephone stood, thrust his hand in his pocket.

"Then keep your distance," he said, drawing a pistol from his pocket. "I've not much to lose, and there are plenty of shots for both of us."

Macdonald sat perfectly still, and his quiet voice was as steady as ever when he replied, looking at the barrel of the weapon pointed at him, "You had a case of sorts, Mr. Stanwood, but that fire put you out of court."

It was the steadiness of the voice which brought Stanwood back to earth after that tense moment when he had been meaning to press the trigger and blow the other man's brains out.

"A case?" he said. "We'll argue that in the hereafter, you the hunter and I the hunted! Do you realise why I did it, you who stand by the law? A life for a life! Ruth Surray's life! Ruth Surray—pampered, idolised, brutal arbiter of life and fortune that she was. She killed my wife, killed her as surely as I killed Ruth. Do you realise that? I'd have burned the whole brood of them as I'd have smoked out a wasps' nest!" He was shouting now, still with the pistol gripped in a hand that was strangely steady. "You're going to produce your famous piece—anything I say will be used in evidence against me! Say it! Begin to say it and you'll get no further. What I've got to say won't be used as evidence against me anywhere on this earth!"

Macdonald remembered Stanwood's voice saying, "There's madness about." At this moment Stanwood was mad himself, but still Macdonald sat in his place, leaning back in his chair with that surprising air of coolness.

"I have no choice in the matter," he replied. "When you took the law into your own hands you knew what the consequences would be if your scheme miscarried."

Stanwood suddenly laughed, and the frenzied look went out of his eyes for a moment as he replied, "Do you realise that this is funny, you sitting there like a judge with eternity yawning before you?"

"No, it's not funny," said Macdonald. "It's the grim anticlimax of your own actions. I've a right to say this much in common humanity before I put you under arrest: I have enough imagination to realise the provocation you suffered."

Remembering the queer scene afterwards, Macdonald felt that those words were drawn from him by the realisation of the facts which had turned the brain of the man before him. He had been driven to hideous acts by the recollection of long drawn-out suffering which he had been powerless to assuage. Macdonald had measured his own wits against the murderer's, tricked him into giving himself away, and yet could see the wretchedness which had inspired the crime.

"I arrest you for the murder of Ruth Surray."

He got no further, for a report filled the room like thunder, and as the smoke cleared away Macdonald was on his feet. Unhurt, he dodged the pistol which was hurled at him as Stanwood realised that his shot had not taken effect, and next second the two men were grappling together, crashing back and forth in a grim struggle. It was a fight between a madman and a trained athlete, and the maniacal strength of the smaller man had a violence which Macdonald had never before experienced. Stanwood's hands gripped his adversary's throat with a hold which could not be loosened, and Macdonald, the blood singing in his ears, his vision blurred with balls of fire, swung his weight forward so that the two crashed against the heavy table with Stanwood undermost, and suddenly the throttling hands went limp.

A voice spoke beside Macdonald, but for a while he could make no sense of the words. With sweat pouring down his face, he drew in great gasps of air into his lungs, conscious that he had been as near death as a drowning man.

"All right, Chief? You wanted to do it on your own account, but, by heck, it nearly ended your career as well as his."

"Poor devil!" Macdonald gasped out the words, and then he and Reeves bent over the limp body which had slipped to the floor. Reeves had thought Stanwood was only stunned, but it was the man's maniacal fury which had killed him. A blood vessel burst in the brain which had so cunningly planned Ruth Surray's death.

Before they left the flat, Reeves picked up the pistol which Stanwood had fired. It was, in Macdonald's words, a "grim anti-climax." The flat had been searched before Stanwood returned to it from the nursing home, and the ammunition had been removed and blank shot substituted. Macdonald, waiting for the assurance that he was not wrong in his own conclusions, had had no intention that Stanwood should claim another life to satisfy his own vengeance.

It was to Robert Surray that Macdonald outlined the evidence which was finally docketed at Scotland Yard.

"Stanwood? But why?" cried Robert. And a moment later, "And how? That fire—he wasn't anywhere near the place."

"He had no need to be. But we'll take your questions in their proper order. Why? You could have answered that question yourself; you had all the data. I had it, too, but other things intervened. When your brother first told me about Keith Brandon, the latter's shadow seemed to obliterate everything else. What did you know about Stanwood? Three things. One: he had been writing for years, with no recognition, struggling against poverty and injustice. Two: he had a wife who died of tuberculosis shortly before he himself leapt into fame and fortune. Three: a copy of one of his early books was found by you in the library of your sister Ruth. You can argue everything else from that."

Robert pushed his hands up through his thick red hair. "I don't think Ruth had ever read that book," he said slowly.

"No, I don't suppose she had," said Macdonald. "I made a guess about it that afternoon just before we heard that Stanwood and your brother had been poisoned, and I have since learnt—from Elsa Wentworth—that my guess was right. When Mrs. Stanwood first became ill and Stanwood was desperate for money to send her away to St. Moritz or Leysin, he sent a copy of his book to your sister, and asked her to help him by giving it a favourable notice, knowing how great was her influence in the world of letters. She sent him a curt letter of refusal, indignant at being solicited in such a manner."

"Yes," said Robert slowly. "I can believe that. Ruth was high-handed. She took herself seriously."

"Stanwood never forgave her that high-handedness," said Macdonald; "but he might have forgotten it if Ruth Surray had not suddenly done the very thing he once asked of her. She, admired and firmly established at the top of the ladder, chose to exert her influence on his behalf just after his wife died. Stanwood accepted her patronage with gratitude on his lips and murder in his heart. He had lost his wife, and he chose to put her death to Ruth Surray's account."

"No," said Robert, breaking in indignantly; and Macdonald replied:

"Don't think I'm holding a brief for him. I am not; but I do understand his bitterness a little. Whichever way you look at it, he hadn't had a fair deal. It's admitted now that his early work is as good as that which was acclaimed at long last. It was enough to warp any man's mind."

"I'm glad he's dead," said Robert slowly. "It would have been horrible to..." His voice died away, and Macdonald nodded.

"I'm glad, too. It was all horrible. However, no use brooding over it. You wanted to know 'how.'"

"Yes," said Robert. "It's queer, isn't it? One's sense of curiosity is stronger than one's sense of horror."

"During the short time he knew your sister, Stanwood must have worked at his own plan. He probably found out that she took thalmaine by telling her of his own insomnia. Then he drew her attention to that much-debated book, *Last Leaves*, which your sister Ruth deplored and which your brother admired. Can't you imagine Stanwood saying, 'How would you like that to happen to you? A slip in the street and one dies, and one's loving relatives publish one's leavings down to the last scrap.' The fact that Dr. Surray had liked *Last Leaves* would have had influence in making her rewrite the will and delete his name as executor. As we know from Brandon, Stanwood learnt from your sister's own lips that the will had been rewritten."

"And the message?"

"That was originally a sheet—probably the last in a short story. Stanwood cut it down to remove the numbering at the top, so that the sheet was identical in size with the block your sister used for her letters. He cut it with the 'plough' in the workroom and so obtained the accurate edge necessary to deceive the experts. Hence the fire in the workroom—to conceal the fact that a plough knife had ever existed."

"But, damn it, the man was in London when the fire began," expostulated Robert, and Macdonald nodded.

"Yes, he was in London all right. He managed that fire by the simple expedient of a piece of string. It was simple enough, but I was very slow in tumbling to it. You remember that the maid, Gladys, gave evidence that she shut the door of the workroom when it was ajar? If you fastened a strong piece of string to the power switch, led it through a screw eye in the floor and then fastened it to the handle of the door, and left the door ajar, when the door was shut the string would go taut and pull down the switch. Stanwood had an hour to himself that afternoon. He knew I was busy over the Montague and Fellowes story. All he had to do was to avoid being seen by the servants, and that he managed quite successfully. Once he had got away from the workroom unseen he was safe enough. If anybody had gone into the place and seen the string there was nothing to give him away."

"That fire was a devilish idea," said Robert fiercely, and Macdonald agreed.

"Yes. I find that unforgivable."

"What made you hit on Stanwood? Had you guessed before Brandon told his story?"

"I could only see the possibilities. There was the motive—I groped after that uncertainly. When I hit on the idea of the faking of the farewell message and saw the plough knife I groped a bit more wildly. Then I learnt—what you knew already—that Stanwood was the son of a small printer. Every working printer knows all about bookbinding and the use of a plough knife. It's one of his most familiar tools. Next, in Stanwood's flat I found a tin of coffee substitute—the sort of thing which sufferers from insomnia prefer. If he had taken the stuff with him to Upwood, he might easily have made your sister a cup of it that night, advising her to try it, as people do who suffer from a like disability. That would have explained the coffee cup which was removed from her room. The dose of thalmaine was in the coffee cup—probably in a first cup which Miss Surray drank downstairs. He doubtless went to her room, found the copy of the will and placed it with the faked farewell message at her bedside."

"What did you make of the suicide essay which was found in her flat?"

"I've only guesswork to go upon. I think that Stanwood wrote the essay, typing it on a new portable, similar to your sister's. He may have given it to her to criticise, and she wrote in the pencilled criticisms and signed a note at the end, put it among her own papers until she had an opportunity of discussing it. I gave it to her publisher to read, and he is certain the style is not that of your sister."

"Good God! To think of the elaborate preparations the man made!" cried Robert aghast.

"Yes—and you haven't realised all of them yet. Why was the portable typewriter found in your brother's room? Stanwood must have borrowed it—or just taken it—from Miss Surray's flat. Then, when his plan of fire-raising went wrong, he sought to place clues involving your brother in the murder. The presence of that typewriter gave you—and me—a nasty few minutes."

Robert broke out into a sudden sweat at the recollection of his own fears, and then he said, "Well, you've accounted for most of it. What about the atropine? Did he mean to kill himself as well as Richard?"

"No, I don't think so. He could have killed himself so much more easily—with thalmaine, for example. The street corner at which he collapsed was a rather useful spot—close to an oculist's and a toxicologist's. If a man collapses on a physician's doorstep, it's twenty to one that the said physician will be called upon to render first-aid. I think the whole episode was nicely calculated, with special reference to the timing. Incidentally, Miss Elsa Wentworth—poor unhappy thing—is employed in a firm of manufacturing pharmaceutical chemists in Birmingham. It was through her that he got both the atropine and the thalmaine. When he collapsed he still retained enough presence of mind to say that there was no one at his flat to be told of his illness. It seems pretty obvious that his brain was not working normally by this time. He was unbalanced, and couldn't work out cause and effect."

"I was convinced that Montague was responsible for the poisoning business," said Robert. "My brain wasn't working normally either."

"Nobody's was," said Macdonald dryly. "Your brother, for instance—the shock of Miss Surray's death obscured his judgment. He was so obsessed by the possibilities of Brandon that he could not see the problem as a whole. As a matter of fact, Montague seemed a probable enough suspect at one time. The business of Fellowes' accident looked pretty fishy. It's a curious thing, Fellowes believed that he had heard Montague downstairs on the Sunday night, because he heard him cough. What could be easier to imitate than that little dry nervous cough of Montague's? I expect that Stanwood got an idea that he was heard as he went downstairs. He coughed—with the intention of letting others believe that it was Montague who was on the move."

"And if Fellowes had spoken out to begin with—as he should have done—Montague might have found himself in the dock?"

"It would have been a case of one man's word against another's, and the inquiry would have gone forward just the same. Incidentally, Stanwood unwittingly produced a few nebulous pieces of evidence when I first questioned him. He spent the afternoon of the first Tuesday in July at Miss Surray's flat, and he laid discreet emphasis on the fact that she was depressed and weary. It happened that Dr. Surray had told me that on the same date he saw your sister dining with Keith Brandon, looking the very reverse of unhappy. In those first days of her acquaintance with him it seemed illogical to suppose that she would have been depressed in the afternoon when she was going to dine with a man with whom she was in love in the evening. Not a very strong argument, perhaps, in the case of a complex woman like your sister, but it seemed odd to me when I thought it over. It also seemed odd that Stanwood, who had told me that he always slept well, should keep Medinal tablets by his bedside in his own flat."

Robert puffed thoughtfully at his pipe.

"Here a little and there a little," he observed. "It's hard for a murderer to see the implications of every word he utters."

"It's hard for anybody to foresee the implications of their own words," said Macdonald, "or of their own reservations either, wherefore the requirements of the law—the truth, the whole truth, and nothing but the truth. The intellectual who acts on his own judgment, and the devoted adherent who suppresses certain facts out of loyalty, are as much a stumbling block in criminal investigation as the downright liar."

"It sounds simple enough," said Robert, "but you've got to make allowances for human loyalties and susceptibilities."

Macdonald laughed. "I'm acting the heavy elder, as Brandon told me, but you needn't instruct me in the complexities of human loyalties. I spend my life studying them, and they're responsible for the devil of a lot of mischief sometimes." He got up and stretched out his hand to Robert. "Good-bye. It's only in the nature of things that you should hope that you won't ever be called upon to see me again."

"I don't feel that way about it myself," said Robert. "Won't you come and dine with me after the holidays—and talk about something remote from all this?"

"With all the pleasure in the world, if you'd like me to," replied Macdonald, and then added, "I was terribly sorry that your mother had all this additional misery. I did realise how bitter it was for her."

"She was like the rest of us—not normal," replied Robert. "She told me only to-day how grateful she was to you for keeping Naomi out of it, and she will never forget that you saved all our lives on the night of the fire."

Macdonald looked back at Robert with his thoughtful grey eyes.

"Whenever I'm feeling particularly fed up with my own inability to see through a brick wall, I shall console myself with the recollection that on that evening I happened to be at the right place at the right time," he replied, and Robert answered with a flash of his old gaiety:

"The child's guide to detecting—be at the right place at the right time. What you call routine, I take it?"

And Macdonald replied, "That's about it."

THE END

If you've enjoyed *Murder by the Book*,
you won't want to miss

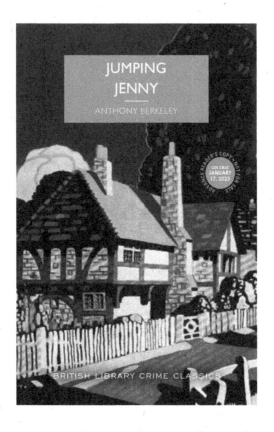

the most recent BRITISH LIBRARY CRIME CLASSIC
published by Poisoned Pen Press,
an imprint of Sourcebooks.

poisonedpenpress.com